By Dean Murray

Reflections

Broken

Torn

Splintered

Intrusion

Numb

Trapped

Forsaken

Riven

Driven

Lost

Marked

Dark Reflections

Bound

Hunted

Ambushed

Shattered

Burned

The Awakening

Reborn

Immortal

Endless

A Broken World

The Society

The Destroyer

The Warlord

The Founder

The Desolation

Reflections

(Dean Writing as Eldon)

The Greater Darkness

A Darkness Mirrored

The Guadel Chronicles

Frozen Prospects

Thawed Fortunes

I'rone

Brittle Bonds

Shattered Ties

Driven

Dean Murray

&

Eldon Murphy

Driven is a work of fiction. Names, characters, places and incidents are the products of the author's imagination or are used fictitiously. Any resemblance to actual events, locales, or persons, living or dead, is entirely coincidental.

Published by Fir'shan Publishing

ISBN 978-1-9393632-7-5

www.FirshanPublishing.com

First Edition

For Katie, Sage and Alayna

Because fast forwarding is a terrible crime.

Chapter 1

Jasmin Bianchi
I-40
Santa Rosa, New Mexico

I first realized that I was being followed somewhere outside of Albuquerque. I probably should have noticed the black SUV an hour before that, but I'd been paying too much attention to Ben and not enough attention to the other cars sharing the dusty freeway with me.

Ash is the kind of treasure trove of information that only comes along once in a great while. I hadn't spent as much time with him as Dominic had, but I'd still managed to pick up an awful lot of information and tradecraft during the short time between when he'd joined the pack and when Alec had scattered us to the four corners of the country. That meant that I knew enough to realize I was being followed, but I hadn't learned enough from him to be able to lose a tail in an unfamiliar city.

The SUV posed a bigger problem than I wanted to admit, but I ruthlessly forced myself to be rational about things. The tinted windows meant that there was no way to know how many people were inside. It could be as few as one or as many as seven or eight. I was betting on a lower number simply because shape shifters, especially the big hybrid bruisers favored by the Coun'hij, tended not to play very well with other people.

If someone had really been stupid enough to pack seven of my kind inside of that vehicle, then all I needed to do was stay on the road for another hour or two and wait for the boredom of the chase to make them try and kill each other.

The members of the Coun'hij were a lot of things, but stupid wasn't one of them. The SUV wasn't going to be full, but while I could beat one other hybrid or two wolves, anything more than that was pretty much a guaranteed loss for me.

I didn't want to have to backtrack because I didn't know how much longer Ben had. He'd been doing better since before the pack all split up, but he was once again getting weaker. The process was so slow that I could almost convince myself that I was imagining it, but it was happening.

I sighed, partly in anger, partly in resignation, and then pulled my phone out and called the number I was hoping would still put me in contact with Alec. He picked up on the second ring and I started talking before he could get a word out.

"I've got a problem. A black SUV has been tailing me for at least the last few miles. Heck, they could have been back there for hours for all I know."

"Join the club. I've had more than a dozen other people report in during the last hour with the same problem."

Alec sounded tired, but that wasn't too surprising. It had to be hard to run a war, especially when your troops consisted of a bunch of stubborn, erratic shape shifters.

"That's it? There isn't any brilliant master plan for getting me out of this particular jam?"

I almost said more than that, but I managed to get ahold of myself at the last second. My temper had been harder to control for a couple of weeks now, but ever since I'd manifested a hybrid form my beast had wanted to throw down against every single person I ran into.

"If you want help you're not exactly going about asking for it the right way."

Barely suppressed rage bubbled in the back of Alec's throat and it was all I could do to force myself not to respond in kind.

"You're right, I'm...I'm sorry. Please can you help me out here?"

Alec was silent for a second. I couldn't tell whether he was reinforcing the fact that he was the one holding all of the cards, or if it just took him that long to calm down to the point where he could respond without causing a reescalation of the situation.

"Where are you right now?"

"Half an hour west of Albuquerque."

The silence stretched out to nearly a full minute before Alec finally responded.

"If you've been driving for two or three hours then you don't have enough range to make it to anyone who could help."

I silently counted to five in an effort to keep my cool, but it didn't help much. My tone might not have been quite as challenging, but my words were still pretty close to the line.

"Seriously, there isn't anyone else from one of the coalition packs within a hundred miles of me?"

"No, there are others that close to you, but they've all got tails of their own, Jas, and everyone is headed north in an effort to meet up with one or more other groups who have a chance of helping take out whoever is following them. You knew when you started down that direction that I was trying to keep our people out of there. The cats are already applying a lot of pressure to the remaining border packs."

I wanted to yell or scream, but that wouldn't buy me anything. I'd known Alec as far back as I could remember; if he said that there wasn't anyone he could send to help then it was the truth.

"How did this happen?"

"I'm not honestly sure. I've got some of the best hackers in the country on my payroll right now, and contacts that will let me bring in half a dozen other guys if I'm willing to fork over the money required to keep them interested. They told me that their security on this one was bulletproof."

"Define bulletproof."

"They were supposed to have all of the satellites taken care of. They've got the actual feeds redirected to their servers and are sending back a ghost feed that is mostly all the right data, but with select parts of the map blurred out and replaced with footage from hours ago."

I wasn't any kind of hacker myself, but I'd spent enough time in conversations with Alec, Ash and others to have at least a passing understanding of some of the high-level stuff the black hats did.

"How is that even possible, Alec?"

"My guys are tracking everyone's cell phones and making sure that any attempts to locate our people returns bogus location data. There wasn't any other way to keep in contact with everyone, burner phones wouldn't work with this many people in the mix. It would be more than a full-time job for three people to keep track of who was using what number and then you'd still have a central point of failure that the Coun'hij might be able to capture."

"So your guys are using the location data from the cell towers to erase our cars from the satellite maps?"

"Yeah, only they aren't sure it's working now. I called two of the ringleaders when I started getting reports that people were being followed and they tore their methodology apart and found some possible holes."

"Someone could take the ghost feed and analyze it for those moving discrepancies."

"In theory, but that would take a huge amount of computing power and an incredible amount of access to the systems of the various intelligence agencies. There are a couple of holes in their control of the phone companies too. I won't bother trying to explain them though because it gets into the kind of stuff that nobody is sure is possible. That means that there's no way to prove whether or not we've actually been counter-hacked."

"That's bad news, Alec. I mean bad news even beyond the fact that I'm about to go up against an unknown number of Coun'hij bruisers."

"I know. Honestly I'm hoping that we were hacked, because if we weren't, then it means that the Coun'hij have recruited or found another weapon—one capable of keeping eyes on us in some other way."

I could feel a headache starting to build. "Right, and that's worse because we won't know how to counter that. Even assuming that it can be countered."

Alec's response was more certain than I could have managed in his shoes. "Everything can be countered."

"Only if you know what you're really up against. How bad do you think my odds are?"

This time I could tell he was trying to balance the truth against the need to keep me from losing hope.

"You've got a chance. Nobody has actually engaged yet, so I don't know how many people everyone else is up against, but the Coun'hij only has so many people working for them. They can't have each and every vehicle full; they just don't have that many bodies."

"That's something at least. I guess it's time to roll the dice."

It was dark by the time I stopped, and my car was running on little more than fumes by then. I found a tiny town that wasn't much more than a gas station and a couple of houses, and then pulled off behind a massive red barn that had seen better days.

It wasn't much, but it would screen me so that nobody on the road would be able to see me, and the darkness should take care of any other prying eyes.

I glanced over at Ben as the car rolled to a stop. He looked so small in the passenger seat like that. His IV bag had run dry an hour or so before and I hadn't been able to stop and hang a new one for him because of our pursuers.

It was one more reason to hate the Coun'hij, but things were past the point where a little extra injustice made much of a difference. I was fighting for survival and an extra smidgen or two of anger wasn't going to change the odds one way or the other.

His red hair had gotten longer than normal. I should have asked Rachel to help me give him a haircut before everything fell apart back at the manor. I brushed a stray strand back behind his ear so that it would be off of his face and then opened my door. There wasn't time to just wait around, not if I wanted to avoid being trapped inside of my car.

The Coun'hij SUV was approaching slowly. Whoever was driving was overconfident, which meant that I was outnumbered. I stepped well away from my car in case they decided to try to run me over, and then waited.

I could feel possible courses of action stretching out before me in an almost infinite set of paths, but I didn't let myself get too focused on any one of them. There might be an almost unimaginable number of different ways to get there, but there were only two possible outcomes to this fight and getting too attached to a specific route of attack would just increase the chances that I wouldn't be walking away from this particular fight.

If James had been driving that SUV, he would have come in fast and we would have bailed out of the car at a run as soon as it dropped down to thirty miles per hour. If Jess had been driving, she would have stopped soon enough to leave plenty of room between her and the target. Luckily the recruiting standards for the Coun'hij enforcement group had gotten lax enough that the actual driver didn't do either of those things.

As the SUV rolled to a slow stop less than twenty feet away from me I reached out to my beast and she responded with the white-hot rage that only a threat to someone we considered to be *ours* could spark.

The change from human form to hybrid took only a tiny fraction of a second, but it was still new enough for me that it hurt in ways nobody who wasn't a shape shifter could ever understand. Having your muscles tear free of your bones and then reattach themselves somewhere else is an incredibly painful experience, but that was just the start.

For a heartbeat pain was the whole sum of my existence, and then scraps of my clothes were fluttering through the air, falling in a circle around me like some pagan symbol designed to trap a beast whose only resemblance to humanity was the fact that it had two arms and two legs.

My hybrid form was more than seven feet of muscled fur and each of my fingers was tipped with a seven-inch semi-retractable claw capable of scratching steel. If there'd been any humans around to observe what I'd become they would have run away screaming, at least they would have done so if I'd held still long enough for them to get a good look at me.

I didn't hold still though, instead I bounded forward, the rocky ground blurring from the speed of my passage, and put my left fist through the driver-side window. There was a rush of power as the driver tried to transform, but even if he'd had time that wouldn't have saved him. There wasn't room for a hybrid inside of the SUV, and shifting to a wolf would have just resulted in him being trapped on his back against his seat.

My claws wrapped around his throat, severing arteries and veins in the split second before the momentum of my charge slammed my left arm into the unyielding metal of the car and spun me around so that my right hand shattered the last window on my side of the car. I missed the guy in the back seat by less than an inch.

He was still moving with human slowness, but killing the driver had taken me just long enough that he'd managed to throw himself to the other side of the vehicle. Now that the windows were shattered I could smell the occupants of the car. There had been three of them, but I'd accounted for the driver already, which meant that I still had a chance of surviving the fight as long as neither of the other two were hybrids.

The two surviving attackers bailed out of the other side of the SUV in a graceless approximation of what they should have done a few dozen feet further back. The vehicle was between us, but it only took me an instant to release the driver, who was now hanging partway out of the car despite his seatbelt, and lunge around the back of the SUV.

I'd had my hybrid form for mere hours rather than months or years, but the massive muscles and long arms already felt *right* in a way that I couldn't explain. I was fast, faster in some ways even than when I'd been a wolf, but the two guys I was chasing had both shifted to wolf form and they'd split up so that I couldn't go after one of them without giving the other one an uncontested shot at my back.

I feinted at one of them, more to keep them off balance than for any other reason, while I tried to decide what to do. I'd gotten a sense of their power when they'd both shifted. They'd felt weaker than I'd expected them to be, but that wasn't a guarantee that they were just wolves.

A whisper of sound was the only warning I got. One of the wolves had seen through my abbreviated lunge and had decided he had an opening. He threw himself at me with the kind of speed that had to be seen to be believed, but what I lacked in experience fighting as a hybrid I made up for by the fact that I'd spent thousands of hours trying to figure out different ways for wolves to take a hybrid down. It hadn't been an abstract exercise for me either, it had been a matter of life and death, and I'd put everything I'd had into becoming the best killer I could given the constraints of my frailer wolf body.

Coming at me from the side like that meant that the first wolf, the one lunging at me, only had a couple of decent targets, and I could *feel* that he was coming too high to be aiming at my legs or arms. I ducked forward, something most hybrids wouldn't have done because it meant that there was a chance that the wolf would be able to still latch on my back where I wouldn't be able to reach him. I knew it was a risk, but I stepped forward anyway because it was the only option that let me also spin to the left so that I could deal with the second wolf.

The second wolf had assumed that I'd be in a slightly different spot than where I actually ended up and it was easy to sink my claws into his side as I ripped him out of the air. I'd overbalanced slightly to get him though and had to put both hands on the ground to keep from falling over.

The action of catching myself drove my claws further into the second wolf who yelped weakly before going limp. I tried to spin back around to intercept the first wolf, talons digging deeply into the red soil beneath me, but he was just too fast. I managed to throw his aim off slightly, but he still got his teeth into my shoulder.

He couldn't reposition for a better hold and I couldn't reach him, but I could feel his teeth grinding together, searching desperately for a vein that would allow him to bleed me out. We weren't quite at a standoff, but neither of us had particularly good options open to us.

I threw myself back into his SUV, trying unsuccessfully to crush him, but he managed to reposition his body enough that most of the force of my blow missed him. I staggered away from the vehicle, my motion accompanied by a squeal of protest from the metal that was partly a result of the impact and partly from the way my claws had ripped and bent the metal.

In my normal shape I never could have hoped to bend a piece of steel like that, but my hybrid body was strong enough to do it without evidencing any overt signs of effort. It was a small advantage, but it was enough to allow me to bend a section of metal up and out so that it formed a ragged spear pointing away from the SUV.

It was another risky move, but I knew exactly how hard it was to see anything once you had the kind of death grip on someone that my opponent was currently maintaining. I threw myself into the side of the barn, snapping thick boards like they were toothpicks, but that wasn't any more successful at scraping the wolf off of me and a wave of weakness washed through me as blood loss started to make itself known.

I almost lost my balance as I came back out of the barn, which wasn't a good sign considering the lethal mess I'd just made of the SUV. Hybrids are tough, but I still wasn't sure how far I could push this body before I'd become too weak to continue fighting.

I stumbled back toward the SUV, but at the last second I realized that I didn't need to blindly throw myself backwards on the spear. Instead I simply got close to the side of the vehicle and then spun around so that the spear passed only inches from my back.

The wolf never even saw the attack coming, but even if he had there wouldn't have been much he could have done to avoid the shard of metal that impaled him through his ribs. He let go of my shoulder with a yelp of pain, but I couldn't think poorly of him for that. I'd already started pulling away from the SUV—if he hadn't let go he would have been torn in half.

Trapped as he was dangling from my improvised weapon, it was only the work of another second or two and then he was dead as well.

I shifted back down to my primary form and made my halting way back to my car. I was sorry to give up the unassailable constitution of the hybrid, but the act of shifting helped staunch most of the blood pouring out of my shoulder. Besides, I knew I was going to need hands if I was going to get myself bandaged up.

There was a first-aid kit in the trunk along with more clothes and a replacement ha'bit, the stretchy undergarment that all of the Sanctuary pack wore under their clothes. I had vague plans to steal the plates off of the SUV before lighting it on fire and heading to the gas station that was a few miles down the road, but all of that could wait for a few minutes.

The first thing I needed to do was check on Ben. He was the only reason I was out here instead of safely with the rest of the pack. If Ben wasn't okay then all of this was pointless.

Chapter 2

Geoffrey
South Side
Chicago, Illinois

Geoffrey had been wandering more or less aimlessly for days now, but there weren't very many chances to see the kind of gorgeous architecture present at the Holy Name Cathedral. Since he'd left New York he hadn't stopped in any one place for more than twenty-four hours. Sometimes he'd stretched his stay out in a particular city to a few days by moving around and spending each night in a different hotel or hostel, but even that left him feeling vaguely uneasy.

The trip he'd taken earlier that morning to see the cathedral had been a worrisome departure from the low profile he'd been maintaining, but he hadn't been able to resist.

He'd gone heavily disguised and he'd stayed for less than an hour, but it had still been a foolish thing to do. It was one more sign that on some level he was losing hope of being able to maintain his freedom.

It had only been a few days ago that he'd finally realized what had been worrying at his mind. He'd left New York, fled from Imastious, the vampire elder who'd been his master, but he'd never actually expected to make it very far.

That kind of thing could very easily become a self-fulfilling prophecy. Conviction that he would shortly be recaptured could lead to making the kinds of mistakes that led to being located. Geoffrey knew that, but he still hadn't been able to stop himself from making the unnecessary trip to the church.

He needed a new anchor, something to keep him from slowly giving into the despair waiting in the wings, the despair that needed only a couple of heartbeats to rise up and strike him without any warning.

Geoffrey's memory only extended back over a period of time measured in weeks rather than months. He knew a lot of facts, he knew how to do things, but there wasn't any context for much of what he knew. The popular culture references that the kids in the hostels threw back and forth at each other might as well have been code for all the meaning Geoffrey got from eavesdropping.

The only non-mundane conversations that had made any sense to Geoffrey had been the discussions on morality. It had been astonishing to him how many of them said that they were 'spiritual' while at the same time decrying concepts like good and evil.

Geoffrey spent the odd minute or two wondering how kids like that were going to survive in a world where evil was so prevalent and concentrated that it had created people like Imastious. Geoffrey still woke up sometimes in the middle of the night from nightmares where Imastious was torturing him, nightmares where Geoffrey was being pushed to do terrible things.

It was the kind of thing that should have made him bitter. He was pretty sure that it would only be a matter of days, or perhaps a couple of weeks, before Imastious caught up with him, but he found that he wasn't as jealous of the kids around him as he'd expected to be.

In many ways Geoffrey had earned his place in hell. All that was left was to hope that the teenagers who'd surrounded him like an ever-changing sea of faces ever since he'd left New York would be able to find their moral absolutes in time to save them from a fate like his.

The despair wasn't his only concern though. The hunger had been steadily growing for the last few days. It was dangerous for a vampire to go too long without feeding, dangerous both for the vampire and for any humans in the vampire's vicinity.

Geoffrey hadn't wanted to believe Venice, the gorgeous blonde vampire who'd taught him nearly everything he knew about living in the shadows, when she'd told him that blood starvation could cause him to lose control and kill people indiscriminately, but he hadn't been able to deny the truth of her words after his one and only experience with the hallucinations that had led to the death of an anonymous mugger weeks ago.

Geoffrey hadn't pushed the limits of his endurance very often like this since then, so he didn't know exactly how much longer he had before he'd lose control, but he suspected that his time was almost done. Fortunately he had a...target...in mind.

He'd noticed the couple when he'd first arrived at the hostel earlier that evening. The young man was obviously deep in the throes of an oxycontin addiction, but not so far gone as to make his girlfriend abandon him.

A few minutes earlier Geoffrey had watched the drama play out in one of the public areas of the hostel as the boy had promised he didn't have any drugs and then had snuck off to get high as soon as the girl had left to use the bathroom.

Geoffrey intercepted the girl before she made it far enough down the hall to be able to see her boyfriend who'd just stumbled back in from the kitchen area.

"Do you really care about that guy you are with?"

A barrage of emotions flashed across the girl's face so quickly that anyone else wouldn't have been able to categorize them all, but Geoffrey had an advantage that others lacked. Tendrils of thought had started reaching out to the girl as soon as she'd left the bathroom.

She reached up to slide a lock of black hair back behind her right ear and then her face settled into an impassive mask. The expression was the hard-won trophy of the kind of life no parent would want for their child, but her emotions all but leaped out of her mind and threw themselves at Geoffrey. She didn't just love the guy she was with in the casual, here-today-and-gone-tomorrow manner of most of those he'd run into lately, she loved him with a fierceness that caused Geoffrey's breath to catch.

By almost any rational measure it wasn't healthy to be that attached to another person, but there was a purity and strength to the emotion that had a beauty all of its own. The emotion was at the forefront for only a split second before other feelings took center-stage.

"Yeah, I guess I do. I must to put up with everything he puts me through."

The words were a brave front, but Geoffrey could feel the longing she wouldn't vocalize. She saw goodness in her boyfriend that she'd never found in anyone else, not in so much abundance, and she'd made it her personal mission to try to drag him back from the edge of ruin, even if he came kicking and screaming.

"What would you say if I told you I could help?"

"I'd ask you what your angle was. Nobody does something without having something in it for them."

"That's a pretty jaded worldview..."

She didn't want to tell Geoffrey her name, but he sent a tiny pulse of power through one of the tendrils he'd inserted into her mind. It wasn't enough to compel her to do anything, but it did soften the hard core of resistance that he sensed inside of her.

"Aly. My name is Aly."

"Okay, Aly, that's a pretty jaded world view, but I'm not going to try and dispute the fact that I'm hoping for a trade of sorts. Is your boyfriend really worth saving?"

"Keith, his name is Keith and he's all I have left in the whole world. He's tried not to use. He made it for an entire month a little while ago. We moved out of our old neighborhood, but eventually his dealer tracked him down."

She was fighting the hope he could feel building inside of her, but her strength was too brittle to successfully quash all of what she was feeling.

"I won't be able to help him if he doesn't really want to change, but if he does then I can make it so that he won't ever go back to the drugs again."

Her laugh had an edge of hysteria to it. "You must not be very good at conning people. Don't you know that you're supposed to promise to fix him no matter what?"

Geoffrey gave her a smile that he was pretty sure was tinged with more sadness than he meant it to be. "I could promise that, but it wouldn't be the truth. I'm only offering to do what I'm really capable of delivering on."

"Right, payments in advance, no refunds given."

Her melting determination, her softening core, had given Geoffrey the access he needed to skim off some of the surface thoughts he otherwise would have been unable to access while still carrying on a conversation.

"Your favorite color is yellow, but you haven't worn it since you first caught Keith using. You had a canary named Sunshine when you were little, and I remind you of...your butler."

Aly opened her mouth, doubtlessly to ask him how he knew all of that, but Geoffrey didn't give her a chance to interrupt him.

"I'm going to make you say springtime now. You're going to try to stop yourself, but you won't be able to."

Even as he said it, Geoffrey poured some more of his precious reserves into a surge of power along the tendril that he'd lodged into her speech center.

"So what, you're some kind of *springtime* hypno..."

Under other circumstances her expression would have made Geoffrey laugh. She looked like someone who wanted with all her heart to believe. The hope that she'd been doing her best to keep in check had just surged through her like the crescendo of a world-class orchestra.

"No *springtime* way...how are you doing that? I meant to swear, but the wrong word keeps coming out. I can feel it on the edge of my mind. Every time I go to say...well, you know, springtime pops out instead."

"What I do is better than hypnosis, but it still has limits. Do you believe me now?"

She nodded, not like someone who was unable to speak, but like someone who was worried that speech would shatter the illusion and wake her from a dream.

"What do you want? What is your price? We...we don't have any money."

"What would having Keith back be worth to you? What would you be willing to give up in order to have things be like they used to?"

"Anything."

Geoffrey's emotions surged up in a tidal wave that nearly cracked his composure. He was so adept at interpreting other people's emotions, but sometimes it was all but impossible to properly categorize his own.

Relief was certainly a huge component, but it was more than just that. He'd sworn never to feed from someone unwillingly again, but a part of him knew that what he was doing wasn't any better than abducting Aly in the dead of night and tearing the side of her throat open. She was so obsessed with Keith that she wasn't fully capable of making the decision Geoffrey was offering her. Despite all of his efforts, Geoffrey wasn't sure that he was all that much better than Imastious.

"Are you sure? Anything?"

Another nod and this time Geoffrey couldn't have missed the certainty washing through her mind. She was imagining the worst possible things she could think of and yet she was still willing to pay that price if it was what Geoffrey demanded.

"I can't promise to fix him, it all depends on whether or not he really wants help. Are you still willing to pay anything for just the *chance* that he'll come back to you?"

"Not death, and I don't want to be a cripple. If there is a chance that this won't work then I'll need to be around to take care of him. Beyond that whatever you want is yours."

Geoffrey had been planning on asking her if she was the kind of person who took her promises seriously, but there wasn't any need. He could feel her commitment surging through the tendrils connecting their minds. She'd already risked everything she was or could become on a promise to Keith, this was just an extension of that original promise.

"We'll need privacy; do the two of you have a room?"

Aly nodded and went as though to pick Keith up. Geoffrey slung Keith's other arm over his shoulder and a couple of minutes later the pair had safely deposited Keith on the bed in a small white-walled bedroom one floor down from where Geoffrey would be sleeping.

"I'm going to close my eyes for a few minutes, it's important that you don't disturb me while I'm working."

Aly nodded. "I understand."

Geoffrey took a deep breath and then closed his eyes and inserted a mental probe into the front of Keith's head. Hours of practice paid off as Geoffrey strengthened the probe, forcing it to a thickness that made it seem as though his mind broke free of his body and traveled down the probe and into Keith's mind.

Geoffrey hadn't been sure what to expect from deep contact with the mind of this particular kind of addict. He'd expected to find a torrent of destructive energy, all directed inward, he hadn't expected to find that the torrent had been frozen into motionless suspension by the drugs coursing through Keith's system.

Swimming downward through the surface levels of Keith's mind was a new experience as well. His thoughts didn't actively resist Geoffrey's efforts to go deeper, but there was a stickiness to them that left Geoffrey feeling like he was being coated with an unpleasant residue.

Geoffrey's reserves of strength weren't what they should have been. He'd known that before setting out, but he hadn't realized just how depleted he was from the combination of being on the run and the blood starvation. The realization triggered a wave of almost panic, but Geoffrey was disciplined enough to keep the emotion from leaking into Keith's psyche and he was experienced enough to know that once he was this deep there was no course open to him but continuing to dive deeper.

He would either have the strength to make it to the seat of Keith's reason, the metaphorical eye of the storm, or he wouldn't, but turning back now would just guarantee his destruction.

Just as Geoffrey became convinced that he'd misjudged, that he wouldn't have sufficient strength to arrive at his destination, he brushed up against something hard, something unyielding, the only unyielding thing he'd yet found in the sticky sea surrounding him.

Matching his essence to the barrier was more difficult than usual. The same stickiness he'd noticed in Keith's thoughts was also present in the barrier, but eventually Geoffrey was able to pass through the barrier and into the calm center of Keith's mind.

As always, Geoffrey was astonished at the way the thoughts and beliefs in the center of Keith's mind formed a coherent, beautiful latticework of glowing crystal. Aly had been right, there was an incredible amount of goodness in what presented itself to Geoffrey. Keith was a person who had great creative capacity, but there was a black fissure running through one side of the arrangement of light and glass.

The beliefs and habits located here in the center of Keith's being had only minimal ties to the memories outside of the room, but Geoffrey still got vague impressions of a soul-crushing loss that had happened at some point in Keith's past. There was just enough to that thread for Geoffrey to formulate a plan for fixing the flaw he was examining.

As always, creating constructs inside of this place was a heady but difficult experience. The mental commands and impulses Geoffrey was leaving would have a staying power exponentially longer than anything he could do on the surface of Keith's mind, but it was hard to work simultaneously with thoughts and emotions all the while seeing the fruits of his labor visualize as part of the living forest of crystal before him.

Even working here in the near-absolute calm that made what he was doing possible, Geoffrey still knew that he wouldn't be able to fix everything that needed to be fixed before he ran out of strength. He arrived at a compromise as he was working, a compromise that *felt* right even though he had no way of being sure that it would work.

Creating an aversion to the drugs that were ruining Keith's life was easy. That construct was equal parts aversion to poking himself with needles and a healthy fear of the long-term effects of what the drugs were doing to his body.

If Geoffrey had been able to stop there he would have returned to his own body still with a large portion of his energy reserves intact. Unfortunately that was nothing more than a short-term fix. Unless Geoffrey could correct the underlying problems Keith would just find a different way to self-destruct.

Geoffrey laid out a series of patches designed to hold the damaged part of Keith's mind together. An acceptance that loss was part of life, that without the bad parts of life the good parts wouldn't be quite as good, was one glowing shard that connected the two halves of Keith's psyche and then contracted to pull the edges back together.

An ability to forgive himself, a deeper understanding of what his actions were doing to those around him, especially Aly, a desire to interact with others, the constructs sprang into existence one after another and stitched themselves into the fabric of Keith's beliefs like life-saving sutures.

Looking at the clean vista around him, it would have been easy for Geoffrey to believe that he'd solved the problem, but he knew it was still there, a fissure of weakness running underneath the patches that was just waiting to break back open.

Geoffrey marshaled what was left of his strength and sent a single tiny tendril of thought back out into the sludge of Keith's thoughts. He'd never tried this particular experiment before, but it seemed to be working. Geoffrey let his probe skitter from thought to thought, memory to memory, until he finally found what he thought was the key.

Keith had lost someone important, but it wasn't just anyone, it had been someone very similar to Aly. The similarities had been a blessing at the start of his relationship with Aly, but as time had gone on they'd become a curse. Their relationship had progressed to the point where Keith should have told her about the other girl, the girl Aly reminded him of, but he hadn't been able to bring himself to tell her precisely because of how much she reminded him of what he'd lost.

Geoffrey placed one more construct inside of Keith's mind. He created a certainty inside of

Keith that he could talk to Aly about anything. Once again there wasn't any guarantee when Geoffrey started the construct that it was what was required, but when he saw the way that it settled down over the very start of the damage, the way that it seemed to join core supporting threads of Keith's personality together, the fact that it seemed to have tiny tendrils already growing further into the damaged area, Geoffrey knew it would do what he wanted it to do.

Keith wasn't cured any more than a single session of therapy would have cured him, but the foundation had been built. If Keith talked to Aly, and if he could avoid any serious shocks to his life for a few months, then things should heal completely. Even after he healed he'd still be just as vulnerable to loss and damage as anyone else, but at least he'd have a chance at happiness.

Geoffrey created another construct, a fragile one that started fraying away as soon as he set it down, and then launched himself out of the protective bubble and into the full fury of Keith's conscious mind. The final construct did its job, creating a fissure of calm that ran all of the way out to the furthermost edge of Keith's mind.

Geoffrey expertly followed that fissure, racing along it at the mental equivalent of a sprint, but even so he barely made it all of the way free before the thoughts closed back together. Geoffrey came back to himself with a gasping breath that was unlike anything he'd ever before experienced.

"Are you okay?"

It took Geoffrey a few seconds to get his breathing under control enough to respond. "Yes, I think so."

Aly looked at him doubtfully. "Are you sure? I think you stopped breathing for a minute there."

Geoffrey had known that his strength was running out, but he hadn't realized that he'd pushed things that close to the edge of disaster. Even now he could feel that his mental strength was exhausted, that it was pulling against the reserves of physical strength that were keeping his heart beating and his lungs working.

"Did you save him?"

"I think so. I've done all I can, right now at least. Are you ready to make your payment?"

Aly was obviously scared, but she didn't let that stop her from nodding, and if the nod was the tiny movement a small animal might make when in the sights of a large predator, well, she could hardly be blamed.

"It's important that this remain a secret, Aly. That's part of the price I need from you."

"I'll never tell anyone."

Geoffrey felt the hallucinations dancing just outside the edge of his field of vision. He was running out of time. He reached over and gently took her by the wrist.

"I'm not human. I need to feed on your blood, but I promise not to take so much that you'll die."

Geoffrey didn't have any tendrils out probing her mind, but her emotions were so powerful that they seemed to pour into his mind of their own accord. She was relieved that he wasn't going to demand what she'd feared he wanted, but she was also terrified. There was no doubt inside of her but that he'd just told her the truth.

For the briefest of seconds she resisted the gentle pull of his hand, but it only took one look at Keith, who was already resting more peacefully than he'd been when they'd brought him into the room, for her to remember her promise.

"You really did everything you could for him?"

Geoffrey's nod seemed to reassure her, but she still needed something else.

"Is there anything else you can do to help? Not now, but later?"

"It's possible, but I can't stay here and it will take a few days for me to recover enough to do that again."

Aly thrust her wrist at him, suddenly eager for him to proceed.

"Take it, however much you need. I'll give you my cellphone number. You can call me whenever you're ready and we'll meet you anywhere in the country."

Geoffrey nodded hesitantly, not sure why he was agreeing to tangle his life up further with theirs, but unable to deny her obvious need, not when it was paired with such a willingness to pay whatever price was required.

Positioning his mouth carefully to avoid damaging any tendons or nerves, Geoffrey bit down on the pale skin of her arm and had to fight off a tremor of relief at the first taste of her blood. Geoffrey had fed dozens of times that he remembered and hundreds, maybe even thousands of times in the section of his life that had been stolen from him by his amnesia, but he couldn't remember any other feeding like this.

Her blood wasn't just sweet, it tingled with power and energy. Geoffrey could practically feel his reserves of energy filling back up in time with the slow pulse of her heart.

Ever since he'd left New York, Geoffrey had refused to give into the darker aspects of his nature. He hadn't killed anyone, but more importantly, he hadn't taken from anyone without giving something back in return.

Back in New York he'd traded money for blood, albeit with unwitting victims who had no idea what they were agreeing to. He no longer had any method of replenishing his funds, not with the way he was forced to constantly move from place to place, but he'd still found ways to provide value in return for what he took from his victims.

Many of the homeless people he'd encountered had been suffering from different kinds of psychosis and he'd cured them, or at least lessened their symptoms, before drinking from them. This however was different. Geoffrey always felt an odd sense of connection to those he was feeding from when doing so wasn't just a kind of predation, but this was something more than that.

Aly seemed to hum with energy and he established a link to her mind without even meaning to. Geoffrey had never experienced both sides of a feeding before, but that was what he was feeling in that moment.

He could feel her warm blood trickling down his throat, feel the strength pouring into his limbs and mind, feel the hallucinations and the blood hunger being chased back to a distant corner of his being, but at the same time he could feel the warmth of his mouth on her wrist. He could feel a tingle that masked the pain of his bite, feel the heat spreading up her arm and a sense of euphoria that was only partially dulled by the weakness slowly stealing through her body.

Always before, even with Melody, it had been hard to tear himself away from a blood donor. He'd loved Melody. He'd tried to tell himself at the time that it was some kind of obsession, that she would be better off without him, but even if that had all been true it hadn't changed the fact that he'd loved her. Even when he'd fed from her he hadn't been able to release her this easily.

Geoffrey pulled his mouth away from Aly's arm and then pulled a square of gauze from his pocket and taped it to her arm to stop the bleeding.

"Are you okay?"

She nodded wordlessly, almost seeming as though she were in shock. After nearly a minute she managed to speak again.

"Is it always like that?"

"No, that was a first for me."

"I could feel you inside of my mind. I could see some of what you did to try and help Keith. I wanted to believe so badly, but I couldn't quite bring myself to. Now I know though, I know that you are everything you said you were, that you did everything you said you'd do."

"If you didn't really believe me, then why did you agree to let me feed on you?"

Geoffrey already knew the answer, at least most of it, but the question tumbled out of his mouth regardless, not seeming to care that it was unasked for.

"I did it because there isn't anything I wouldn't give for Keith. I know that's probably not healthy, I know that I'm giving too much of myself to him, for him, but I can't help myself. It's just how I am."

"Do you wish things were different?"

"Are you asking me if I want you to fix me?"

"I'm not sure. I guess maybe that is what I'm asking. Do you wish things were different?"

Aly shook her head as she ripped a sheet of paper off of the tablet on the desk next to the bed and wrote a number on it.

"I don't want to be different. Maybe if you told me that there wasn't anything that could be done to save Keith then I'd want to change, but things were so incredibly perfect for the two of us back when we first met. Back before he started using."

Geoffrey accepted the folded sheet of paper. "It's possible that he won't need any more help than what I've already given him. If you can get him to talk to you about who he lost then he might be able to recover. No matter what happens he won't be using for at least a little while, but with a little luck he'll recover enough that he won't stumble into some other kind of self-destructive behavior."

"I know; I really did see part of what you did to him. I...well, I guess I'm volunteering. If he needs more help then I want you to come help him, but even if he doesn't, I want to do my part."

"Your part for what?"

"My part to keep you alive so you can help other people. Most vampires aren't like you, are they?"

Something very much like terror started to grow inside of Geoffrey. It had happened once before with Melody. She'd been able to see inside of his mind at the same time that he'd been inside of hers. Having someone else inside of his mind didn't have to be a terrifying evil, but the fear operated as a reflexive thing that engaged and disengaged at a level of consciousness far below anything he had control over.

Imastious had scarred him too badly for things to be any other way. Maybe he'd get past that at some point, but it wasn't going to happen anytime soon.

"Did you see that too?"

Aly gave him a sad smile and the expression implied that his fears weren't unfounded. "No, not really. It was more along the lines of vague impressions. I could tell that you came from somewhere terrible though. Even if I hadn't seen that I'd still know that most vampires weren't like you. The world is too bad a place for things to be any other way. If there were hundreds of people like you running around helping people like Keith and me then the world wouldn't be as bad as it is."

Not trusting himself to speak, Geoffrey simply nodded and then left the room. He was almost back to his room before they struck. Exhaustion had made him grow careless or he would have had enough probes out to feel them coming.

Geoffrey rounded a corner in the dingy hallway leading to his room and was suddenly confronted by a slender, almost skeletal redheaded woman. Even before Geoffrey's reflexive probes skittered off of the blank wall of someone who was actively trying to make sure that their thoughts couldn't be read, he was backing away. It was an unplanned movement, triggered by something that knew she was wrong on levels that he couldn't consciously identify.

It would have been foolish to turn his back on her, but Geoffrey didn't need to turn around in order to make sure that he'd be able to retreat. He burned up some of the strength Aly had lent him as he sent out a network of fine thought-tendrils behind and to either side of him.

He brushed up against two more shielded minds, and then something struck him from behind with enough force to knock him to the ground.

Geoffrey didn't realize that the blow had been to his head until he noticed that he was surrounded by an inexplicable blackness. The voices he was hearing seemed to be coming from a long ways away.

"You're sure that's him?"

"Yeah, he's a little worn around the edges, but he matches the picture that Imastious sent over."

"Good, let's get out of here then."

A third voice chimed in with what sounded like a hint of mocking laughter dancing between the spaces in his words.

"Still scared that some big monster is going to tear your throat out?"

"Laugh all you want, ever since we arrived here I've felt like someone is watching us. Chicago is the only major city where Imastious doesn't have at least some kind of contact with the local power structure."

The woman sounded like she'd heard the same argument a dozen times already and was bored with it.

"It's fine. Either Imastious is telling us the truth and there isn't any kind of significant concentration of vampires here, or he's lying and we could run into some kind of hunter-killer squad at any moment. We're going to be careful either way, so it's not like it matters."

The scared guy muttered something under his breath before responding loud enough for the other two to hear. "Right, but the real question is what could cause this entire city to be vampire-free like that. We now know that there is such a thing as werewolves; who knows what else is out there hunting us."

As the darkness reached up to fully claim Geoffrey, the despair that had been threatening to consume him for days finally enveloped him. He was Imastious' prisoner once again.

Chapter 3

Jasmin Bianchi
McCleary Gas and Grub
Great Bend, Kansas

I ended up in Kansas less out of some kind of grand plan and more because it was hard to get much more centrally located. That and because I needed to keep moving. I'd sent Alec a text once I made it back to the car and got myself bandaged up. There hadn't been a response, not that I'd particularly expected one. If I'd been further north he probably would have tried to get me to go up and help out one of the other groups that were being tailed, but I wasn't so he didn't.

At the time I'd been relieved that he wasn't trying to sidetrack me into doing him a favor, but now I wasn't so sure. I was out here driving around with no backup, just Ben and I, on nothing more than faith in Rachel and an unhealthy measure of rapidly-diminishing hope.

Right before she'd disappeared she'd found me and told me that I needed to find someone named Geoffrey. Rachel had been acting weird lately, and she'd been at her weirdest that night, but it had been a convincing performance, convincing enough at least to get me out here.

I looked over at Ben and frowned at what I saw. His health had been steadily declining for weeks, ever since I'd rescued him from the vampires who had been holding him captive. Alec had paid for some of the best doctors in the state to take a look at him, but nobody had been able to explain his coma.

That was why Rachel had only needed to provide me with the barest glimmer of hope to convince me this idiocy was actually a good idea. When there aren't any other options, it's amazing what a person will do to try and save someone they love.

Ben had actually been doing pretty well right before we'd left. It had gone against everything I knew about his condition, but it had been an undeniable fact. He'd spent nearly two hours disconnected from the machinery responsible for monitoring his condition, two hours without an IV drip, two hours of smoke and terror where none of us had been sure we'd survive. That should have caused his condition to deteriorate sharply, but instead he'd seemed almost to the point of waking back up on his own.

He'd started swallowing on his own. I'd actually been able to feed him some broth in the RV right before I'd said goodbye to Alec and the others. I'd kept him on an IV drip since then, initially more just to be on the safe side than for any other reason, but over the last couple of days he'd started getting worse again.

Now I kept him on an IV because there wasn't any other way to ensure that he got enough calories in to keep him from starving to death.

Despite dozens of hours spent poring over every scrap of medical information I'd been able to find on anything that might be related to Ben's condition, I still didn't know enough to save him. I could run an IV, but I couldn't do anything to fix his breathing, which was steadily getting worse.

He was still on the course of antibiotics that he'd been prescribed just before everything had fallen apart back at the estate, so I knew the cause wasn't bacterial. Honestly it probably didn't matter what the cause was. Every time we got one symptom under control something else flared up.

It was like his whole system was shutting down and there didn't seem to be anything that anyone could do to save him. Unless you believed Rachel, in which case somebody named Geoffrey had the key to a complete recovery.

I was driving, so I'd only looked over at Ben for a second, but it had been enough to confirm my suspicion that his IV bag was nearly empty. It was actually not terrible timing, we were only a few miles away from an exit, and the car was down below half a tank, so I figured I should just kill two birds with one stone.

Driving fast is practically part of the job description for your average shape shifter. Even in human form I had the kind of reaction time that any professional racer would kill for. Despite Ash's statement that it was a dangerous hole in my skillset, I'd never put in the time required to develop the kind of driving reflexes that he and Alec had. Even without their vaunted skills, I could usually do twenty or thirty over the speed limit without putting myself or anyone else on the road in any danger.

With the radar detector blinking its reassurance at me that there weren't any cops in the area, there wasn't any reason for me not to push the Mercedes up to triple digits, but I'd stopped driving so fast sometime the day before. I didn't have an ultimate destination in mind, so it didn't matter whether I did a hundred and twenty or if I did thirty. Either way I was still headed nowhere.

I pulled off at a Chevron and reached into the backpack on the floor behind Ben for another IV bag. I was starting to run low. It was too late to text Alec and ask him to have someone arrange for me to get some more, but I made a mental note to do so first thing in the morning.

Actually, I wasn't even sure if what I had in the bag was a controlled substance of some kind or another. Some things you had to be an honest-to-goodness doctor to get, while other things could be purchased from a medical supply company by anyone. For as long as I could remember, first Donovan and then Alec had made such considerations less than nothing. If we needed something, regardless of the legalities involved, we had it.

It was incredible what money and influence could do for you, but in the end it could only do so much. It could help protect the ones you cared about, but some forces couldn't be bought off with hundred-dollar bills, and once someone was gone there wasn't any power wielded by Alec or anyone else that could bring them back.

I managed to get the new bag hung without disturbing Ben. One of the nurses Alec had brought in to give Dominic and me some time off hadn't been able to tell the difference. To her a person in a coma was for all intents and purposes dead to the world. Maybe that was how it worked for other people, but not for Ben. I could tell when he was comfortable and when he wasn't.

Sometimes it was nothing more than the barest shadow of a crease on his forehead, sometimes it was a subtle change in his breathing, other times it was a weak almost-movement of an arm or leg. It was hard to catch sometimes, but it was possible for anyone who cared enough to learn.

Needless to say that particular nurse hadn't lasted long.

Satisfied that the new bag was properly secured to the handle above Ben's head, I wadded the old bag up so I could throw it away while I was waiting for the tank to fill. I didn't even get my car door open before my phone rang.

It wasn't a number I recognized, but that didn't mean much these days. Even with Alec's hackers running interference for us there were times when you had to ditch a sim card and replace it with a burner card so that you could throw someone off of your trail.

"Who is this?"

I tried to keep the exhaustion and borderline hostility out of my voice. I hadn't slept since the attack down in New Mexico. It was dangerous and I was going to have to stop and rest soon, but I hadn't been able to shake the feeling that I had a target painted on my back.

Apparently I did a worse job disguising my state than I thought because the voice that responded to me sounded like its owner was only a heartbeat away from breaking into hysterical laughter.

"You really should have taken a nap earlier, Jasmin."

"Rachel! Where have you been and why haven't you called before now to tell me what's going on?"

"I've been going where I was needed, Jasmin. I thought you, of all people, would understand that."

"Ben needs you. Hell, I need you."

"Yes, I'm afraid you're right about that, but you're not ready yet."

I fought down a wave of anger, but it was hard. My beast spent more time in the driver's seat than I would have admitted to any of my friends. It was like I was thirteen again all over and trying to adjust to having an alien presence inside of my head, a violent presence that I wasn't completely sure I could control.

Things had been bad enough after Chicago, when Alec had killed Agony. There wasn't any reason that my beast should have gotten more difficult to control at that particular point, but she had. I'd struggled with my temper almost as soon as we flew back home, but it had gotten twenty times worse since I'd manifested my hybrid form.

I liked Rachel, most of the time at least, and once upon a time my beast had taken a pretty laid-back view of her too. Right now my beast was pissed. She didn't like anyone telling her what she was or wasn't ready to deal with, but it was even worse coming from someone my beast viewed as being weaker than us.

I knew that there was more to being strong than just who could hit the hardest, but my beast didn't think like that. I told myself for the thousandth time that I controlled us, not her. If I hadn't learned anything else from my dad, I'd learned that you had to maintain control.

He'd been the perfect example of what happened when you let the beast run unchecked. Donovan said that my father hadn't ever really recovered from what happened when Agony tore through the pack the first time.

The way that Donovan said it always made me feel like he was trying to cut my dad slack, like he was trying to make excuses for him. The truth was I knew there wasn't any kind of justification for what my dad had become.

He'd lost a lot when the pack was shattered. My mother, his wife, had been killed by some anonymous Coun'hij enforcer that night. He'd lost nearly everything he cared about when she bled out on the rocks, but so had everyone else. Some people had lost even more. James' mom had lost a spouse, Andrew had lost his wife and been crippled to the point where he was confined to a wheelchair. Neither of them had turned into a child-abusing monster.

I knew I had my own set of problems, but I wasn't my father and I forced my beast back into the darkest corner of my mind where she would have a harder time influencing my thoughts and feelings. From the outside all I did was take a couple of deep breaths, but that didn't do justice to the sheer amount of effort involved. It was like dragging an elephant through a field with nothing more than my fingernails and sheer willpower to see the job done.

There wasn't any way that Rachel could have known what I was doing. Once I spoke she'd be able to hear the difference in my voice, but she didn't wait for that before speaking herself.

"Good, Jasmin. You're going to need more of that control if you're going to be able to save Ben."

"I thought you said I needed my rage."

"I did, and you do, but you're past that now. Your rage helped you get where you are today, but now it's just going to get in the way unless you manage to control it."

"Fine, I'll work on my temper. Now *please* just tell me where I can find this Geoffrey guy."

"I have an address for you, Jasmin, but you're not going to like what happens next."

"Yeah, I know. You've said that already. Just give me the address. If Geoffrey can save Ben then it doesn't matter what happens to me."

Relief made my limbs weak as Rachel finally complied and rattled off an address. It was some tiny city in Nebraska that I'd never heard of before, which meant that my instinct to come here had paid off. I wasn't very far from the help that Ben needed.

"Thanks, Rach. I'll fill the car back up and then I'll head straight there."

"No! Don't wait to fill up the car. Go now, put the address into the GPS on your phone and drive as fast as you can."

"That's stupid, Rach. I'm below half a tank already. Five minutes isn't going to make a difference."

"That's where you're wrong. Five minutes will make all of the difference in the world. Do it my way or you're going to be sorry. You're going to need more help from me than just this address before all is said and done."

"What does that mean?"

"Geoffrey isn't just sitting there waiting to talk to you, he's a captive and you're going to need my guidance to get him out."

"How do you know all of this, Rach?"

"It's hard to explain, I just know it. Now go. Seconds matter right now."

I took off like a bat out of hell. I wasn't just driving aimlessly like I had been before. I had a destination and I positively shattered the speed limit. It was especially dangerous to drive this fast in the dark. Any set of headlights, no matter how good, couldn't let you see as far ahead as you could during the day. At slower speeds that was less of an issue because it took you longer to cover the ground that you could see. At a hundred and twenty it was a very real problem. I had my brights on, and even in this form my vision was quite a bit better than a human's, but it was still taking a risk.

I told myself that Rachel would have known if I was headed towards an accident, and I just poured on more speed. I'd thought that I had my anger under control, but as the miles rolled away underneath my tires I felt it growing again. Rachel had no right to be toying with me. It was ridiculous to expect me to go into everything blind like this.

By the time an hour had passed, my rage had grown to the point where it was all I could do to stop from ripping the steering wheel free from the dashboard. I wasn't actually sure that I was strong enough to do that now, but it had already creaked alarmingly a couple of times over the last few minutes, so I was doing my absolute best to stop from stressing it even more.

The computer on the dash started warning me that the tank was nearly empty when we were still more than forty miles away from the address Rachel had given me. The computer was predicting that my tank would be bone dry within the next twenty miles. I couldn't change the laws of physics, there was no way for me to make it there without stopping for gas, but the anger bubbling just beneath the surface had a lot to do with my choice to stop when I did.

I pulled off at a tiny gas station in the middle of nowhere and did a double take when I realized that there wasn't a credit card reader at the pump. I'd switched over to prepaid credit cards, the closest thing there was to the equivalent of a burner phone, when it became important to remain anonymous, but it looked like I was going to have to dip into the store of cash Alec had given me when I'd left.

I pushed the button that put me in touch with the attendant in the tiny store a few dozen feet away, and then waited for a couple of seconds.

"Yeah, what can I do for you?"

"I need some gas."

"How much? We've got a cash-first policy for anything over forty bucks."

"Forty should be fine."

I was pretty sure that it would take more than that to fill the car up completely, but I didn't want to make two trips into the store, one to pay and another to pick up any change. The clerk made a noncommittal kind of grunt, but a few seconds later the pump lit up and asked me to select a fuel grade.

While I was waiting for the tank to fill up I looked at Ben through the window. He looked cold, and I made a mental note to try and remember to turn the thermostat up. Ever since I'd gained my hybrid form I'd been running hotter than normal, but Ben didn't have the same kind of metaphysical space heater.

The pump shut off promptly at forty dollars' worth of gas. I racked the nozzle and then started towards the store at a quick jog, locking the doors to the Mercedes with my key fob.

The clerk had a TV on. It looked like one of those extreme reality shows, but it must have been pretty enthralling because he barely looked up as I handed him two twenties. As I turned and walked out of the store I realized that three guys had appeared at the edge of the area lit by the large overhead lights that surrounded the pumps.

Most girls would have been nervous at the sight of three rough-looking guys this late at night, but I wasn't most girls. Even in this form I was more than able to defend myself from guys much stronger and dangerous than these guys looked to be. My biggest worry was that they'd slow me down and put me even further behind Rachel's schedule. At least that was all I was worried about until I saw the way that the lights were flickering.

Flickering lights weren't a sign of trouble in and of themselves, but the lights inside of the store hadn't flickered at the same time as the outside lights. There was only one thing that could cause those kinds of selective power problems. Werewolves.

If there'd been any doubt left in my mind of what I was up against, it would have vanished when I saw the expression on the closest guy's face. There was a kind of savage craziness to it that I'd heard described more than once by others who'd run into werewolves before the animals had shifted out of their human forms.

My options were so few as to practically be non-existent. They were between me and the car, which meant that I couldn't get to Ben without going through them. I couldn't fight them. One werewolf would outclass me all by itself, three would mow me down so quickly I wouldn't even know what hit me.

I could run—in wolf form I should be faster than them—but if I did that there was still a risk that one of them would stay and hurt Ben. If I was going to run then I needed to make sure that they would all follow me.

I slipped my key fob and money clip into one of the two tiny pockets in my ha'bit and then confirmed that my phone was safely tucked away in the other pocket before taking a couple of steps towards them, angling away from the shop so that I'd be out of the clerk's field of vision if he happened to look up from his show.

Werewolves would kill a human if there wasn't a better target around, but they would almost always bypass humans if there was a vampire or a shape shifter in the area. Nobody was quite sure how werewolves were able to pick shape shifters out of a crowd of humans, but their ability to do so was uncanny.

Their ability to find vampires was less mysterious. They probably did it the same way we did—scent tracking the characteristic old-blood smell that vampires all seemed to have coming out of their pores. The smell was strong enough that we shape shifters never had any problem identifying a vampire, and it only made sense that werewolves had similarly sensitive noses.

Whatever mechanism they used kicked into high gear as I took yet another step towards them. All three werewolves looked at me simultaneously with an expression that told me they knew exactly what I was.

They all sprang towards me at the same time, but I'd been waiting for that to happen and I shifted and tore off across the fields in a blaze of speed that only my wolf form could muster. I couldn't risk looking back at them, not when I was in full flight, but didn't need to. I could hear that all three of them were chasing me.

I could hear them, breathing hard, their footsteps getting heavier as they shifted into the huge, hybrid-like forms that made them so deadly. I was faster than they were, but not by much. Werewolves were the single deadliest predator in existence, and it was more than just their phenomenal size and strength that allowed them to occupy the apex spot. They had an energy and endurance that was unnatural, even in comparison to a hybrid.

The only way for shape shifters to defeat werewolves was to fight them on our terms. If we outnumbered them and could bring the fight to a quick conclusion then we could bring them down, but everything about this encounter was stacked against me. I was the one outnumbered and my only hope of survival was to stretch the run out long enough to put a significant distance between us.

Their supernatural endurance was going to make that an extremely tough challenge. It had been done before, if not by me, but there was only a very tiny window in which it could work. I was going to have to run in a long arc, far enough to create the kind of lead I needed, but not so long as to let exhaustion set in and rob me of the precious inches and feet I was currently building into the cushion that was my only chance.

I'd been running for less than a minute before I realized that the ground was working against me. We were traversing fallow fields and the partially frozen dirt was soft enough that it robbed my feet of some of the energy of each lunge. If the werewolves had been likewise slowed then it would have been a non-issue, but their talons seemed to be digging deep enough into the ground that they were catching ahold of something harder and the earth wasn't robbing their movements of energy in the same fashion.

My beast knew we were in trouble. I'd half expected her to be urging me on to greater speed, but she remembered our last encounter with a werewolf and she knew just how close we'd come to beating it by ourselves. I was big, even for a hybrid, and I was stronger than any of the other hybrids who'd been following Alec.

I still came up short against the mountain of muscle and claws that was a werewolf, but with some more experience and with intelligence up against savage cunning I knew I'd eventually be able to give at least the smaller werewolves a run for their money.

Unfortunately the operative word was eventually. As things stood right now, turning and fighting like my beast wanted to do would be a quick kind of suicide. The only good thing about fighting off my beast's urges was the fact that it gave me something to do other than just panic.

By the time I'd bound my beast back down to my will, I had a plan. I needed terrain that favored me, which meant something that would slow the werewolves down, speed me up, let me lose them, or provide me with some kind of respite.

A forest, one with thick underbrush, would have been the best option, but the empty farmland didn't offer any natural phenomenon that would suit. As far as the eye could see was nothing but the faint light of tiny plant life. The only trees, brightly-glowing behemoths that otherwise would have served admirably, were miles away and they were nothing more than a single line meant to serve as a windbreak.

Instead I turned towards the large black area to my left. From this far away it was hard to be sure what I was headed towards. I thought I could see the black bars of bare structural steel, but I'd have to get closer before I'd know for sure.

Things were as desperate as they were going to get. By the time I got close enough to find out what I was up against, I'd be too tired to try for an alternate destination, but the decision was surprisingly easy despite that. I simply didn't have any other options.

Three more heart-pounding, exhausting minutes passed with the werewolves losing ground on me far too slowly for comfort before I was able to see the partial ruins of some kind of factory. It was the last thing I would have expected to see out here.

Structural steel, large girders designed to defeat the forces of gravity and corrosion, could serve as a kind of artificial forest to slow down my pursuers, but that kind of density wasn't what you'd usually find in most building designs.

It looked like the factory had caught fire at some point and the owners must have taken the insurance money and cashed out, that or maybe the insurance payout hadn't been enough to rebuild. Either way, the lack of artificial lighting indicated that they'd left the undamaged section of the building just as vacant as the smoke-stained sections that had ultimately brought the factory to its knees.

I didn't particularly want to get caught inside the hallways and offices of an unfamiliar building, not when I was being followed by three times my own number of pursuers, so I angled to the right, darting into the blackened ruins.

I was in luck. The wreckage contained dozens of machines that had been ruined in the fire, too big and heavy to justify moving out, and they were more than substantial enough to stop the headlong flight of werewolves which each weighed the better part of half a ton.

I slipped between two of the largest machines, vast monsters that were set less than four feet apart from each other and which the werewolves would have to detour around. It bought me a few seconds, long enough to cross halfway across the manufacturing area.

I waited until I could hear the werewolves' talons scraping across the concrete floor and then dodged through another bank of machinery. I'd never slowed down, but I knew I hadn't bought myself enough of a lead.

I turned to the right and the werewolves took the bait. All three of them sounded like they were headed straight for the open ground, correctly thinking that they would make better time there than trying to navigate through the densely-packed rows of machinery.

I continued streaking towards the far end of the building until I heard them crash through what was left of the exterior walls and then I cut left as hard as I could, heading straight towards the undamaged part of the building.

It was another risky choice, but the concrete was slick enough that the werewolves would start catching up to me again unless I could get onto carpet. Two more bounds took me into the non-manufacturing section of the building.

I was in a long, straight, carpeted corridor and I stretched out into nearly a full sprint. I'd gained a much bigger lead on the werewolves than I'd ever had before, especially during those precious few seconds where they'd been running towards the outside edge of the building. Those few steps had taken them almost directly away from my current direction of travel, the direction I'd been planning on traveling ever since I'd made it into the building. Each of those steps had bought me a three-step lead and now I had a very real chance of making it back to Ben and the car with enough time to get in and drive away before the werewolves could catch us.

Everything now rode on whether or not I could correctly pick my route through the corridors and offices of this part of the building. The best option would be to turn left and head back directly the way I'd come because it would mean that I'd get the benefit of the carpet for the longest time possible while the werewolves would have to take the long way around the building.

Less appealing would be if I had to continue straight for some reason or other before finding a door or a window and then cutting left to head back towards Ben, but even that should still give me a fighting chance.

Turning right, or turning around and heading back towards the manufacturing area, would pretty much guarantee that I'd be run down and killed well out of sight of Ben and the car. I couldn't afford to let that happen.

The building was huge, and more than a dozen doorways flashed past me so quickly that I got only vague impressions of the rooms they opened up into. There were a lot of empty offices on the left, but the right side of the corridor seemed to contain nothing but a long series of storage rooms, packed to the ceiling with the kind of soft, sound-absorbing panels that I'd last seen when Alec had asked Donovan to have part of the manor renovated and modernized with better soundproofing than they'd had available when the house was built.

The panels here seemed to have encased me in a bubble of near silence. I could hear a single werewolf behind me. It had apparently come back through the exterior wall and started across the concrete again, but I couldn't hear anything from the other two werewolves which were apparently still racing around the outside of the building.

My nose was assaulted by something nasty up ahead as I approached an opening on the left side of the corridor that was more than twice as big as the doorways that I'd been flying past.

It was one of those split-second decisions that can make or break a violent confrontation. If I kept running straight then I'd be heading towards the outside wall and the windows that would provide me with an escape route, but every step I made in that direction was effort wasted in that it didn't get me any closer to Ben.

Taking the opening had the benefit of sending me in the direction I actually wanted to be running in, as well as turning towards the source of whatever was causing the stench, a stench that would go a long way towards masking my scent and making it harder for the werewolf behind me to continue to scent-track me.

It was that last point that decided things for me. I knew I was accepting a bigger risk in some ways by turning before the end of the corridor, but I also knew that it gave me a chance to get out of sight before my pursuer could see me. It might even give me a chance to lose it altogether, which meant it would be as good as out of the chase.

I darted to the left without slowing down in the slightest and lost traction for the barest of moments. My hips and legs swung around, doing their best to continue in the direction I'd been running despite the fact that my front half had changed directions.

I slammed into a stack of large barrels that had been invisible until I was almost to the corridor. Those barrels shouldn't have toppled like they did. They were full of some kind of heavy liquid, and only the fact that they'd been stacked with an unbelievably reckless abandon allowed the force of my collision with them to send the top several barrels crashing down, spilling the liquid as they went.

I'd been almost certain that my flight was going to end right then, either to a sprained appendage, or from being crushed by the barrels. All of my concentration was focused on staying upright, on outrunning the cascade of metal cylinders, and my efforts still almost weren't enough.

One of the barrels struck me a glancing blow as I bounced off of the far wall and then shot forward less than half a step ahead of the liquid that the barrels had just splashed everywhere. I was half a dozen steps further into the new corridor before I realized that the barrels had been at least part of the cause of the stench, and that what I was in wasn't actually a corridor.

My heart was already working as hard as it possibly could, but it stuttered in an attempt to go even faster as I took in the cavernous warren of rooms I'd just inadvertently chosen as the location of my final stand.

It was no use going back the other direction. Even in the poor lighting I could see the slick film that coated the water behind me. It was slick, and not just in a transitory way either—if I stepped into that it would slow me down for long painful minutes as well as making me stink so badly that the werewolves wouldn't need to see me in order to know when I exited the building.

I was out of other options, and even as I raced deeper into the maze of rooms I was looking for a place where I'd have a chance of taking out at least the closest werewolf. Nothing looked very promising.

From the outside I'd thought that this section of the building had escaped damage from the fire that had destroyed everything else. Now that I'd stopped running quite as fast and was taking the time to examine my surroundings, I was realizing how far off base I'd been. This part of the building had been damaged too, but the fire had mostly been confined to the roof and tops of the walls.

In fact, the faint starlight coming in through the gaping holes up above me was the only reason I was able to see anything at all. At first glance the walls seemed to be coated with the sound-absorbing panels I'd noticed earlier in the hall, but as I brushed up against one of the walls I realized that wasn't quite the case. The panels were exactly what I was expecting, but they were backed with something soft and flexible that made them give more than they would have otherwise.

I still sometimes had a hard time going directly from wolf to hybrid form. For whatever reason it was easier for me to shift to human form first, so I shifted to two legs as I walked ever deeper into the testing area.

It wasn't until I started referring to it that way inside of my own mind that I realized it was the perfect description of what I was inside. The factory had apparently manufactured soundproofing material and this had obviously been where they'd tested out new products. There was even a complicated metal framework in the ceiling with what looked like attachment points for microphones.

In some ways I'd just found the perfect place from which to launch an ambush of the werewolf that had been following me. The stench meant that it wouldn't be able to smell me waiting for it, and the panels robbed the sound from my steps before the vibrations had a chance to travel more than a foot or two through the air.

That was the difference between Alec and me though. I was capable of improvising on the fly, of using my rage and riding it to victories, but Alec could do that and more. He was a much better tactician than I was.

Alec would have already come up with a dozen different scenarios that offered at least a possibility of him being able to come out on top of what was following me, but all I could think about was just how fast and strong the last werewolf I'd faced had been.

I was tired and despite the anger bubbling up from my beast, I was scared, but I found a dark corner room that seemed like it was going to be my best bet and prepared to shift again.

My heart nearly stopped when my phone started buzzing. I practically tore a hole in my ha'bit trying to get it out before it could vibrate a second time.

Jasmin, it's Rachel. Don't worry, it can't hear you or me right now. I'm calling you now, it's vitally important that you take my call.

Almost before I'd even had a chance to finish reading the message the screen lit up with an incoming call. I answered it out of little more than reflex. I hadn't had a chance to finish processing the implication of her words, but I couldn't bear to let a chance to talk to her slip through my fingers.

"Rach, now isn't a good time."

"I know, you've got three werewolves chasing you and you're cornered inside of a series of soundproof rooms."

"How can you possibly know that?"

"I know a lot these days, Jasmin. In fact I went to quite a lot of trouble getting you here at this exact instant. There were a lot of other ways this could have gone down; I had to work really hard to make sure that you had a chance to survive this."

Something about her words made bits and pieces of information click into place for me that I hadn't realized still needed to fit together.

"The only reason that I'm here is because of you, Rach. If I'd just gotten gas when you called last time, or if I'd taken a slightly different route, I wouldn't have ever run into these three monsters."

"You're right. Believe it or not, I had to go to a bit of effort to make sure that they were here too."

"Are you *trying* to get me killed?"

Rachel continued the conversation without missing a beat, almost like she didn't even hear my question.

"Are you ready to go get Geoffrey?"

"Yes, but I've already told you that, and you didn't seem to believe me then. I'm not sure what else I'm supposed to do to convince you that I'm ready to do whatever it takes to save Ben."

"It's not me you have to convince, Jas, not really. It's you. Once you're really ready to do whatever it takes then you'll find him."

My beast was pushing against my control and my vocal cords started to thicken as she tried to force a change in response to Rachel's tone.

"If you don't stop screwing around, Rach, I swear that I'll..."

"You'll what, kill me?"

A tiny part of me wanted to respond in the affirmative, to yell my answer at her despite the danger it would represent, despite the fact that a werewolf was doubtlessly prowling through the testing lab even now.

"I don't know. Maybe. Ben doesn't have much time left. If something doesn't change soon he's not going to make it, and if you let him die when you could have stopped it from happening I'm not sure I'll be able to control my beast the next time we meet."

Rachel sighed. "Your beast understands what's at stake, Jasmin. You need to be willing to abandon everything else to save him or this isn't going to work out. Every time you and Ben start to get close one of you backs off because you're scared of what might happen, because you're not fully committed to the idea of the two of you. Somebody has to break the cycle, and it's going to have to be you."

It was like someone had draped a black cloth around my insides. Everything was suddenly dark and dying inside my core. Rachel had no right to be lecturing me about relationships. She was wasting my time after having led me into a trap. I was spending precious seconds talking to her that would have been better spent coming up with a plan on how to get out and back to Ben. Some of the emotions that defined me, Jasmin, as a separate entity from my beast shriveled up.

"I don't know why you care about Ben and me getting back together, Rach, but you just pushed me too far. If I get out of here then I want an address for Geoffrey without any more of this screwing around. If you cross me again

I'm going to hunt you down and I'm going to kill you, but I won't do that until after I've killed your mom and Donovan and anyone else who means anything to you."

"I don't care about you and Ben, Jasmin. At least not like I used to. I still care, but I have a lot more to care about now than I did back in the day. I need you to reach your potential though, or things are going to go very badly."

"For Alec?"

"For everyone."

There was another pause and then Rachel seemed to remember that I was only heartbeats away from a fight that I couldn't win.

"Stuff your phone back in your ha'bit, but leave me on speaker."

I slipped my phone back into the little pocket that had been designed for it. Rachel resumed talking as soon as it was in place.

"Okay, now shift into hybrid form and start climbing up the wall."

"That's the dumbest idea possible, Rachel. The walls are tall, but they aren't tall enough to keep me out of the reach of a werewolf. I'll be a sitting duck up there."

"Just do it. Think of it as part of the price of saving Ben."

I forced out an affirmative response and shifted in a hot flare of power. Climbing the wall was harder than I expected it to be. My claws sank through the wall panels and the soft backing behind them, but they just tore through all of that like so much tissue paper. There was no way that anything that fragile was going to support my weight.

I struggled to find something with more substance inside of the wall. I tore off a huge chunk of the wall covering, but the metal studs underneath weren't much better. I needed a bearing wall, not one of the fragile walls that were used to partition off interior sections of commercial buildings.

"The wall on your right, and hurry!"

I turned and ripped another section of panels away and was rewarded with a structural steel girder that ran at an angle from the floor all of the way to the ceiling.

"You could have just told me that to start out with."

The words came out with a kind of breathless anger that was all I could manage while hauling my massive hybrid body up towards the ceiling.

"It wouldn't have worked. There's nearly enough room for you to be able to slip through what's left of the metal framework there. It's rusted, just give the inside corner a good tug and it will bend out of the way."

Rachel's voice came out of the cell phone in a staccato rush, but I hardly noticed. My attention was focused on getting up above the ceiling, and Rachel was only important in as much as she could help get me out of there alive.

She was right; the heavy metal was rusted through so badly that it warped without much effort at all on my part. As I scrambled up through the hole I'd made and onto the heavy metal framework that formed the ceiling, I noticed just how thick the insulation was. The mounting points for the microphones hung down more than a foot below the actual framework, a silent testament to just how much insulation was required to muffle whatever sounds they'd tested with.

"Run towards the center of the room! Now!"

For once my beast didn't protest Rachel giving me an order. Instead she threw all of her energy into the effort of complying with what we'd been told to do. It took me only two steps to cross the room I'd just been inside of and another two were all that were required to put me almost directly in the center of the long corridor that ran through the center of the testing area.

I saw Rachel's error partway between my third and fourth steps. The rust that had allowed me to bypass the microphone framework was endemic through the whole system. Sheer chance had allowed me to step on some of the few crosspieces that were still sound enough to bear my weight, but the chains that supported the framework weren't up to the same standard.

I felt the two chains on my left give out at the same time, and reflexively looked down to confirm that the ground beneath me was clear of obstacles. It wasn't, instead I saw the werewolf that had been pursuing me. A section of the soundproofing material had fallen away at some point in the past, leaving a hole that let me see my enemy, a hole that allowed sound free passage down to the werewolf.

The werewolf must have heard me running across the framework. It was the only explanation for why it had stopped right there, but my mind examined that theory with only a fraction of my processing power.

The end of the framework I was on hurtled towards the ground, pivoting on the two chains on the other end like a pendulum. I would have jumped free, but there wasn't anything to push against, and I suddenly knew for certain that I wasn't going to survive Rachel's supposed help. The last thing I saw before the movement of the framework carried the werewolf out of my sight was it turning to meet me, arms outstretched, wicked claws ready to rend my body.

I was still trying to push off of the framework when the werewolf's claws pierced the soundproofing material. Werewolf claws were harder than steel and sharper than a razor blade, there was no possible way that they could fail to tear through even my massive hybrid body like I was nothing more than a rotting apple.

Only somehow they missed.

I was so sure that I was going to die that I didn't realize the werewolf had missed me until after the framework had completed its descent and swung back and forth like some kind of child's toy. I'd ridden it down, talons on one crosspiece and my left hand curled around another, but that wasn't the astonishing thing. Even the fact that the werewolf had missed me paled in comparison to the fact that those same claws which had come within inches of killing me were now dangling lifelessly to either side of me.

The mounting points for the microphones had pierced the werewolf in half a dozen spots, and apparently half a ton of metal with several hundred pounds of hybrid thrown into the mix for good measure had been sufficient to drive those metal spikes deeply enough in that they'd struck something vital.

"Do you trust me again, Jasmin?"

"I…I guess so. You really knew that was what was going to happen?"

There was a long pause as she considered my question.

"Would you believe me if I said yes?"

"I'm not sure. It was hard enough to believe that Kristin could see a few hours into the future, and what she sees is so limited that half the time it's not much use anyways. What you just did here is godlike."

For a second I thought she was going to actually answer my question.

"There still isn't much time, Jasmin. You need to climb back up onto the metal framework and use it to make a beeline back towards Ben. The exterior skin of the building is nothing more than sheet metal. Tear through that, let yourself down and then run back to the car as fast as you can. The werewolves are both inside of the building now looking for the one you just killed. If you go now you can make it back to Ben and drive away before they can catch you."

I was already moving, climbing up past the werewolf, but this time I had plenty of breath left over to ask her questions.

"Why did this have to happen, Rachel? Why didn't you just send me directly to wherever Geoffrey is?"

"You're headed to New York next, Jasmin. Don't shatter any speed limits, but don't waste any time either."

"Why did you set me up like this?"

The pause lasted so long that I crossed over to the far end of the building before she finally responded. I was starting to think that she'd hung up on me, but then as I punched through the metal and threw myself towards the ground I heard her voice again.

"I didn't have a choice, Jasmin. I always thought that more vision would equate to more options, but the truth is it's the opposite. That werewolf needed to die or the whole house of cards would have come crashing down. I had to at least try, I'm sorry."

My legs hit the ground hard enough that I sank several inches into the topsoil, far enough that I would have had to really work to get myself free, but I simply cheated and shifted a split second after I landed.

My wolf feet were skinnier than my hybrid feet had been. I easily slipped out of the deep holes I'd created in the ground and raced away through the darkness.

Chapter 4

Geoffrey
Unknown location
New York, New York

There wasn't much light in the cage holding Geoffrey, but what little bit there was sent shooting arcs of pain through his head. It was hard to decide whether the pain was the result of a concussion or side effects from being drugged, but Geoffrey already knew that he had other, more important, things to worry about.

The cage holding him was a known quantity. Geoffrey's superhuman strength wouldn't make any difference when pitted against the shining steel bars. Imastious bought them from a manufacturer who specialized in creating containment enclosures for big game, and once the door was closed and locked Geoffrey wasn't any more able to escape than a lion or a rhinoceros would have been.

The room was vaguely familiar, almost as though Geoffrey had once spent a long time here in the past, but he got the feeling that he'd been on the other side of the bars previously. Something danced just below the level of his consciousness, less than a memory, more like a feeling with visual components if such a thing was actually possible.

Geoffrey let his mind churn away in an attempt to force the impression into something more concrete, but after a couple of minutes he abandoned the effort and instead tried to get up.

He'd been so motionless up until that point that for a second when he couldn't move he almost thought that Imastious' people had left him in restraints as well as having locked him in the cage. Geoffrey's head and neck seemed to more or less function, so he turned to the side far enough to confirm that he was resting on nothing more than an aluminum-framed cot.

Reassured that there wasn't any way to restrain him against such a flimsy bed, Geoffrey tried once more to roll off of the cot and onto his feet. He wasn't restrained, but he was the weakest he could remember ever being. All of his effort barely sufficed to slide one foot off of the bed so that it could thump against the floor.

Geoffrey rested for nearly a minute and then tried to force his other foot off of the cot. The effort was too much for him and a few seconds later his head collapsed back against the nylon of the cot. He was dizzy, much more so than the drugs or concussion could explain.

Once the dizziness passed, Geoffrey craned his head around until he found the two full bags of blood that had been used to bleed him out. They were sitting on a small table safely on the other side of the bars where Geoffrey wouldn't be able to reach them. Imastious hadn't tortured him, at least not yet, but the older vampire had taken every other precaution to make sure that Geoffrey would face him in as weakened a state as possible.

Geoffrey was still trying to figure out how Imastious had tracked him to Chicago, when the worn, white door opened and a tall, emaciated figure walked into the room.

"I'm glad to see that you're awake, Geoffrey. Normally I would have just been able to pull what I needed out of your sleeping mind, but the combination of the drugs and the concussion made that impossible. Now that you're conscious again, let's get started."

Imastious had probes arrowing towards Geoffrey's mind even before he finished speaking and they burrowed into his skull with alarming quickness. Imastious had hundreds of years of practice behind his efforts, as compared to Geoffrey's few months of experiences, but Geoffrey had fought him to a standstill once before.

Geoffrey hardened the outside layers of his mind at the same time that he used a blade of mental force to shear through the two probes that had penetrated the deepest. Imastious countered with a blow of force that sent tremors through Geoffrey's entire mind, but Geoffrey patched up the cracks almost as soon as they appeared and visualized a wave of fire rolling across the surface of his mind, burning the remaining probes to a crisp before Imastious could launch another attack.

The first few exchanges of the fight happened in exquisite slow motion to Geoffrey, but they took less than a second of real time. For all of their speed and brutal simplicity, they served as a very pointed object lesson that Geoffrey was operating at much more of a disadvantage than the last time he and Imastious had faced off.

The exhaustion would have been enough all by itself, but it wasn't the only burden he was operating under. Something, either the drugs or the blow to his head, was slowing his response time and making it feel as though he was fighting Imastious off from underneath a layer of water. The battle was taking place inside of Geoffrey's mind, thereby giving him a kind of home-court advantage, but Geoffrey couldn't escape the feeling that it wasn't going to be enough this time.

Imastious sent a dozen new probes at him, but the hard, slick surface of Geoffrey's mind allowed them little if any purchase and all but one of them went skittering away. The last one, the one that didn't ricochet away, wormed into his mind faster than he would have believed possible, sprouting decaying roots that expanded like dark balloons.

Geoffrey tried to cut the tendril of thought off at its base, but another hammer blow of force crashed into him just before he managed to launch his own attack. Geoffrey's aim still felt like it was true, but the thought-blade that struck Imastious' probe was dull and brittle. It bounced off of the rapidly thickening line between them without doing any apparent damage.

Before Imastious could respond to the opening provided by Geoffrey's failed counterattack, Geoffrey launched a blow of force of his own, one that came from the center of his mind and pushed everything outwards. Geoffrey's thoughts rippled as the blow ripped its way up towards Imastious' beachhead, a three-dimensional mental wake like a submarine moving through water at impossible speeds.

Geoffrey didn't just expect this effort to succeed, he knew it would, just as he knew that the strength of his conviction was part of what had transformed this blow into an irresistible force. Geoffrey tensed up in anticipation, but although his effort succeeded in uprooting the black weed of Imastious' probe, it nearly did so at the cost of Geoffrey's sanity.

There was more to Imastious' tentacles than Geoffrey had realized. They didn't end cleanly as he'd thought, instead they expanded into millions of feathery lines that had burrowed more completely into his mind than anything he'd ever seen before.

The force of Geoffrey's effort was too strong to be denied, but the act of ripping the roots out tore huge furrows inside of his own mind and left wounds that bled energy. Geoffrey tried to create a new shield over the top of the damaged portions of his mind, but Imastious had already reacted and now there were a dozen probes exploiting the hole in his defenses, expanding out into portions of his mind in a violation that turned Geoffrey's stomach.

The deeper Imastious' probes went into Geoffrey's mind the slower their progress became, but they were still progressing. Geoffrey needed a new kind of mental construct, something he could create and let loose without having to constantly monitor it.

Nothing he'd ever done before quite fit the bill so he acted on instinct and what was left of the reflexes he'd developed before losing his memory. Geoffrey envisioned a swarm of mental insects, a silvery metallic horde that multiplied at an exponential rate. The swarm became a plague of biblical proportions in less than a heartbeat and then scurried upwards.

Geoffrey's newest attack bit into Imastious' probes, devouring them from the bottom up. The deepest tendrils of Imastious' attack were consumed almost instantly, but the thicker roots closer to the surface of Geoffrey's mind proved more resistant, growing back nearly as quickly as they were being destroyed.

It was disheartening to see just how much stronger Imastious was, even inside the peripheries of Geoffrey's mind. It would have been enough to make Geoffrey give up but for the fact that his insect constructs seemed to be doing more than just attacking Imastious' constructs. They were somehow feeding off of Imastious' work. They weren't increasing in numbers, but they were healing the damaged portions of Geoffrey's mind with the sustenance that they'd stolen from Imastious.

Under other circumstances it would have been better than a stalemate. Geoffrey could feel the jagged, brittle edge of his concussion fading away into something he could work with, but it was too little, too late.

Imastious pushed harder, cracking open another section of Geoffrey's mind with another blow of force. This time the tendrils that Imastious inserted into Geoffrey's mind didn't grow roots. Instead they each fractured into dozens of angular constructs that scurried from place to place like spiders with nothing but a dark, nearly invisible, gossamer thread connecting them back to Imastious.

Geoffrey had seen this attack before, but his exhausted reflexes were a heartbeat too slow in responding to it and a sticky spray of apathy coated everything inside his mind. The insects were still worrying away at the thick roots Imastious had put into his mind; they were hundreds of thousands of points of fire that were slowly trying to burn away the feelings of lassitude, but even they couldn't stand against the constructs that were now ranging freely through Geoffrey's mind, dousing his will to fight with every action they took.

A few seconds were all it took before Geoffrey's defenses melted away with an odd mental pop and then Imastious was fully inside of his mind. Imastious was like an oil spill, slowly coating every part of Geoffrey's mind, and Geoffrey would have thrown up if not for the way that he'd been disconnected from his feelings.

Imastious crept through the outer reaches of Geoffrey's mind, moving with a speed and surety that was one more piece of evidence as to how completely he overmatched Geoffrey. Once the exterior thoughts, feelings and memories had been catalogued, Imastious moved deeper.

He was moving more slowly now, but that seemed to be at least partly because he was taking more care with his examination. Imastious dropped deeper and deeper until Geoffrey could feel him right outside the bubble of calm that was Geoffrey's inner psyche.

Geoffrey was expecting Imastious to match his essence to the reflexive barrier that was all that separated Imastious from what had to be his goal, but instead Imastious started wandering back and forth across the metaphysical floor of Geoffrey's mind, his attention like an evil searchlight that illuminated the darkest corners.

The search seemed to take hours, but eventually Imastious withdrew from Geoffrey's mind. Geoffrey opened his eyes and found that the shadows in the room hadn't lengthened appreciably. Only minutes had actually passed, but Geoffrey felt like he'd been running for hours.

Imastious had collapsed against the bars of the cage, putting himself as close to Geoffrey as possible without actually entering the cage with him. That in and of itself might not have signified anything, but when Imastious looked up there was a trickle of blood running out of one of his nostrils.

Geoffrey tried to search his memory for another instance where Imastious had been forced to exert so much energy and effort to break through anyone else's defenses, let alone Geoffrey's defenses. He couldn't be sure; the effects of the apathy constructs hadn't run their full course yet. His mind was simply too listless to be certain that he'd searched every memory, but he couldn't remember Imastious ever being pushed that hard.

Imastious stood and looked at Geoffrey for several seconds.

"You're an interesting puzzle, my child. You thought you could defeat me, but you forgot about the negative spaces. Only time will prove whether or not there is enough left there for my purposes, but it won't make any difference one way or another to you. You're far too dangerous to leave alive now any longer than absolutely necessary."

Chapter 5

Jasmin Bianchi
Journey Youth Hostel
New York City, New York

I'd never run faster in my entire life than I did from that factory back to the car. Once I got back to the gas station I didn't even stop to pick up the scraps of clothes that had been left as a result of my transformation to wolf form.

I had my Mercedes in gear and moving within a couple of seconds of getting to it, and I didn't drop below eighty until I was almost a hundred miles away from there. The gas station clerk probably thought I'd lost my mind, but that was okay. As long as he hadn't seen the werewolves or me running by on four legs, I didn't care what he thought.

The trip from Kansas to New York took another day and a half. I slept for an hour in the car somewhere outside of Columbus, Ohio. I didn't want to stop, and not just because I was worried about making whatever schedule Rachel had in mind.

I'd been ambushed twice since leaving Sanctuary and the rest of the pack. I'd always known that the outside world was dangerous, but that kind of thing wasn't all that relevant when you had someone like Brandon trying to kill you closer to home.

Back in the day I'd actually looked forward to the few trips Alec sent me on to help mind his business interests. Back then a trip away from home had meant getting away from danger. Sure, there'd been the possibility, even then, of running into a couple of vampires, but vampires are so easy to pick out by their scents that I'd been pretty sure I'd be able to avoid getting caught by any of them.

Alec's business interests had been carefully selected to make sure that they were well outside the territory of any of the other shape shifter packs, which meant that my biggest worries had always been the dispossessed, shape shifters who didn't belong to a specific pack, and the werewolves.

Back then Puppeteer had been doing a better job of keeping the werewolves in line and the dispossessed mostly wouldn't have messed with me once they knew that I was part of the Sanctuary pack. Don't get me wrong, some of the dispossessed are super dangerous, but even the really dangerous hybrids among the dispossessed know better than to screw around with an entire pack, even a pack as small as ours had been.

Ulrich Bishop had been very careful up until recently to keep the Chicago pack from getting involved in politics, but he and the rest of the pack leaders took an especially dim view of rogue hybrids eliminating entire packs. It had happened a few times in the past, but even the Coun'hij understood that the rank-and-file wolves needed at least the illusion of security, so they'd usually helped put down anyone really dangerous who killed outside of the formalized bounds of the challenge law that dispossessed hybrids could use to take over a pack.

Besides, anyone that dangerous didn't usually stay dispossessed for very long. If there was any way possible to work someone like that into the structure of a pack and keep the pack even remotely healthy, someone like Ulrich would snatch them up before too long. If it wasn't possible for someone to function as part of a pack then the Coun'hij usually found a way to use them, or barring that to turn them into a weapon that could be pointed where they would do the most damage possible before being brought down.

For a while suicide squads sent after targets south of the border had been all the rage. After a decade or two of that the dispossessed had figured out that causing too much disruption just got the person creating the stir assigned to a suicide squad. Things had died down quite a bit after that. Now the dispossessed mostly just posed a threat to each other unless you were part of a pack that was vulnerable to a hostile takeover of some kind or another.

There were other threats of course, but most of them were so rare that even we shape shifters half believe they are nothing more than legends. I'd enjoyed the freedom of being safe, enjoyed the liberty of being able to walk down the street and not worry that someone was going to try to kill me.

That had all changed now. With the Coun'hij actively trying to kill us and Puppeteer having unleashed dozens, possibly even hundreds, of werewolves to run loose in an effort to intimidate the unaligned packs, I was in constant danger. When you threw in the fact that Alec had opened up something like a third of the southern border with a corresponding increase in the number of jaguar shape shifters flooding across the border from Mexico, it was starting to feel pretty astonishing that I'd survived even this long.

I'd stopped in Columbus and slept for an hour, but I'd stopped during broad daylight and I'd parked right outside the busiest section of town I'd been able to find. I really should have slept for longer than that. Shape shifters don't need as much sleep as normal humans, but the sleep we do need is correspondingly more important.

I'd been riding the ragged edge of safe for a couple of days now. That hour-long nap had bought me a few more hours, enough time to make it the rest of the way to New York City, but I was running a much bigger risk than I wanted to admit to myself by waiting this long to sleep.

For humans sleep deprivation is dangerous enough—it leads to mistakes, impaired driving, and in extreme cases death when the organs of the body started to give out. It's practically impossible for a shape shifter to get to the point where their body starts failing as a result of sleep deprivation. The danger for us is that we usually lose control of our beast long before that happens.

For the beast there was only one legitimate reason to go without sleep, being chased by a predator even more dangerous than us. The best-case scenario for a shape shifter who gets so tired that their beast wrestles away control from them, is for other shape shifters in the area to beat them into submission before their beast goes into some kind of killing spree.

I didn't have the benefit of other shape shifters around, so I was operating without a safety net. Given the strength of my feelings for Ben, I didn't think my beast, even in full-on kill-every-threat-in-sight mode, would hurt him, but it wasn't the kind of chance I should be taking. Not with Ben, not with anyone really, but not with him most of all.

My phone had been working only intermittently for the last few hours. I was pretty sure that meant that someone was looking for me and Alec's guys were having to kick me off of the grid while they shut down the trace attempts. It had made life extra difficult, if not as difficult as dealing with another squad of Coun'hij enforcers would have been.

Despite the difficulty, I'd managed to find a youth hostel on the outer edges of the Bronx, one that was close enough to reasonable parking for me to be able to get Ben out of the car with my normal 'my friend is too drunk to walk on his own' trick of throwing his arm around my shoulder and supporting his weight with my arm around his waist.

I managed to secure one of their few remaining open double rooms, which was a bigger stroke of luck than I'd realized. Apparently it was best to call ahead and reserve a room by phone. The only thing that saved me was that we weren't quite to the heavy tourist season because it was still so cold outside.

I put Ben in the black metal bunk that was mostly hidden by the door so that I'd be able to enter and exit the room without people in the hall seeing that he was just lying there as unresponsive as always, and then made him as comfortable as I could. Once a new IV had been run and he was as well off as I could make him, I locked the door and went out to grab something to eat.

I needed something that was as energy-dense as I could get it without just going straight sugar, so I jogged over to a fast food joint and ordered two meals to go. I was back in the room with Ben less than fifteen minutes after I'd left.

"You know, Ben, I think if I'd been living on sugar water for as long as you have been that just the smell of this food would wake me up."

I waved a golden fry underneath his nose, but got absolutely no response at all. If someone else had been around I would have pretended that I was just joking around, but the truth was that I would have done much more foolish things than that if it would have woken him up.

"Don't worry, Rachel will come through. She always has before. She's crazy now, like halfway out of her mind, but she does seem to know stuff that she shouldn't be able to know. Maybe I'm being stupid, maybe she's gone completely bonkers or she's just using me for some nefarious purpose of her own, but I don't think so. I think this Geoffrey guy really exists, and I think that she'll lead us to him sometime soon."

My beast was still edgy just due to the lack of sleep, but she'd calmed down a little once I started getting some food into my stomach. Getting too hungry was almost as bad an idea as going without sleep. None of us in Sanctuary had ever lost control and eaten something…or someone… we shouldn't have, but there were plenty of stories about people who had, and I was pretty sure that not all of them were urban legends.

Discussing Rachel got my beast worked back up, and for a moment it was all I could do to hold onto my shape as a wave of anger and otherworldly energy crashed through me.

"Wow, that was a close one. My beast has always been so protective of Rachel before now. It's always viewed her as being *ours* in a way that most people wouldn't understand. It's my fault though; my beast is just taking its cue from me."

Ben was still just lying there as silent and motionless as ever, but I could feel his attention, feel that he was listening to me. I knew it was selfish, knew that he'd run away precisely because I'd accidentally addicted him to my touch, but I couldn't help myself. I reached out and took his hand in mine.

"The truth is that I'm not really even pissed about how flakey Rachel has gotten lately. Don't get me wrong, I'm not a fan, but the thing that really has me so mad at her is the fact that she's calling me on my crap. While I was stuck in that factory, not sure whether or not I was going to make it back to you, she told me that the reason that you and I hadn't ever been able to make it is because we've never put each other first."

My voice started to break, but I cleared my throat and forced myself to go on. If this was part of the price of bringing Ben back to me then I would pay it.

"I've spent the last day or so telling myself that she was wrong, that I couldn't have done anything differently, but the truth is that she is right. I knew that you needed me. You were stuck there in the hospital, going through the worst withdrawal pains you'd ever experienced, and I wasn't there for you. I could have been, but I was scared. I know, right? Big bad Jasmin, scared. I'm not sure that anyone in the pack other than maybe Alec and Dominic would have even believed that was possible."

I'd spent weeks now with tears only a couple of heartbeats away. I'd mostly managed to keep them at bay, but they were even closer to the surface now and a single tear broke free of my right eye and trickled down my face.

"Actually, that's not fair. Rachel probably knew at the time—she just had too much else going on right then to come talk to me about it. It's crazy, but it's the truth, I was scared out of my mind. I was scared of Agony and the rest of the Coun'hij. I could have gone to you, but that would have been a calculated insult to Agony and doing that might have pushed Alec into withdrawing the protection of the pack."

I'd grown up surrounded by Agony's handiwork. Reminders of the extent of his power had been carved into the flesh of all of the adults in my life. Donovan's limp, Andrew being confined to a wheelchair, even Addison had scars from the night when Agony had killed more than half of the pack.

"I had a good reason to be scared of Agony, but the truth was that I was most scared of you. I wanted to be with you so badly, but I was scared of what you'd say to me. You'd worked so hard trying to clean yourself up, and I'd just sucked you into a new addiction, one that was stronger than anything else you'd ever had to fight. I was afraid that you'd reject me like you had so many times before, only this time you'd be rejecting me despite the Ja'tell bond, and I wasn't sure I'd be able to survive that. I didn't want to know that you found me so repulsive that not even the flesh addiction could overcome your dislike of me."

That first tear had been joined by others, but I didn't wipe them away, didn't try to pretend that they weren't there. Ben deserved better than that. He deserved a girl who didn't suppress her feelings like some kind of emotionless cyborg. He deserved a real person, not some battered abuse survivor who barely functioned from day to day.

"I just wanted to tell you that I'm sorry that I let you down. I've always let you down, but I'm going to do better now. There isn't any reason for you to believe me, I know that, but I'm going to prove it to you."

I fell asleep in my chair, still holding Ben's hand.

I woke in a state of high alert. My muscles were charged with energy and my beast was pacing back and forth at the edge of my mind. It took me a second to figure out what had caused me to wake from the sleep I so desperately needed.

It was quiet, far, far too quiet. I was used to the quiet of the manor house, but it had been built with shape shifters in mind. Even in the older parts of the house, the parts without any kind of modern sound proofing, it was still usually dead silent simply because everyone's rooms were positioned so that there were empty rooms on either side of us.

The hostel hadn't been that quiet when I'd fallen asleep, but it was nearly as quiet as the manor house now. It was dark outside, but my phone said that it was only a little after midnight.

It was too early for everyone to be asleep, but the only sound I could hear was breathing from the two rooms that were closest to us. I was still trying to figure out what might be the cause of the sudden change when an incredible feeling of lassitude settled over me.

Suddenly I had no desire to get out of my chair, no inclination to deal with whatever danger lurked just outside of our room. All I wanted to do was go back to sleep. It was like alien tendrils of exhaustion had wrapped themselves around my mind and sucked away all of the energy that my brief rest had infused me with.

The human part of me wanted nothing so much as to give in, to follow the insistent demands that I drop back off, but my beast roared to life an instant before I would have closed my eyes again. She recognized the fact that the influence currently working on us was alien. It had bothered me, but it infuriated her.

My beast didn't particularly like the fact that she was subject to me. If I'd been a little less strong-willed, or if I hadn't been part of her in some indefinable way, she would have taken over control a long time ago. She suffered my rule, but she wasn't going to suffer the rule of anyone else, at least not without fighting, not without forcing them to prove that they were dominant to her.

The flare of otherworldly energy from my beast pushed, at least momentarily, the foreign presence out of my mind. I was out of my chair and headed towards the door before my conscious mind had finished the threat assessment that told me that my most likely adversary was a group of vampires.

I paused for the barest moment at the door. Even through the white-hot rage of my beast I knew that I didn't want to leave Ben here alone and undefended, but the only alternative would be to cower inside of our room and wait for them to come murder us.

Even if it had been a smart choice it still wouldn't have been the kind of thing that I could have forced myself to do. I stripped off my clothes in quick, smooth motions and then slipped outside, making sure that I heard the lock click shut behind me.

The narrow hall was lit by nothing more than safety lights as I ghosted down it, my ears questing for some clue as to where the vampires were. I could feel the alien presence lazily pushing against my mind, but the mental intrusion was still a blanket, undirected kind of thing. I knew that I'd be in trouble if the mentalist realized I was awake and coming for them. If he was strong enough to cover an area as big as the hostel and put everyone inside it to sleep then he was strong enough to read my mind in the middle of a fight. If the presence just outside of my mind started to really push it would be a sign that things were just about to go from bad to worse.

I was able to smell them after taking only a few steps forward. The air inside the hostel was too still to guarantee that I was able to scent all of the vampires involved, but it smelled like there were four different vampires in the building. It was sometimes hard to identify different vampires by scent though, the incredible stink of old, rotting blood is generally strong enough to overpower almost everything else about them.

I stepped around a corner and saw the first open door of the night. As I got closer my nose and a set of soft sucking sounds confirmed what I'd suspected. The vampires, at least two of them, were inside and already feeding.

If I was in luck the strongest vampire, the mentalist who had sent everyone into a deep slumber, would be in that room and I would be able to take him by surprise and kill him before he could bring the full wrath of his powers against me. I couldn't remember whether or not vampires were capable of sensing the energy bleed of a shift the way that the moonborn could, so I decided not to take any chances.

I went through the door at something that was very nearly a full run and shifted as I went, exploding into my hybrid shape with a surge of power that preceded me like an angry wave. It was too much, I was moving too fast as I shifted, and I stumbled as I went across the threshold.

I was off balance and in an unfamiliar room. It was a recipe for disaster, but I'd taken the two vampires inside of the room completely by surprise. They managed to get their mouths off of the girls that they'd been feeding on, and one of them even managed to get his sword halfway out of its sheath, but I killed them both within milliseconds of each other.

For several long, painful seconds I stared at the two girls the vampires had been feeding on. They were both white from blood loss, with their eyes rolled back up into their skulls. I wanted to save them, wanted to apply direct pressure on the holes in their wrists, but I forced myself to turn away.

They were as good as dead and I couldn't afford to stay in one place. The drowsy pressure behind my eyes hadn't gone away. There were other vampires in the hostel and if I didn't keep moving, didn't keep hunting, then I had no chance of surviving. The two girls had been dead the moment the vampires had walked into their room, it was just going to take a few more minutes for nature to run its course.

I didn't bother shifting back down to human form as I stepped out of the room. My choice was little more than habit. My hybrid shape was the most deadly form available to me and shifting back and forth between forms wouldn't make me any safer, it would just risk a debilitating set of muscle spasms in the middle of the fight.

It hadn't been by design, but the fact that I was still wearing my hulking hybrid body as I took my first step down the hall was the only thing that saved me when the mentalist realized something was wrong and brought his full strength to bear against me. Frozen daggers of ice stabbed into my temples as the vampire pried at my mind in an effort to find out who and where I was.

If I'd been in my human shape he would have succeeded, but in my hybrid shape my beast was closer to the surface of my mind. She had more leeway in this shape because a small but definite portion of my human reason was sublimated to her savage instincts. This was a new arena, one that she wasn't used to fighting in, but she was ready and willing to fight anywhere and at any time.

The shards of ice trying to pillage my memories melted away when faced with the heat of her anger. I could still feel the vampire's mental fingers trying to pierce my mind, peeling back the outer layers of my psyche, but my beast met every attack with biting, spitting defiance, and for now she seemed to be holding her own.

I took two more steps down the hall and a tremor of something very much like fear ran through me. The artificial exhaustion hadn't gone anywhere, I'd only thought I was facing the mentalist's full powers. I'd been wrong—he was still making sure that the other residents of the hostel wouldn't wake up and cause him and his companions any problems.

I heard hushed voices up ahead.

"...no, we haven't heard anything...a *presence*? Can't you be more specific than that? Peters isn't answering his phone? Bollocks, that means it's got to be nearby. We'll finish up here in a second and then go hunting."

This time there were three of them. I could hear them moving around inside of the suite just ahead of me. This one was designed to sleep four, and I already knew that all four of the kids who'd been sleeping there were dead or dying. The vampire wouldn't have been on the phone otherwise.

I crept forward, desperately hoping that vampire hearing was human dull. I made it almost all of the way to their door before the pacing steps moved towards me.

The first vampire came out of the door with a pair of long knives in his hands, but I grabbed him before he'd made it far enough into the hall to realize that I was right there next to him. My right hand grabbed hold of his wrist, controlling the closest weapon, and then I punched the claws on my left hand into his chest.

He was a big man, he probably weighed nearly two hundred and twenty pounds, but that was nothing to my massive hybrid muscles. I picked him up, using his body as a shield, and charged into the room.

A woman had been only a few feet behind him, but I hit her hard enough to knock her over and then threw the first vampire at the one who was just now returning his phone to his jacket pocket. The female tried to get back on her feet, tried to get her sword into play, but I stepped on her sword hand and then sank the talons on my other foot into her stomach.

A casual flick of my wrist across her throat ended the threat she represented and then I was fully inside of the room and facing my first prepared opponent, a vampire who was old enough that his telekinetic power had been sufficient to knock aside the body that I'd just thrown at him.

He had a sword out, a long, straight duelist's weapon, and he'd obviously had plenty of years in which to learn how to use it. He almost got me on the first pass despite my best efforts. I wasn't used to dealing with a stabbing weapon. Hybrid combat was all about slashing attacks, and this was something entirely different.

His weapon darted forward, aimed at my chest, but when I went to slap the blade away with my claws I instead found that my arm had been encased by some kind of invisible force. It was as though I had two hundred pounds of weight dragging at the appendage. I was strong enough still to move against that kind of force, but even a hybrid as big as me couldn't move that kind of weight and still be quick enough to block the lightning-fast strike of the vampire's sword.

I knew my original plan was futile, so I simply stepped to the side. His telekinetic gift pushed at me, trying to stop me from moving, but a mere force of a few hundred pounds wasn't enough to even slow my bulk by very much. I didn't move enough to avoid the strike completely, but I'd known that I wouldn't be able to, so I hadn't even tried.

His sword entered my chest three inches to the left of where my heart would have been if hybrids kept their hearts in the same place as humans did. It hurt with the dull almost-pain of a hybrid's nervous system, a nervous system designed to transmit information without allowing pain to stop us from doing what needed to be done. It hurt, but not enough to stop me from stepping into the blow and shoving the claws on the end of my left hand into his chest.

He was dead before he hit the ground and I stepped away wounded and bleeding, but still more than capable of making sure I took a few more vampires with me.

The vampire stink got stronger as I got closer to the front door, but the blood smell was still too strong to allow me to pick out how many vampires I was up against. I looked at the door for a couple of seconds and then grabbed one of the utilitarian steel chairs scattered about the foyer.

My claws made short work of the seat and back, and then I tore the frame apart and wrapped one of the longer pieces around the door handles where they came together. It was crude, but I'd just locked the door against anyone who didn't have the strength to bend steel.

I felt a moment of regret at the action. I'd just locked all of the humans inside with the vampires. They could still go out the windows, but that would slow them down and potentially cost lives if I didn't manage to kill all of the bloodsuckers. It was regrettable, but it would also help keep the vampires imprisoned with us here as well.

It was the kind of decision I'd seen Alec forced into, especially when Agony had made his visit to Sanctuary. I'd hated him at the time for some of the things he'd made us do back then, but I knew this was the right decision to make, and for more reasons than just the twin jets of hate and rage burning inside of me. The only thing that was holding the vampires back from taking over the heartland of the United States was the fact that we shape shifters preyed on them like they preyed on the humans.

They didn't know we existed, which allowed us to stalk and kill them in small groups. If that ever changed then the advantage would swing irrevocably the other way. The vampires could reproduce with a speed only found in truly parasitic organisms and the mentalists inside of their ranks would be able to find our packs one by one and destroy us by bringing overwhelming numbers against us.

I needed to win tonight for more than just Ben and I.

I pushed the elevator call button with a knuckle and then waited with my heart in my chest as it came down. I half expected a dozen vampires to come streaming out of the car once the doors opened, but it was thankfully empty. I wedged a chair between the open elevator doors to make sure that it wouldn't be of any use to the vampires, stuck my head inside to confirm that they hadn't used it yet, and then turned for the stairs.

The mentalist attacked again when I was halfway between the first and second floors. My beast fought back, but this time the vampire had let the blanket exhaustion he'd been maintaining drop back to nothing more than a hint of what it had been. The change freed up resources that he used to hit me with an attack that had all of the subtlety of a falling anvil.

I stumbled on the stairs, dropping to the ground for a second as I tried to function in a world where I couldn't see or even tell which way was up. For long moments I couldn't do anything more than just stay there, crumpled to the ground, and hope that none of thc other vampires would happen upon me.

I was completely defenseless to physical attack, but that didn't worry my beast, she was much more concerned with the fact that oily fingers were rummaging through my mind like it was nothing more than a series of file folders. My beast attacked with fire and the mental equivalent of fang and claws.

Exhaustion pulled at me, real exhaustion, not just the mentalist's working, but my beast seemed fresh and eager to continue fighting. I could feel a shining golden line running from her off into a place that was simultaneously far and close, a place that existed but couldn't possibly exist. It was the first time I'd ever noticed the slender thread, but I could tell it was important. Energy rolled down the line, feeding her an unnatural vitality that I could tap only the barest fringes of.

A starving man takes what he can get, so I did reach out for that golden conduit, skimming off something that was less than a tithe of a tithe of those terrible energies. Even that little bit of power kindled a fire that went raging through my insides.

My hybrid nerves didn't dull this pain, but I forced it below the level of consciousness and threw all of my efforts to supporting my beast. She clawed and bit, but I was more than just a savage animal, I had reason at my beck and call. Man had been building in one form or another since we'd first stacked two branches on top of each other to form a windbreak. I called upon those skills and began building a fortress inside of my mind.

Brick by immaterial brick, I built up a translucent wall and with each course of bricks I felt the pressure inside of my mind lessen. The mentalist tried to undo my work, tried to break down my wall, but my beast was there shredding his attacks, chasing him off while I continued to encircle us in a tower that was impervious to anything he might try to do to us.

It seemed as though my work lasted for hours, and even the energy I'd siphoned away from my beast was gone, consumed in the effort, by the time I finished, but when I was done we were alone inside of my mind.

I opened my eyes and pulled myself to my feet, heading for the heavy metal door only a few steps above me. My beast paced back and forth on the inside of my mental wall. She didn't like being caged, even when the cage was for our protection, but now she had the measure of our enemy and she knew we couldn't defeat him on the terrain of our own mind. She would leave the wall be for now. She wanted him dead at least as much as I did.

I paused just outside the gray door to the second floor, sniffing to confirm that the vampires were all on this level. Nobody had gone up to the third story, which meant that I'd probably contained them to this one floor unless they'd already started fleeing down the fire escape.

A series of deep breaths oxygenated my blood and then I threw open the door and dashed into the corridor beyond it. It was past the point where I could hope to sneak up on the vampires, instead it was time for boldness and speed.

Two vampires were waiting for me a dozen feet down the left-hand corridor. They looked like twins. Two men, both golden-haired, tall and slender. The weapons in their hands were likewise matched weapons, huge swords that were meant to be wielded with two hands. I closed with them and hoped that neither was old enough to have developed any kind of power, telekinetic or otherwise.

Their weapons were fierce, heavy things that would easily take off even one of my massive limbs, but they weren't the ideal choice for fighting in such close quarters. I jumped back out of range of the first slash and made as if to follow along behind the sword so that I could bowl the lead vampire over, but the second vampire launched an attack only a heartbeat behind his fellow.

Instead of advancing forward I found myself forced further and further back. They were used to fighting together, displaying a skill and speed that would have been beautiful to watch if it hadn't been directed towards the job of ending my life.

The wound in my chest continued to ooze a slow flow of blood. Strategically positioned muscles inside of my body had already contracted in an effort to direct most of the blood in my body out and around the damaged section, but even for a hybrid that wasn't enough to completely stop the bleeding.

The weakness that I'd felt before had all been mental, though it hadn't been any less real because of that. It hadn't vanished, but it was quickly being joined by a physical exhaustion that threatened to make me clumsy and slow, easy prey for the vampires who were still pressing me.

The blades came at me again, slicing through the air with inhuman speed as I ducked and retreated, occasionally knocking them to one side with my claws in a spray of sparks. We were approaching a decision point.

I was tired and getting slower, but it was more than that. The corridor was too narrow for both of them to get at me like they would have liked. Instead of coming at me from multiple angles they were forced to trade off on who led, one aggressively attacking me while the other waited to strike if I tried to close and kill the lead vampire. They had driven me far enough back now that it would only take another step or two and I would be in the broad junction of corridors next to the elevator. If they surrounded me I was as good as dead.

There was a chance that I could slip under the reach of one of them and kill him while the other was still too far away to help, but it was an infinitesimally small chance. It was much more likely that they'd just bleed me out, safe behind the added reach that their weapons granted them.

I stepped backwards as a blade licked out in an effort to cut me across the neck. I knocked the strike from the second vampire away with my claws and then had to step backwards again to avoid the backstroke from the first vampire which otherwise would have taken off my arm.

The second step was the proverbial straw that broke the camel's back. I was far enough back into the junction now that the first vampire started forward at an angle, anxious to flank me by getting into the other hall so that they could pin me against the elevator.

The *smart* thing to do, the thing they expected me to do, was to rush the first vampire while they were spaced slightly further apart than they had been. Failing that, I probably should have retreated more quickly, angling backwards myself so that I ended up in the other corridor and kept the fight from changing drastically one way or another by denying them the room they'd been hoping for.

I did neither. Instead I retreated, but rather than heading towards the other corridor I backed right up against the corner they'd hoped to trap me in. It was suicide except for the fact that during one of our last couple of exchanges I'd caught a glimpse of a heavy wooden chair next to the elevator.

It was one of those chairs that you sit *in* rather than *on*, a huge monstrosity that weighed close to a hundred pounds. I hooked it with the claws of my right hand and then hurled it at the first vampire with all my might.

The vampires hadn't exactly become complacent, but they'd thought that the parameters of the fight had been well established. They were fast, skilled, and with their swords they had a reach that exceeded even what I was capable of. They'd forgotten about the fact that I was many, many times stronger than either of them.

The chair shot across the empty space between me and my target, a target who had been so eager to box me in that he'd already made it to the other corridor, a corridor that helped limit his options for evasion. He tried to dodge the projectile, but I'd thrown it at waist level, too high to jump, too low to duck. His sword couldn't deflect this blow and his best efforts still ended with the chair clipping him in the shoulder, splintering in a spray of wood and fabric as it knocked him to the ground.

The second vampire pressed the attack in an effort to buy his companion time to get back up and help him, but he was too used to me retreating. A hybrid is capable of moving backwards with incredible speed, but that's not what we are really built for.

I was done retreating. I shot forward with the kind of vision-blurring speed that I'd always loved as a wolf. I checked his arm with my right hand, stopping his sword as he tried to swing it, but it was merely a safety precaution. I was already inside the arc of his weapon and my jaws closed on his neck before he even realized just how badly he'd misjudged me.

I let the body drop away and turned back to the vampire I'd hit with the chair. He was back on his feet, sword at the ready, but it was obvious that the chair or the fall had hurt his shoulder. He stepped forward and slashed at me, but the attack had only a shadow of his previous speed and grace. I stepped back out of range of the attack and then darted forward before he could recover.

He was still trying to bring his sword back around at me again when I grabbed his wrist and threw him into the wall behind me with enough force to break even a vampire's neck. I made sure of him with a couple well-placed slashes and then started down the dimly-lit hall.

I knew that there was at least one more vampire. I couldn't smell him, but none of the vampires I'd killed yet had been the mentalist who had come so close to incapacitating me just a few minutes earlier. I continued down the hall on the left, the hall where the twin vampires had been standing, and found the mentalist in one of the rooms in the middle of the hall.

I'd expected the leader of the group to be a man. I'd had the feeling that the mental intrusions I'd been dealing with had been too heavy-handed to be the work of a woman, especially not a delicate, thin woman with long blonde hair and large, innocent eyes.

The illusion of innocence lasted only an instant and then I took in the devastation she'd left in the room. The occupants were dead, gone to feed the vampires and fill half a dozen blood bags that currently sat in an open cooler at her feet.

"What are you? Can you even talk?"

My lips pulled back, revealing enough fang to make most normal people shake in fear, but the vampire just stood there expectantly.

"You know what I am, you pillaged enough of my memories and thoughts to have at least a basic idea."

Another layer of the illusion was stripped away as her eyes took on a self-satisfied, sadistic look. "You're right, I know what you are. I'm astonished that you've managed to keep your existence a secret for so long. I never would have expected that level of sophistication out of mere beasts."

"Better a beast than a soulless monster who murders innocents."

There was another flicker of emotion on her face. I'd just told her something that she'd needed to know, but I didn't see how she'd taken any kind of advantage out of what I'd said.

"I thought you'd deny being a beast."

"I would have, but I don't actually care what you think. I'm just here to end you."

She looked down at the sword in her hand, another long rapier, and then shrugged. "You might find that more difficult than you expect it to be, but that's not what I want to talk about. I expected you to deny the fact that you're an animal; I was prepared to prove otherwise. Your mind was too alien to be human. I suspect that's why you were able to shake off the sleep construct in the first place. Even when I invaded your mind I still had a hard time understanding most of what I saw there."

She was stalling, but I didn't know why. I needed to end this so that I could go back down and get Ben. We needed to disappear before anyone woke up and called the cops. I moved forward, testing her defenses, but she stepped back, smoothly keeping herself out of range.

"I can save him, you know, but if you kill me you're going to have a very difficult time keeping him alive."

A chill ran up my back and lodged in the base of my skull. "Who?"

"Ben. That's his name, isn't it? He's going to just continue getting weaker. It won't matter what you do. Put him on antibiotics and his liver will fail, or his kidneys. Put him on dialysis and his heart will stop beating. You're fighting his own body now, it doesn't want to continue living."

It was the only thing she could have possibly said to stop me from pouncing. I opened my mouth and this time I was the one who was stalling for time. "How do you know that?"

"I was in your mind. I've seen everything about you. You've loved Ben for years. He was taken by vampires and when you saved him he dropped into a coma."

"You're lying, there's no way that you could have pulled all of that out of my mind that quickly."

She shook her head. "You're nothing more than a child, you haven't even seen two decades come and go, and you'll be dead in another sixty years. I've lived for thousands of years. You're fortunate really, there are only a handful of vampires who can save him and you've stumbled into me, someone who can help you."

I let my hands drop slightly and did my best to look confused. It was only partially an act. Most of my attention was directed inwards, searching, scouring my mind for something I couldn't feel, but which I suddenly knew had to be there.

It took less than a second to find them, a network of clear threads inside of my psyche. They'd grown through the seams in my wall where the blocks butted up against each other. They were so tiny and blended in with their surroundings so well that my beast hadn't been able to distinguish them as being alien, as being something that needed to be destroyed.

Her probes had buried themselves in nearly every part of my brain, but they hadn't penetrated the section where my beast was anxiously pacing back and forth. I looked out at her and knew just how precarious my situation was.

For all I knew she could read my thoughts as I had them, maybe not all of them, but certainly she'd know if I started to attack. She'd know which attacks were feints and which were real. She'd know where I was going to be as soon as I decided on a course. Fighting her would be like trying to fight my own shadow, a shadow that could kill me at any instant.

I let my mind dwell on her words, and it was only partly a ploy. I knew that she expected me to be considering her offer. She knew how much Ben meant to me, she'd trolled out the best possible bait imaginable.

A week before, even a day before, I would have said that I wasn't capable of making any kind of deal that resulted in a murdering parasite like her walking free, but I'd changed at some point over the last twenty-four hours. I *needed* for Ben to survive, had to have it in ways that defied reason.

In the grand scheme of things Ben's life wasn't any more valuable than anyone else's. If every life is precious like I'd been taught in school then how can you put one life in front of any other life? It was like picking between priceless paintings, only I was ready to pick, ready to discard one to the flames if it meant I could save the other.

I knew most people wouldn't agree with me. Some would probably even say that I was picking the wrong life to save. Ben had been a drug addict. He was a high-school dropout. Most people would say that if you stacked him up against an *average* person that they should live and Ben should die.

If I were to let this vampire go in return for her healing Ben's mind then I'd be condemning hundreds, possibly thousands of other people to a slow, painful death at her hand. There was no way to know how many more years she'd live before someone else stopped her. Even worse, each person she changed over into a vampire just made the math worse. She was the terrible, parasitic seed and there was no way for me to know how many apples of death she'd be responsible for as a result of me letting her go now.

As I worried at one of the clear threads inside of my mind, she interrupted my thoughts. "You've found my probes. You know you can't win, that I can read your thoughts as you have them. Give up, take me down to your friend, to Ben, and I'll heal him in return for you letting me go."

She was right. In that instant she knew me better than anyone else...and she knew me not at all.

I couldn't hope to destroy her network of probes, I knew that. They were too extensive and I was too tired, so I didn't even try.

Instead I grabbed a single thread and thrust it at my beast. I forced her to see what had invaded our mind, forced her to see past the camouflage that had hidden them from her. My beast went crazy. She ripped through the probes with a speed I never could have hoped to match on my own, and she showed the kind of animal cunning that sometimes defeats even the brightest intellect.

She didn't try to destroy the network of threads from the inside out, she went along the inside of our mental wall and cut them off even with the wall. She pulled them up by the root and left what remained to wither and die.

The vampire sensed my actions as soon as I started them, but it didn't do her any good. She attacked, lunging forward with a speed and grace that was greater even than what the twins had demonstrated, but knowing what I was going to do wasn't sufficient to overcome my even greater speed.

If I'd attacked her, moving towards her in an attempt to kill her, then I would have been spitted like a pig. Instead I backed away from her, springing backwards so hard that I sailed through the doorway behind me and shattered the sheetrock of the corridor wall.

The vampire knew I'd been committed to retreating. She'd thrown herself forward with every ounce of speed she possessed. Under normal circumstances it wouldn't have been out of line for her to commit so strongly to an attack because she would have known what I was going to do in plenty of time to foil any attack I might launch.

This time was different though because my beast had thrown her out of my mind. I bounced off of the corridor wall and moved forward myself, dodging slightly to the side as I advanced. I could feel her pressing on my mind, furiously trying to work her way back in so that she'd once again have the upper hand. My beast was still doing the best she could to keep the vampire out, but the parasite's efforts were almost sufficient.

The vampire brought her sword around, aiming her sword at the center of my chest, the spot where I was *going* to be. It was a remarkable display of mentalist power, but it was too little and much, much too late.

I swept the point of her sword out and down, so that it took me through the stomach, and then slashed her across the chest with the claws of my right hand. She collapsed to the ground as her sword dropped from hands too weak to hold it.

"Why? I could have healed him. Without me he'll die."

"I can tell when I'm being lied to. You aren't thousands of years old and you weren't as omnipotent as you wanted me to believe. You pulled a lot out of my mind, but you didn't know that I'll live for another three hundred years."

She was having a hard time talking around the blood leaking out of her mouth, but my hearing was still good enough to make out what she was saying.

"Something so small…you were ready to give up everything for him."

"I still am. I wasn't before, but I am now. I'd give up everything for him, but only if I *know* that my sacrifice will pay off. I couldn't have guaranteed that you were going to help him. You had the upper hand and we both knew it. You had to die and I'll just have to take my chances that Rachel will come through for me."

Chapter 6

Jasmin Bianchi
Near the corner of Nassau and Liberty
Manhattan, New York

Once all the vampires were dead I went back to Ben and found to my relief that he was unharmed. I texted Alec and then gathered up our stuff and carried Ben out into the darkness outside. The text to Alec was probably a waste of time, but somebody needed to know that I was leaving behind a massive problem.

Alec didn't have the resources to scrub the hostel clean, but the Coun'hij did. It was a long shot, but maintaining the cloak of secrecy that had protected us from humans and vampires was the one thing that the Coun'hij had demonstrated a commitment to over the years.

I moved us to a very pricy, very exclusive hotel. It meant that I only had a few days before my money would run out, but it also guaranteed a level of privacy and security that I wasn't going to find anywhere else in the city. I expected to hear from Rachel the next day, but almost forty-eight hours passed before she contacted me.

Go to Nassau Street by yourself. Look for the red neon circle.

By the time her text arrived, my injuries from the fight were almost completely healed, which was the only thing that allowed me to keep control of my beast. If I'd still been weak and hurt, my beast probably would have shifted us into a hybrid and destroyed half the room. I maintained control, but that didn't mean that I liked the order, didn't mean that I was willing to go on letting her do this to me indefinitely.

I saw to Ben before I left, hanging a new IV bag from the golden light fixture above the bed and brushing his hair back so that it wouldn't be in his eyes. He seemed to sleep better that way.

I hung the 'do not disturb' sign on the door and started down towards 25th Street. It took me an hour and a half to find the spot Rachel had been talking about. The red neon circle was barely an inch across, practically hidden behind a window display in the store where it was located. I was debating whether or not to go inside the store when Rachel called me.

"Hi, Jasmin."

"Hi, Rach, more wild goose chases?"

"That depends on you, it always has."

I expected my beast to be unruly, but instead I just felt tired. It had started raining a few minutes before, a light, freezing drizzle, and I wanted nothing so much as to just go back to the hotel and curl up on the bed next to Ben.

"Whatever. Just tell me what you want me to do so I can get it over with and go back to Ben. He doesn't have much longer. I should be spending this time with him rather than running around doing your dirty work."

"Tell me about the hostel."

I snorted. "I suspected that was more of your handiwork."

"Not my handiwork, no more than a gentle nudge to make sure that you were there to stop them."

"You already know everything you need to, then. I killed them, nearly getting killed myself in the process, and then we left."

Rachel was silent for a few seconds and then she sighed. "I know some, but not all. I know what happened, but not how you felt."

"Pain. I felt a lot of pain. That happens when you get stabbed."

"Is that the only pain you felt?"

It took a couple of tries to get my voice working. "No, that wasn't the only pain."

"Why don't you tell me about that?"

I wanted to tell her that it wasn't any of her business, but I forced the beginning of anger back down where it wouldn't explode, at least not yet, and leaned against the window behind me.

"They were a bunch of vampires, a bunch of worthless, bloodsucking parasites, but you already know that. There was this mentalist, a pretty powerful one. She said that she could save Ben, that she could reverse whatever the vampires he was working for had done to him. She said that there weren't very many vampires strong enough to save him, but that she could."

"Did you believe her?"

"Yeah, it only makes sense, at least the bit about a mentalist being able to save him. A mentalist messed him up, it only stands that another mentalist might be able to fix him."

There was something about Rachel's voice, it almost seemed like I was talking to another person for a minute. "That's very logical, Jasmin. Logic can be a harsh mistress though, it doesn't have any room for exceptions or mercy."

"Whatever. Are we done now?"

"No, not quite. You said just now that Ben doesn't have much time left. She wasn't able to help him?"

"I don't know if she could have helped him. I killed her a few seconds after she offered to heal him."

"Because she was a vampire? I thought you were ready to do whatever it took to save Ben."

"Yes, I killed her because she was a vampire, but not for the reason you mean. I couldn't trust her. For all I knew if I let her close enough to work on Ben she would have just made him worse."

"So you would have let her live? You would have taken responsibility for all of the blood she would have shed if you let her go? You would have spared her?"

I felt like a traitor to my own kind, but Rachel kept saying that she needed more proof that I was ready to go however far it took to save Ben.

"Yes, damn it. I would have let her live if I'd been able to guarantee that she would fix him in exchange. I would have traded however many faceless, anonymous people it took in order to keep him alive."

"So you're saying that not all lives are equally valuable?"

I closed my eyes and nodded even though I knew she couldn't see the gesture.

"Yes, is that what you want to hear?"

"Honestly? I'm not sure. I guess I can see both sides of that particular argument right now."

My patience was exhausted, just like my body. I turned and started down the road, heading back to the hotel.

"Where are you going, Jasmin?"

I didn't bother asking how she knew I was moving.

"I'm headed back to Ben. I don't need to be standing here in the rain to play twenty questions with you. We can do that just as well if I'm warm and dry in my hotel room."

"You're right, we could talk just as easily there, but you can't save Ben from there. Geoffrey's in the building you were just standing in front of."

It was suddenly hard to breathe. It took everything I had to manage a response to her. "You're not screwing around with me again?"

"No, he's really there, and you're going to break him out in a few minutes."

"Break him out? He's captive?"

"Yes, he's being held against his will…by vampires."

My stomach clenched tight at the word. Vampires…I'd killed vampires already once in this city. I'd walked away without any kind of serious wound, but it had been a closer fight than almost any other I'd ever had.

"How many?"

"That's not important, Jasmin. It doesn't matter how many there are there, you're going to win him free, I've seen it."

I took a deep breath and then nodded. "How will I know when I've found him?"

"He's the only one there who's chained and bound."

"Okay, which suite is he in? I'll go to him now."

"No, not quite yet, it's not time yet." There was a pause, almost like Rachel was consulting notes or something. "He's on the twenty-third floor, in Suite A."

"Suite A, on the twenty-third floor, okay. What else do I need to know?"

"In a few minutes you're going to see a woman in a red dress walk by, you need to follow her. She'll go to an elevator, but you don't want the same elevator as she takes, you want the next one over. You'll know it's the right one because it will open at the same time as hers."

My mind felt like it was simultaneously reeling in shock and hyper-focused. Every single word she was saying engraved itself on my mind in fire.

"Your elevator will have a vampire on it. He's headed towards Suite A. Follow him, but make it look like you're going to go past him to another suite. As soon as he opens the door to Suite A, kill him."

"Is that all?"

"No, you need to kill everyone there but Geoffrey. It's very important that none of them survive, even the ones who aren't vampires."

The world swayed slightly. I closed my eyes to keep from throwing up. "I'm going to have to kill humans too?"

"Yes. They aren't any more innocent than the vampires. They know what they are working for, at least a little bit. They need to die or else you'll have an execution crew after you before you can make it back to the hotel. In hybrid form the evidence you leave will look like the attack was done by a werewolf, but if there are any eyewitnesses they'll know that they were up against something else."

"Okay, I'll do it."

"Jasmin, this is the most important part. You have to make sure that Geoffrey survives. No matter how badly you get hurt, you can't afford to lose control and let your beast kill him."

"How badly am I going to get hurt?"

"Does it matter? I thought you were willing to pay any price to save Ben."

My breath caught, but I still managed a response. "You're right, all that matters is that I survive so that I can get this Geoffrey guy back to Ben. You've seen how this all ends up, so I don't need to worry."

"I never said that, Jasmin. Even in those instances when you can see things, it doesn't mean that there isn't anything to fear. The man who saw the truck coming at the last second is just as dead as the man who never even saw it before he was killed."

Rachel hung up on me before I could say anything else. I called her back. I wanted to demand an explanation, but she didn't answer and before I could try again, I saw the woman in the red dress.

I wrapped my trench coat tighter around me and then followed her inside, trying to look casual. The stately building, fully of marble and mirrors, reeked of vampires. It was so bad that the stench burned as it traveled through my nose and down into my lungs.

The stainless-steel elevator doors opened exactly at the same time, just like Rachel had said, and I got into the second elevator. I'd never seen such a big elevator, and by the time the doors closed it was so full that I almost felt like I couldn't breathe.

The certainty I'd felt at the start of the conversation with Rachel evaporated as I considered her last statement. I knew Rachel better than almost anyone else. She'd been warning me there at the end. She hadn't wanted to lie to me, but she also hadn't wanted to tell me the whole truth.

There was no way for me to prove it, but I suddenly knew that she couldn't see everything. Her vision was infinitely more powerful than Kristin's dreams, but it was still somehow limited, still somehow constrained such that she didn't know how the next few minutes would go. She'd talked in absolutes—the woman in the red dress, the elevators opening at the same time. She'd acted like she was reading from a script, but that was an illusion.

I fought to keep my pulse steady. It was ludicrous to worry about something so small—the fight at the hostel had proved that the vampire hearing wasn't as sharp as shape shifter hearing, and even if he could hear my heart hammering away inside of my chest he wouldn't be able to pick me out of the crowd as the person who was scared out of her mind. It was silly, but that didn't stop me from doing my best to keep my breathing steady and any trace of concern off of my face.

I might die, but I couldn't control that, all I could control right now was the small things. Breathing, keeping a smile on my face, those were the things that were inside my power right now. I just prayed that I wouldn't have to kill any of my fellow passengers.

That was when I realized just how far gone I was. Killing humans on nothing more than Rachel's word that they weren't innocent, that they knew what they were involved in, was bad enough. Killing innocents who just happened to be in the wrong place at the wrong time was the kind of thing that I'd always despised the Coun'hij for doing.

I would still despise the action, even if it was me that did it, but I was finally ready to kill anyone who got in my way. I would save Ben regardless of the cost, the only question was whether or not I'd be successful. The question of whether or not I'd be able to look him in the eye once this was all over didn't even enter into it, not yet. I'd rather have Ben alive and hating me than see him dead. If that happened then the fact that my hands were clean wouldn't save me from the despair I'd felt stalking me for weeks now.

We made it all the way up to the twentieth floor and without losing much in the way of passengers. A trickle of people got off on the twenty-first, but not enough to make a real difference. I'd nearly resigned myself to the impending murders, but everyone else got off on the twenty-second floor, leaving me with the vampire, a gaunt-looking man, dressed all in black, who made my skin crawl.

A couple of seconds later the elevator slowed and the doors slid open. I could hear Rachel's warning thrumming inside of my head.

I needed to make sure that he thought I was going somewhere else. I slipped out of my trench coat and fished my phone out of my pocket, walking the same direction as him as I pretended to be looking up an address.

The door to Suite A was a large metal affair that was only a few steps from the elevator. The vampire pushed a button and looked at the camera as though expecting to be buzzed through. I spun slowly in place as though trying to figure out which hall led to wherever it was I needed to be going.

I caught the vampire looking at me out of the corner of my eye, but he seemed to have dismissed me as any kind of threat. He stepped closer to the buzzer, entered a code on the number pad next to it, and then slid his finger across a biometric sensor.

As the door clicked with the emotionless sound of a remote unlock, I struck. I'd pulled my trench coat off because I hadn't wanted to walk back to the hotel wearing nothing more than my ha'bit, but I hadn't come up with a solution that would let me save my shoes.

I stepped into the vampire as my beast ripped free of the chains I'd placed around her. My massive hybrid body hit him hard enough to make sure that the door wouldn't shut and lock us back out, and my right hand tore into his back, killing him before he'd even realized that I was anything other than the harmless girl I'd worked so hard to look like.

Just inside of the door was a security booth, but for whatever reason it was empty. I let the corpse drop off of my right hand even as I shook my trench coat off of my left arm. There was a huge, obscenely heavy bookcase across from the security booth. I tipped it over, using it to hold the door shut and ensure that nobody would be able to leave, and then I stalked forward into the suite of rooms.

The stink of vampires was too strong to pick out individual scents, human or otherwise, but that was a blessing. I tore through a blur of bodies and tried not to notice any of the myriad signs that would have told me whether a given victim was human.

A stocky, overweight man in a security uniform came around a corner and went for his gun as soon as he saw me, but he was hopelessly slow. I killed him before his weapon had even cleared its holster. A dozen women in pantsuits and skirts went down singly and in pairs, falling as my claws turned them into red ruin.

A big guy who looked like he'd probably played college football at some point came at me with a heavy metal chair in his hands, but he died as easily as the rest. I killed half a dozen more people in less than two minutes, but it wasn't until I made it to the end of a long hall that I started to run into significant opposition.

A vampire—he was too quick to be a normal human—came at me with four feet of naked steel gleaming darkly in his hand. I knocked his slash wide and then backhanded him into the wall with enough force to break his neck.

Two more vampires, females this time, stepped out of what looked like a conference room a second later, probably alerted by the impact as the vampire I'd just killed hit the wall of the room they were in. I slit the throat of the closest female before she even realized how much danger she was in and then was forced backwards to avoid the sword her companion tried to stab me with.

I spun to one side to avoid her follow-up attack and it was a simple thing to pick up the body of the man and use it as a shield to allow me to get in close enough to finish off the third vampire. I could hear heartbeats inside of the conference room, but the fact that they hadn't come out already to face me indicated that they were either especially dangerous or no threat whatsoever.

Normally I wouldn't have been able to locate either of them, not through a wall, even a wall that was little more than two thin pieces of sheetrock with some aluminum supports between them, but one of them made a profound mistake. He bumped up against his side of the wall and told me exactly where he was in that instant.

I spared a fraction of a second to hope that I wasn't about to punch one of the metal supports and then put my claws through the wall. I took my prey through a kidney and then pulled my hand back a split second before it would have been consumed by the sudden firestorm on the other side of the wall. Even so it was scorched and my fur was smoking when I held my hand up to examine it.

The sprinklers inside of the conference room cut loose instantly, flooding the room with water, but I knew that wouldn't save me if the pyromancer set eyes on me. The most powerful pyromancers didn't need to set you on fire from the outside in, they could cook you from the inside out.

Most buildings were wired so that if any single fire alarm was tripped it would trigger a full evacuation. The rest of the alarms inside of the building hadn't gone off yet, which was a good sign, but only an idiot would program their fire suppression system to continue to pour out hundreds of gallons of water per minute into the conference room without eventually triggering some kind of building-wide escalation. I didn't have much time left.

For a moment I was out of ideas and then I saw the huge, metal clock hanging on the wall next to me. It didn't fit my hand very well, but it was heavy and the edges were thin and hard. I pulled it down from the wall, took a deep breath and then spun past the doorway to the conference center, hurling the clock like a giant metal Frisbee in the instant when I was able to see the last vampire inside, just before my momentum carried me safely past.

I'd moved quickly, but once again it almost hadn't been fast enough. The air had shimmered with heat and the walls had started to smoke for the split second that I'd been in view of my enemy. He'd used his dreadful power and he'd come close to burning me, my skin felt crinkly and tight like I had a bad sunburn, but the sound of his heartbeat had stopped now. I ducked inside the conference room just long enough to confirm that the clock had taken him through the chest, and then headed back down the hall.

The last man who tried to stop me attacked with the curved sword of a samurai. He was fast, much faster than anyone else who had faced me, and I had a sneaking suspicion that his slender blade would shear my limbs from my body just as easily as the two-handed monstrosities the twins at the hostel had been using.

His sword equalized the reach advantage I otherwise would have enjoyed, and he moved with quick, economical motions that left no openings in his defenses for me to exploit. His sword licked out half a dozen times and more than half of his attacks landed, albeit for shallow, nonlethal gashes rather than the mortal wounds he'd been aiming for.

My beast was angry that he'd stood us off for so long, but more importantly, I was getting frustrated. I needed to resolve this now, before he bled me out and made me slow and clumsy. We danced down the hall, him always moving forward, me always moving backwards, for another few seconds before I saw the opportunity I needed.

Once again his sword slashed at me in a horizontal blur, but instead of retreating I moved forward. Both sets of claws were down at my side and I used them to form a basket that was harder than steel, a basket capable of stopping his strike cold before it could cut me in half.

It worked, but I'd severely underestimated both the power behind his attack and the leverage disadvantage I was working under. I stopped his blade, but not before it scored a deep gash into my side just above where my floating ribs would have been in human form.

The vampire lashed out with a kick to my legs, hoping to take advantage of the fact that both of my hands were still tangled up with his blade, but I checked his blow with the talons on my left foot and then leaned forward and bit him at the juncture of his shoulder and neck.

I was still bleeding from my side as I stumbled down the hall, but it wasn't enough to kill me, at least not quickly. I searched all of the remaining rooms and predictably it was the last one that contained Geoffrey.

I sheared through the stainless steel lock with my claws and then walked inside the room and saw Ben's savior. He was in a giant cage and his hands were manacled together, but that wasn't what made my beast cut loose with a wave of power that came within a hairsbreadth of shattering my control.

I wanted to deny the truth of what I was facing but there was no denying the scent that had permeated every square inch of the room. Geoffrey, the one man who could bring Ben back to me, was a vampire, a parasitic bloodsucker that I couldn't possibly trust no matter what Rachel might say.

Chapter 7

Geoffrey
Imastious' Nassau Operations Center
Manhattan, New York

The pain in Geoffrey's head had subsided to something nearly muted enough for him to begin using his mentalist powers again, which meant that it was nearly time for someone to administer another round of drugs to him. Geoffrey had been expecting the door to his room to open for nearly an hour, but when it did finally open, it wasn't another vampire standing in the doorway.

For a second as the creature entered his room, Geoffrey thought he was being attacked by a werewolf. Every single time Geoffrey had found himself up against a werewolf he'd survived by nothing more than luck and the experiences had left a special kind of scar on his psyche. Most nights he woke from nightmares where werewolves were stalking him and no matter how fast he ran or how well he fought, they always pulled him down.

The massive beast facing him through the shining steel bars of his cage was so similar in size and shape to a werewolf that for a moment he was positive his nightmares had come true. He'd seen werewolves ferret out nests of vampires before and the werewolves never attacked without a sound advantage, so it was rare that the vampires came out ahead in those confrontations.

It wasn't until Geoffrey realized that the lights hadn't been flickering that he decided he must be facing something other than a werewolf. The hulking, dark figure stepped across the room and came to a stop before his cage. A second later it tore the door to his cage off of its hinges.

"You're coming with me, Geoffrey."

"Who are you?"

"That's not important. Move or I'll kill you like I killed the rest of the bloodsuckers in this little pocket of hell."

Geoffrey had figured out long before that there must be substantial soundproofing around his room. He never heard anyone approaching his door with food until after they opened the door and stepped into his room, and his yells and the times he'd banged on his cage hadn't ever resulted in anyone coming to look for him.

He'd assumed that the soundproofing was because he was in some normal apartment and Imastious hadn't wanted the neighbors to realize anything unusual was going on. He'd never even considered that there might be a permanent, large group of vampires just outside his door.

Geoffrey filed away the fact that this creature was capable of talking, something no werewolf had ever done, and started towards the door.

"Down the hall to your right."

"I don't suppose you'd be willing to take these handcuffs off?"

"No, keep moving, and don't try any of your mentalist tricks on me either. If I detect you trying to influence me with your ability I'll kill you where you stand."

Despite the threats, Geoffrey let a few strands of his consciousness drift free of his physical body and searched their immediate area. He was careful to keep his probes well away from his captor, but even so it took only a few seconds to establish that there weren't any living minds anywhere within several dozen feet of them.

"Stop. Go inside that room."

Geoffrey complied and found himself inside of what was obviously some kind of surveillance room. There were TV monitors stacked in a large bank in front of the room's single chair and behind was a large piece of equipment that had a shield insignia on it and red lettering that spelled out *FastVault Storage.*

"Destroy it."

"What?"

The creature's voice was subtly alien, as if its vocal cords hadn't ever been meant to speak English, but Geoffrey could tell that it was getting frustrated.

"Destroy all of this equipment. I don't want any record of my arrival or our escape to survive."

Geoffrey poked around for a couple of seconds and then started unplugging different pieces of equipment.

"I don't know very much about this kind of stuff, but it seems to me like the key is that storage array over there. If we take it then there won't be any record of anything that's happened…unless it's being sent somewhere offsite as well."

The creature grunted. "I can't control everything; we'll just have to hope for the best. Go ahead and destroy that then."

Geoffrey shook his head. "I don't think anything less than a very strong magnetic field will make that data irretrievable."

"Fine, pick it up and let's go, we'll take it with us and throw it in a river somewhere."

Geoffrey fought the temptation to talk back to his captor and nodded. There was too much he still didn't understand about what was going on, but whatever it was it apparently didn't want him dead. Given the fact that everyone else in the suite of rooms had apparently been killed over the last few minutes, that felt significant.

His best bet now was to go along and hope that he was able to figure out the score before his usefulness waned. For now he was free of the cage that Imastious had put him in. He might be headed somewhere worse, but it would take time for them to get wherever they were going, and his best chance for escape would come once they were outside with plenty of witnesses around.

Besides, it was too soon to even guess at the capabilities of this bestial almost-werewolf.

Picking up the equipment was more difficult than he'd expected it to be, the result of his hands still being restrained and the sheer weight of the hard drives inside of the device. Geoffrey was motioned back out of the surveillance room and complied with the unspoken order. They were several yards further down the corridor before he saw it, his sword, discarded on the floor next to a corpse.

Geoffrey bent forward, intending on setting the storage device down so that he could pick up his katana, and then froze when the tips of the creature's claws drew tiny dots of blood from his back.

"Don't even think about picking that up."

Geoffrey swallowed a couple of times. "It's my sword. I know you won't believe me when I say that I don't want to use it on you, but I don't. I just don't want it left here. It's the only link I have to my past."

"I never expected sentiment from a bloodsucking parasite like you."

Geoffrey turned around with fire in his eyes. "Stop. You can kill me if you'd like, but don't lump me in with the rest of these pieces of garbage. I am what I am, I don't have a choice about that, but it has been months since I killed someone while feeding."

"You expect me to believe that you're a vampire with a heart?"

"Right now I don't care what you believe, but you will treat me like a person or we'll fight to the death right here and now."

"You would lose."

"Probably, but it doesn't matter much whether I die right now or die once we get wherever you're taking me, I'll be dead either way. Honestly I didn't expect to ever get out of that cage, so as things stand right now I'm much better off than I ever imagined I might be."

"Fine. Keep walking. I'll grab your weapon, and I'll get the sheath too."

Geoffrey picked the storage device back up and started slowly down the hall. There was an odd feeling, like an unseen breeze tracing the back of his neck, and then a familiar set of sounds as his beloved katana was picked up and sheathed.

The two of them were nearly to the front door before Geoffrey realized that the steps following him sounded different, lighter and less harsh. Geoffrey turned around and saw one of the most beautiful women he'd ever seen anywhere.

Previously Melody and Venice had always set the bar when it came to his personal standard of beauty, but as disloyal as it felt to both of their memories, this girl was every bit as beautiful and in some ways even surpassed them. Geoffrey got vague impressions of dark brown hair, similar to Melody's rather than Venice's platinum blond, and the exquisite moderately-curved body of a swimsuit model, but it was the eyes that captured him.

Geoffrey knew that blue eyes were always striking when they appeared along with dark hair and dark skin, but this was more than just that. This girl had an exotic slant to her eyes that he'd never seen anywhere else before and the effect was enchanting in a way that he hadn't known was possible.

"What are you looking at?"

"I didn't know that you could shift forms. I guess it makes sense otherwise you wouldn't be able to conceal your true nature for more than fifteen seconds, but I never even considered the possibility."

"Yeah, whatever. Put that thing down and find me some shoes."

Geoffrey looked around. "Where exactly do you expect me to find shoes in here?"

"Take them off of one of the dead women. One of them is bound to be my size. Look for a women's seven and find some kind of coat for yourself while you're at it. It's cold out there and we have a long walk back to the hotel."

"I'm not going to loot the dead."

"Yes, you are. I killed all of them to get you out of here. I did my part and now you're going to do yours. Besides, I'm the one with the sword, not you. And don't even think of trying to grab a weapon from one of the corpses. I'll be half a step behind you and if you even look like you're going for a weapon I'll slice you into multiple pieces."

The girl held up the sword to punctuate her threat. Geoffrey wanted to attack her, but despite the blood trickling down her side he was pretty sure that she was plenty fast enough to kill him with his sword before he'd be able to close with her. He needed a distraction.

"You already know my name; it would only be polite to introduce yourself."

Geoffrey reevaluated the balance of power between them. The girl was starting to look pale, she must have lost more blood even than he'd realized. If he could keep her talking for a few more minutes and if their destination was far enough away, there was a good chance that she'd pass out before they even arrived.

She obviously wanted to bite his head off, but she swallowed down at least a portion of her rage. "My name is Jasmin, and if you don't get a move on we're both as good as dead. More vampires could be gathering on the other side of that door even as we speak."

Geoffrey shook his head. "There isn't anyone else out there yet, I'd be able to sense them."

The point of her sword drooped slightly, and Geoffrey moved up his timetable by a few minutes. She probably wasn't going to make it out onto the street before collapsing. Geoffrey considered stalling some more, but he didn't want to push her too hard. Instead he set down the storage device and started towards the nearest batch of corpses.

Jasmin pivoted in place, keeping the point of her sword aimed at him until a phone resting on the table next to her started ringing. She picked it up and answered it without taking her eyes off of him.

"Yeah, I survived. Are you just calling with more bad news?"

A look of confusion crossed her face and then she tossed the phone in Geoffrey's direction.

"She wants to talk to you."

The handcuffs around his wrist nearly made him miss the phone, but he snagged it out of the air at the last second and held it up to his ear.

"Hello, who am I talking to?"

"Hi, Geoffrey. You don't know me, but my name is Rachel and you're going to listen to me very carefully. I know that you're thinking about getting away from Jasmin right now. You figure that you can wait just a little longer until she's lost a bit more blood and then you can kill her and make your escape."

"I don't know what you're talking about."

The lie came out as a reflex, while Geoffrey looked around the room in an effort to figure out which camera Rachel was using to monitor him. Rachel laughed.

"Yes, you do, but you're not going to hurt Jasmin."

"I'm not? Is this the part where you tell me that if anything happens to her you'll hunt me down and kill me?"

"Nope, this is the part where I tell you that you're going to help her. You're going to do everything in your power to keep Jasmin alive and get her back to the address I'll be texting you in a couple of minutes."

"Why would I do that?"

"Because Melody isn't dead, and I know where to find her. If you do exactly as I say then I'll tell you where she is. If you let Jasmin die then you'll never see Melody again."

Geoffrey's throat had gone dry between one heartbeat and the next. It took real effort to force words past a tongue that didn't seem to work quite right anymore.

"You're bluffing. The fact that you even know Melody's name just means that you're working for Imastious. He's the only one who has had a chance to skim off those memories. I should kill Jasmin right now just to spite you and him both."

Jasmin bristled and raised her sword as though she was going to make him regret that particular threat, but something made her think better of that course of action.

"I'm not working for Imastious, Geoffrey. In fact, I hate him almost as much as you do. The only difference is that you hate him for his past while I hate him for his future."

"What does that even mean?"

There was silence on the other end of the line for several seconds and then Rachel sighed. "It means that when the time comes I'm going to help you and Jasmin kill him, but I'm the one who decides when that happens, not you."

"All I've heard so far is a lot of pretty words. You still haven't given me anything solid enough to make me think this is anything more than just an especially convoluted plot on Imastious' part."

"It's true, when your worst enemy has raped your mind, stealing everything you know, it makes it hard for me to prove myself to you with anything you know, so I'm going to give you your proof in the form of something you don't know."

Geoffrey opened his mouth to tell her she was an idiot, but she talked right over top of him.

"Lucy. That's the name of the girl that Melody reminded you of, the name of the girl from your past life, from the time before you lost your memory."

"That doesn't prove anything. I worked for Imastious before I lost my memories, he would have known that too."

"You're not denying that the name is right though, are you? Even though you didn't know that fact before I said it? It feels right, doesn't it?"

Geoffrey swallowed a couple of times. "Yes, it feels right."

"Then it will also feel right when I tell you that Lucy was so important to you that you would have done everything possible to protect her. Imastious didn't know about her before you lost your memories."

"How could you know that unless you were working for Imastious?"

"The same way that I know where Melody is right now. I see things, Geoffrey. Things that you need to know even if you aren't ready for them yet."

Geoffrey knew that he was going out of his way now to find reasons to believe Rachel. It was a dangerous thing to be doing, but he couldn't seem to stop himself. He turned to Jasmin. "You know Rachel? She's not a vampire?"

Jasmin had her left arm tight against her side, trying very hard to stem the flow of blood from her side.

"Yes, I know Rachel and no, she isn't a vampire."

He turned back to the phone.

"I believe her. She hates my kind too much to be knowingly working with a vampire, but you could be working for Imastious or another Elder and not even realize it."

Rachel's laugh was like the first ray of sunlight cutting through the clouds after a storm. "Someday you're going to understand how funny that statement was. I'm not working for any vampire."

"But you're working for someone."

"A few days ago I would have said no, but now I'm not so sure."

Something about the way she'd responded sent chills working their way up and down Geoffrey's spine, but she didn't give him a chance to say anything else.

"We're out of time, Geoffrey. Hand me back to Jasmin and don't forget to check her phone for that address. She'll have a first aid kit at the hotel."

"I haven't agreed to help you."

"Maybe not, but you will, it's only a matter of time. You aren't going to be able to pass up a chance to see Melody again."

Jasmin took the phone out of his hand and put it on speaker. "You should have just had him put it on speaker, Rach. I don't particularly like being within arm's reach of him."

"It doesn't matter very much either way, Jasmin. You could hear both sides of the conversation no matter what he did, which you just revealed by taking the phone rather than waiting for him to give it to you."

Jasmin swore. "I guess you're right. Sitting here doing nothing while I bleed to death must have made me testy."

"Shift back to your hybrid form, Jasmin. You're going to need the extra strength to move that bookcase off of the door. While you're at it cut that storage thingy in half—you only need half of the drives to make it so they can't reconstruct the data—and then cut through the chain between Geoffrey's wrists, he's going to need both hands if he's going to get you and the storage device back to the hotel."

"It's too late for all of that, Rach. I won't last another fifteen minutes. You should have told me that I wasn't going to survive this one."

For the first time, Geoffrey could hear worry in Rachel's voice. "It's not too late! Change now. The shift will heal your side some more and give Geoffrey time to get you back to the hotel."

"That doesn't always work, Rach, and you know it. One shift, yes, but two shifts doesn't necessarily heal any more than the one, sometime it makes things worse."

"It's going to work, Jasmin. The question of whether or not you're going to survive boils down to this choice. If you shift you'll make it. If not you are going to die and Ben will die with you. If you die you'll just be proving that you're too weak to deserve him."

Geoffrey would have said that Jasmin was too far gone for anything to get her to move. She'd grounded the tip of the sword and she was slumped back so that she was leaning against a desk and the wall behind it.

She looked like she was only seconds away from collapsing, but Rachel's words had kindled some kind of fire inside of her. She looked up at Geoffrey and her eyes had changed somehow. They were harder and the gorgeous blue he remembered from a few seconds before had turned to the cold blue of glacier ice.

Between one instant and the next she shifted forms, the slender, trim frame of a young woman exploding out into the massive monster that he'd first thought was a werewolf. Jasmin moved towards him with the kind of speed and power that had given the werewolves a special place in his nightmares, and for a second he thought she was going to kill him.

It would have been in keeping with the angry hatred she'd displayed so far towards him, but the flashing claws parted the chains between his handcuffs instead of dismembering him and then she was moving past him, shouldering the heavy steel bookcase to one side. Jasmin turned back towards the storage device he'd packed all of the way from the surveillance room and then sheared through it like it was no more than butter.

Jasmin looked back at him and even opened her mouth as though to say something else and only then did Geoffrey see the bright trail of blood that she was leaving behind. Rachel had been wrong, the bleeding had gotten worse rather than healing. Jasmin managed a single step toward him and then collapsed at his feet.

Chapter 8

Jasmin Bianchi
Pinnacle Luxury Hotel
Manhattan, New York

I hadn't expected to regain consciousness, so when I opened my eyes all of the other smaller shocks faded away underneath the sheer astonishment at having survived. I was back in the hotel room with Ben, who looked like he had lost three more pounds that he couldn't afford to lose while I'd been asleep.

My ha'bit had been cut away from my side and bore the expected white second-skin of gauze and tape. I gingerly pulled the tape up and probed the pink scar that was all that remained of the wound that had nearly killed me. A quick survey of the rest of my body indicated that everything else was healed as well so I tried to roll out of the huge bed I'd been sharing with Ben.

I stood too quickly and nearly fell. I'd expected to be light-headed after losing so much blood, but I was even less stable than I'd anticipated. I made a grab for the bed, but I was too far away and my legs didn't seem to want to work. I managed to get them to work for short bursts, but not at the same time. It wasn't pretty, but it was enough. I dropped down onto the thick cream carpet in a semi-controlled rush that was only slightly slowed by my erratically functioning legs.

Once I was on the floor I wanted nothing so badly as to just close my eyes and stay there, but I forced myself up onto all fours and slowly made my way over to the closest chair. I was resting against it in an effort to gather enough strength to try and stand again when I heard movement outside the bedroom door. A second later Geoffrey opened the door.

"Are you okay?"

"Well, it looks like Rachel was right and you decided against killing me in my sleep, so I guess I've been worse."

Geoffrey didn't respond for several seconds and I suddenly realized just how little his face gave away. He'd been less guarded right after I'd freed him, like the shock of no longer being a prisoner had caused him to lower some internal veil, but if so it was back up now.

I took a moment to more fully examine him now that I wasn't moments away from bleeding out. Geoffrey was slender in the way that a marathoner was slender. He wasn't bulky, but there wasn't any wasted weight on him anywhere. He was only a little more than average height, maybe an inch under six feet, and he had piercing brown eyes and short, straight brunette hair. I got the feeling that his face could be wonderfully expressive under the right circumstances, but right now it was an expressionless mask.

"You're probably hungry, Jasmin. I left a sports drink on the table for you. There is leftover Chinese takeout in the fridge, but the sports drink will get calories into your system as fast as possible. While you are finishing it I'll go get the leftovers warmed up."

I'd forced myself to my feet as soon as I'd seen him, not because it had been the smart thing to do, but because some primitive instinct refused to let him see me like that. He'd already seen me as vulnerable as I could possibly get and hadn't acted on my weakness, but it still went against the grain to let him see just how little strength I had right now. It was always possible for him to change his mind when it came to working with me.

There was no telling what combinations of factors would trigger an attack so I simply had to take care of as many as I could. *Control what you can control and try not to worry too hard about everything else.* I practically sounded like Alec now.

The dizziness was back full force now that I was standing up, but my death grip on the table kept me from falling down and once he turned away from me I lowered myself down into the closest chair. I popped open the sports drink and took a sip. It was lukewarm and sweeter than I normally liked, but after that first taste I couldn't stop myself from sucking the whole thing down in seconds.

He'd been right, I'd needed that even more than I'd realized. I sat there for a couple of seconds until the tiny microwave in the main room beeped and then levered myself back up onto my feet and made my unsteady way across the soft brown carpet to the bedroom door.

"I would have brought it in to you."

I shook my head as I gently pulled the bedroom door shut behind me. I still wasn't up to any kind of fight, but some combination of the sports drink or simply just being awake for a few more minutes was doing the trick and I could at least walk without falling over.

"No, it's fine, I need to be up and about. Besides, I'd rather not disturb Ben any more than we have to. How long have I been out?"

"About a day and a half. You're just about out of full IV bags. I used one for you when we first got back here and then have been hanging a new one for Ben every few hours."

I sat down, picked up a fork and started in on the leftovers. We probably would have just sat there in silence for the next hour if my phone hadn't started ringing. I didn't recognize the number, but these days that usually meant it was Rachel calling.

I answered it and then stuck it on speaker phone when she started talking.

"I'm glad the two of you made it back to the hotel safely without any more problems, and that you're up and walking around now, Jasmin."

Geoffrey cut in before I could respond. "You promised to tell me how to find Melody. Where is she?"

I shook my head. "No way, you help Ben and then she'll tell you that."

"What's wrong with him?"

"Do you really expect me to believe that you didn't already ransack both of our minds?"

The words jumped out of my mouth of their own accord. I knew I shouldn't be provoking him, but I couldn't help myself. A couple of seconds passed in silence before I realized that my beast was leaning against the bars of her metaphysical cage. She didn't like Geoffrey and that was bleeding into my feelings, reinforcing my own natural dislike of him.

Geoffrey looked uncomfortable, not like someone caught in a lie exactly, but like someone who was doing something that they weren't sure was in their best interest. "Believe what you will, I haven't scanned either of you. Why don't you give me the benefit of the doubt and just explain what is going on since you're so desperate to have me help you."

"I'm not desperate."

"Fine, let's just sit here for the next few days then. I'm sure that Ben will get stronger rather than weaker while we wait."

Rachel sighed. "Ben was working for a vampire here in New York a little while ago. Once he realized who he was working for he tried to get away but they locked him up. Jasmin and another of our friends broke in and got him out, but he freaked out as soon as they left and Jasmin had to knock him unconscious in order to get him away."

"He never woke up after that, did he?"

My mouth had gone dry. "No, he didn't. How did you know that?"

"It's called a kill switch. The really powerful, really old mentalists implant them in their people as a way of stopping them from running away. Usually they aren't actual kill commands. Mostly they are designed to make it easy for their master to track them down, preprogrammed behaviors and ways of thinking that seem innocuous, but which lead them right back into captivity."

"Usually?"

"Sometimes the person in question is too valuable or dangerous to be permitted to fall into someone else's hands. In those cases they'll program the kill switch to literally kill them.

Sometimes their hearts will stop working, other times they kill themselves for no apparent reason, but usually they just go to sleep and never wake back up."

"Like what's happening to Ben."

"Yeah, like what's happening to Ben."

The room wobbled around me, but my grip on the table with my left hand kept me from falling out of my chair. I had to be strong, for Ben's sake if for no other reason.

"Can it be reversed?"

Geoffrey shrugged. It was an unconcerned gesture, but I got the feeling that he was *trying* to give off that impression.

"Not by the person they are implanted in. Usually a full-on kill switch takes effect so quickly that there isn't any chance for anyone to intervene. It's not like there's a ton of really powerful mentalists running around, and sometimes a kill switch isn't really a kill switch, it's a trap designed to incapacitate or kill any vampire who tries to mess around inside of the victim's mind."

"Can it be reversed?"

I didn't have to try to put a hint of steel into my voice. All I needed to do was stop trying quite so hard to be civil to the bloodsucker sitting across from me. My voice going cold and distant was just the natural result of how I really felt about him.

Geoffrey looked back at me and something behind his eyes told me he wasn't the kind of person I should be pushing right now. "I don't know. I've never seen it done, at least not that I remember, but there have been whispers, legends really, of people managing it."

"Fine, then fix him. Once you're done Rachel will tell you where this Melody chick is and we can all go our separate ways."

Geoffrey shook his head. "No, we do this my way or we don't do it at all. We go get Melody and then I'll go inside of Ben's mind and reverse the damage that was done to him."

A white-hot torrent of anger broke free from my beast and it was all I could do to stop myself from transforming.

"No, I don't trust you."

"You don't have a choice."

His response only fanned the fires inside of me even higher. I could tell that my eyes had changed already and I'd picked up the fine tremble that indicated that I was starting to lose my battle to retain this shape.

"You'll never see Melody again."

"Maybe, but I don't think so. It's possible that Melody is really still alive and that my inaction will result in her dying, but it's also possible that this is all just some kind of farce designed to convince me to dive into Ben's mind. I'm willing to bet on the fact that you care more about Ben, about the prospect of having to watch him die than I care about the slight possibility that you and Rachel *aren't* lying to me."

"I'll kill you myself!"

Geoffrey stepped back away from the table and I suddenly noticed the hilt of his sword. It had been mostly hidden by the trench coat he was wearing, or I would have seen it sooner. My beast wanted me to kill him now before he could stick that sword into us one night while we were sleeping. She wasn't convinced that he could help Ben, but even if he could, she believed in self-preservation above all else.

Rachel's voice sliced through the rising tension like it was nothing more than a mirage. "Both of you sit back down. Killing each other won't accomplish anything for any of us."

I looked down and realized she was right, somewhere along the way I'd stood, knocking my chair over.

Truth be told, I was actually relieved that Rachel was stepping in to defuse the situation. I was pretty sure I could take Geoffrey under normal circumstances, but I was still weak and wobbly from my injuries. As things currently stood, he would probably cut me down without even working up a sweat.

"I'm listening, Rach. What's your compromise?"

There was another long pause before Rachel responded. "You're going to have to take this on faith, Jasmin. I've seen enough to know that Geoffrey isn't going to betray you. You're no less honorable than he is, but my vouching for you doesn't carry any weight with him."

My tremble hadn't disappeared and it redoubled as I listened to Rachel. After everything else we'd been through, after all of the times I'd nearly died, I couldn't believe that she was telling me Ben was going to continue to decay before my eyes while the solution to everything that had been done to him slept less than a dozen yards away from us.

I wanted to protest but Rachel didn't give me a chance. "I promise, Jas, this is the only way. He'll walk before he'll take us on faith and if he walks there isn't any other way to save Ben. There are others who could do it, but they'd kill you both or turn him against you instead of helping."

"You swear, Rachel? Because if you're lying to me I will find you and when I kill you it won't be a clean death. You've already put me through hell twice over."

Part of me knew that I was pushing too hard. This wasn't some bloodsucking vampire I was talking to, it wasn't one of the Coun'hij, it wasn't my archenemy, it was Rachel. In some ways she deserved how I was treating her, but mostly she didn't. I couldn't seem to help myself though. I'd never been the best at keeping my mouth in check and these days I was even worse at it. My beast was just too powerful.

"I swear it. The road isn't going to be easy but if we all do everything just right, this ends up with you both getting what you want."

"Fine, we'll do it your way. Melody first and then Ben gets cured."

Geoffrey nodded, but Rachel wasn't done.

"That's not the extent of the deal. Ben can't die or the whole deal is off, and I don't just mean that I won't help you find Melody anymore, I mean I'll lead you into a trap that is guaranteed to kill you, Geoffrey."

"I can live with that. As long as the two of you lead me to Melody I'll do everything within my power to save him."

There was a new edge to Rachel's voice that I wasn't sure I'd ever heard before. "That's not good enough, not for either side. Melody isn't just sitting in the suburbs somewhere waiting for the two of you to come get her, she's being held captive. The deal is this. Jasmin will help you break into where Melody is being held, and in return you will do everything possible to help Ben, including going into his mind and strengthening whatever needs strengthened to keep him alive if it takes longer than you're expecting to get to Melody. In return I'll do everything I can to move the two of you along towards your goals of saving Melody and saving Ben. That's the deal, take it or leave it."

Geoffrey's poker face slipped a little and I couldn't blame him. The 'deal' that Rachel had just offered him was actually better than what he'd been after. She'd thrown in me helping him free Melody from who knew what kind of nasty beasties and all that I'd gotten in exchange was slightly different language when it came to him saving Ben. Geoffrey was very satisfied with what he'd been offered, but that didn't mean that I was happy with it.

"Hold on, Rach, I never agreed to throw myself into any kind of fight to save this Melody chick."

"Do you trust me, Jasmin?"

"Honestly? For the last week or two all you've done is throw me from one mess where I've almost died to the next bloody snafu. I'm not sure that you really deserve much trust anymore."

For the first time in a while Rachel sounded a little hurt. "You've had a rough go of things, but I've kept you alive so far. I'm not going to throw you into anything you can't win, Jasmin. Everything that's happened so far has happened for a reason, you have to believe me."

I didn't want to agree, but something like fifteen or sixteen years of shared trials pulled an answer out of me.

"Yeah, I guess I still trust you."

"Then agree to the deal. It's the best you're going to get out of him. I promise. I've *seen* it."

"Okay, I agree, as long as you and Mr. Fangs over there agree to hold up your ends of things."

Geoffrey nodded, but before I could tell him that he had to actually *say* yes, Rachel jumped in again. "A nod isn't going to suffice, Geoffrey. Oh, and I agree, or promise or whatever."

"Very well, I agree too. I have to say though that you're a pretty poor fortune teller. Anyone who could really see the future would have found a way to corner me into agreeing to something more along the lines of what Jasmin wanted just now. After the way you've botched this little negotiation you're lucky I'm agreeing at all. I don't know how you're accomplishing some of these little tricks, maybe you've got some kind of video feed here or something, but it's obvious to me that you can't see the future like you've been implying."

Unlike before, Rachel didn't sound hurt, she just sounded tired. "I don't actually care what you believe, Geoffrey. The truth is that there isn't anything important out there that's hidden from me, but that doesn't matter, at least not right now. You still believe me enough that you're going to act. You're going to go after Melody and when the appropriate time comes you'll go inside of Ben's mind and you'll exercise every bit of knowledge and power you have at your fingertips to do what you've just committed to."

Geoffrey hadn't looked particularly mad before, but he was obviously angry now. "I've had more months than I care to think about listening to that kind of all-powerful garbage from Imastious. I'll help Ben after you two take me to Melody, but don't try to double-cross me, and stop lying to me. It's only a matter of time before I figure out how you're doing this. Nobody is omniscient."

"I never said that I was omniscient, merely that I see the important stuff. Maybe you're operating from a false premise, maybe this negotiation wasn't important enough for me to see it."

Geoffrey's laugh was biting. "Maybe, but that isn't the only possible answer."

"You're right, it's not the only possible answer. The other option is that this negotiation needed to happen just the way that it did."

Geoffrey just laughed harder, but I could hear Rachel continue over the sound of his amusement.

"Are you really that ready to dismiss the idea, Geoffrey? Are you really positive that our little discussion just now wasn't the proverbial flapping of the butterfly's wings that creates a hurricane months or even years from now?"

Geoffrey's laughter cut off instantly, but he didn't seem ready to answer her.

"Right, I didn't think so. Just do your part, Jasmin will do hers, and you'll both get what you've asked for once you've paid the price."

I cleared my throat. "So what's the next step?"

"Go find Melody. Puppeteer has her."

Chapter 9

Jasmin Bianchi
Pinnacle Luxury Hotel
Manhattan, New York

Rachel hung up on us before I could ask her where Puppeteer was. I should have gotten my question out sooner, but I'd been so shocked by the revelation that Geoffrey's girl was being held by one of the Coun'hij that I'd just sat there for several seconds.

"How about you tell me who Puppeteer is and why Rachel just made sure that she wouldn't have to tell us how to find him?"

Geoffrey looked calm, but I could hear his heart hammering away at his chest and he smelled like his body temperature was elevated. It wasn't until that point that I realized just how controlled he usually was. I should have been getting all kinds of non-verbal clues off of him before then. Scent, heartbeat, respiration, normally all of that combined to tell a shape shifter what another person was feeling.

Usually I could tell when someone was lying to me, but Geoffrey hadn't been giving off any of the normal cues until right after Rachel hung up on us. Usually you didn't see that kind of thing out of anyone other than a sociopath or another shape shifter, one who'd spent decades training themselves not to betray what they were actually thinking.

It was a bad sign, not because I really thought that Geoffrey was a sociopath, at least not any more or less than any other vampire, but because I didn't actually *know* whether he'd been telling the truth when he'd said that he would help Ben. I was depending on Rachel too much and it had happened without me even realizing it.

"You just realized something, what was it?"

I looked over at Geoffrey and shook my head. "It doesn't have anything to do with Puppeteer."

"That doesn't mean that it isn't important though, and you don't expect me to really believe that you were just thinking about something unrelated to what Rachel just told us."

"I said drop it."

For a second I thought that I'd gone too far. I wasn't any more prepared to fight him now than I'd been a few minutes ago and this time Rachel wasn't available to keep us from going for each other's throats.

"I could find out if I really wanted to."

I shook my head. "If I catch you poking around in my head I *will* kill you, no questions asked. Don't think you can sneak something in there without me realizing it either, my beast is very good at detecting those kinds of things."

I dialed Rachel's latest number again, hoping beyond hope that she'd pick up, but it went straight to voicemail. I sighed in frustration and then looked up to find Geoffrey looking at me, but he looked more curious than angry.

"Your beast? You talk like it's a separate entity inside of you."

"She is. I'm in control almost all of the time, but she's always back there. She's where the power to change shapes comes from, and she doesn't view the world in quite the same way as you or I do."

Geoffrey nodded, obviously filing that information away for later analysis. "So who is Puppeteer?"

"I want your word that all of this stays a secret. My people have worked very hard for a very long time to keep our existence a secret from the vampire community."

"I didn't think that you trusted me to keep any promises."

"I don't, but I'd be pretty stupid not to swear you to secrecy on the off chance that you really do take your promises seriously."

Geoffrey looked at me for several long seconds before nodding. "Very well. I don't actually associate with any other vampires and I'll be doing my best to keep things that way, but if things change for some reason I'll keep your secrets as best I can."

I was going to protest the weak wording he was using, but he stopped me with a gesture. "I'd like to promise that I'd take what you're about to tell me to my grave, but the truth is that I can't guarantee that. I could be recaptured by Imastious at any point, and if that happens it's unlikely that I'll be able to keep anything back from him. It's one of the hazards that come along with being a vampire."

That shut me up faster than I would have believed possible. When Adri had joined the pack she'd commented more than once that pack life was incredibly intrusive. I'd been a part of that life for as long as I could remember; I'd long since become used to just how much everyone was up in everyone else's business, but that didn't mean she was wrong. Pack life was bad enough. Never being able to lie to a direct question sucked in ways that most people couldn't even begin to understand, but that was nothing compared to what Geoffrey was describing.

"Okay, thank you for promising. We shape shifters, the wolves at least, are spread out through all of the continental United States and Canada. Mostly we are just a loose assortment of independent packs that range in size from nine or ten wolves all the way up to eighty or ninety wolves."

"You have a third shape then as well?"

That threw me for a loop for a moment. "Yes. We actually think of our wolf bodies as our second shape and the hybrid form as the third shape, but you're not wrong. I've got a total of three forms."

I waited for a second to see if he had any other questions and then continued. "A long time ago the packs were united by a powerful king. Some people thought a new golden age had begun, but his son was deposed by a group of the most fearsome hybrids then living. Ever since then we've been ruled by an unjust group that calls itself the Coun'hij. Puppeteer is one of the members of the Coun'hij."

"So by stealing Melody away from him we'll be making enemies of your entire people?"

I shook my head. "There is little love lost between many of the packs and the Coun'hij. Even some of the members of the Coun'hij are said not to care much for each other. Currently large portions of my people are in active rebellion against the Coun'hij."

"And yet you're still incredibly scared of the Coun'hij."

I wanted to bristle at the accusation, but the truth was that he was right. I was scared of the Coun'hij and of Puppeteer especially. I was a hybrid, a big, fast, strong hybrid, but I wasn't

Alec or Grayson. I hadn't ever manifested one of the unique abilities that would have allowed me to immobilize or kill dozens of people instantly.

"Yes, I'm scared of them, Puppeteer most of all. Some hybrids manifest special abilities, things that can't be explained by modern physics any more than your mentalist abilities can be. Puppeteer is one of the most powerful of these kinds of hybrids."

When I closed my eyes at night I could still sometimes see the mass of werewolves coming for us, tearing through the manor house, bigger and faster than any hybrid, lethal in ways that most of us could never even hope to match.

"You're aware of the existence of creatures that look like my hybrid form only larger and stronger?"

Geoffrey nodded and for the first time he seemed to share some of my fear. "Yes, there were rumors even before they arrived. Legends among the vampires of things that hunted us, that preyed on us like most of my kind preys on the humans. I suppose, looking back now, that some of those myths might have been due to your kind rather than the werewolves, but even so, some of the other vampires in the city didn't want to believe any of it was really happening when the werewolves started picking us off. There were dozens of them, maybe even hundreds."

This was something new. Werewolves had always preferred killing vampires and shape shifters over humans, but it didn't seem possible for fighting on that scale to take place without the humans finding out about it.

"When did that happen and how did you beat them? Your powers don't work on them so you would have had to kill them with steel."

"You're right to a point. They absorb our powers, but they can only absorb so much. If enough vampires, especially vampire Elders, focus their gifts on a single werewolf they can overcome its absorption abilities and kill it, usually by setting it on fire."

Geoffrey was silent for nearly a minute, but I didn't disturb him. Someone who hadn't been through the hell of battle might have pushed for answers right then, but I didn't. I'd survived the same kind of flickering nightmare and I was more than willing to let him relive those moments if that was what he needed right then.

"As to when it happened, it was just a few weeks ago here in New York. You remember the riots that happened towards the end of the year?"

"Yes. Now that you mention it, I remember that there were reports of widespread blackouts in large sections of the city, but everyone said that some of the city's power distribution infrastructure had been destroyed during the riots."

"No, that was the werewolves. They were hunting us. It seemed like they outmatched us at every turn. They could sense us and they only attacked when they had us outnumbered. We lucked out and killed a few, but it all culminated in a huge fight involving nearly every vampire in the city."

"You guys won?"

"Yes. The individual werewolves were nothing more than cunning beasts, but sometimes it seemed like there was a larger intelligence at work. I outsmarted it by virtue of using humans to help us win. We equipped them with crossbows and they killed enough werewolves for the vampires not to be swept away in the initial rush."

The answer had been there all along, he just hadn't known about the Coun'hij, hadn't known enough to put the pieces together and neither had I.

"The larger intelligence you just spoke of was almost certainly Puppeteer. His power is the ability to control werewolves, vast numbers of werewolves."

The silence between us stretched out again. Geoffrey finally sighed and rubbed his temples. "It all makes more sense now. I wouldn't have thought something like that to be possible, but it explains a lot. He's the one who brought the werewolves out of hiding in such large numbers after so long.

"It doesn't explain *why* he came after us like that, or why he wanted Melody, but it makes sense that Melody would still be with him. The werewolf that took…I couldn't ever explain it before now, but it all fits together too perfectly to be anything but the truth."

My beast still didn't trust him. She would have happily ripped his throat out, and I couldn't blame her. He was a vampire. Regardless of what he'd been before the transformation, regardless of the code he might be trying to cling to now, he was a parasite. It was a biological imperative and nothing he did could change that. He killed people in order to survive.

Still, I felt the slightest bit of kinship with him. "I'm sorry, Geoffrey. I know what it's like to lose someone you care about. My friends and family have suffered at the hands of Puppeteer and the rest of the Coun'hij for centuries. He's a monster and I wish someone had been able to put him down ages ago."

Geoffrey shrugged. "It sounds to me like that would have been impossible. Surely he's the most dangerous individual in the entire world. He must have a constant guard of werewolves, big, strong and impervious to any supernatural ability regardless of whether it is wielded by your people or mine. Where is he?"

"Nobody is sure. The Coun'hij is powerful, but they could never stand up to the full might of the rest of the shape shifters in North America. Their greatest shield is the fact that they have kept their location a secret ever since they came to power. I'm sure that they've been tracked back to their base at some point or another, but they've always been able to seal the leak, kill whomever they needed to kill, and then move to a new location."

"So we're faced with an impossible task then. First we have to find Puppeteer and the rest, and then once we manage that we'll be up against what I can only assume are dozens of your kind and dozens or possibly hundreds of werewolves as well."

My breathing had slowed down the way it sometimes did when I was faced with an especially difficult decision. Apparently all of those years of yoga and breath control meditation had left more of an impact on me than I'd thought when I stopped practicing them.

"I can help with the second problem. I mean I can't make hundreds of werewolves magically go away, but I have...contacts inside of the rebels who are currently trying to overthrow the Coun'hij. If we can find a way to ferret out the location of the Coun'hij's base then my friends will come in force and some of them are pretty big equalizers. We'd at least have a chance of winning, maybe even more than a chance if enough of the independent packs have decided to join the rebellion by then."

I knew I shouldn't feel bad about being so vague where Alec and the others were concerned. Knowing names and numbers wouldn't actually make any difference to Geoffrey, not in any way that mattered, but I still felt bad for some reason.

I couldn't let that sway me though. Alec and the others were already facing off against the combined might of the Coun'hij. If Geoffrey ended up under the thumb of some older mentalist then everything he knew was going to become common knowledge among the vampire community. The last thing I wanted was to put Alec and the rest of my friends in the crosshairs of a bunch of vampires too.

Geoffrey looked at me for a long while, almost as though trying to figure out how far he could trust my promise of reinforcements, and then he nodded. "That's good, that's actually the piece I was more worried about."

"You mean that you've got a way to find the Coun'hij?"

"Yes, I think I do. It's going to require some groundwork before we can even hope for my plan to work, but it's a possibility. The Coun'hij must show their faces from time to time at least. It's impossible to rule otherwise."

"Yes, although as often as not it's merely their enforcers who come through to knock heads together."

Whatever response Geoffrey had planned on making was interrupted by the quiet chirp of the timer on the microwave.

"What's that for?"

Geoffrey was already on his feet and headed towards the bedroom. "It's time to hang a new bag for Ben."

The surge of emotion that shot through me was too complex to identify, and my beast was behind much of it, pushing with all of her might and lending the feelings more power than they otherwise would have had. Ben was *ours* and she didn't like Geoffrey sticking his nose in our business.

I was sure Geoffrey didn't think of his actions in that light, but what he was doing was a kind of challenge to our ownership. It was another reason for my beast to hate him, but I didn't share quite the same view of things. I didn't like what he was doing, but for me it was more about the fact that *I'd* come up short, not that Geoffrey had done anything wrong.

I was ready to kill innocents if needed, had potentially already done so, but I hadn't even thought to check on Ben when I woke up a few minutes ago. I was grateful that Geoffrey had taken such good care of Ben, but I was likewise embarrassed and disappointed in myself that he'd been forced to make up for my lack.

While I was still struggling through my feelings Geoffrey had stepped inside the bedroom and by the time I made it in he already had a new IV bag hanging from the light fixture mounted to the wall just above the bed.

Geoffrey was double-checking the line down to Ben's arm with the deft movements of a professional, but that wasn't what caught my eye. Ben looked content in a way that I'd only rarely seen before. Maybe looked wasn't the right word, maybe it was more about the way that he felt than anything else, but I was suddenly sure that Ben was more at ease with Geoffrey than he'd ever been with anyone else.

I waited to speak until we were back out in the main room and had the door closed so as not to bother Ben. "Thank you. For taking care of him and for taking care of me."

Geoffrey shrugged. "It wasn't like I could just let the two of you die, not if it might have meant that Rachel would refuse to tell me where Melody was. Besides, it's obvious that he means a lot to you. I guess you could say that Melody is my Ben. I understand at least some of what you're going through right now."

"But you're still going to let him sit there and suffer instead of fixing him now?"

"I'm afraid so. I don't take any joy in his suffering, but Ben is the only leverage that I have against you and Rachel. I'm not going to give that up, not if there is any way to avoid doing so."

"You make it really hard not to keep hating you."

Geoffrey acted like he hadn't heard me. "If you can find a way for us to capture one of the

Coun'hij, preferably one of the less dangerous ones, then I can rip the location of Puppeteer and the rest of them out of his mind."

I blinked in surprise. Even with him sitting before me as a constant reminder of what vampires were capable of, it was still hard to think in terms of reading someone's mind. "You're strong enough to do that?"

Geoffrey's nod was a short, choppy motion. "I'm strong enough. The real question is what we'll have to do to them to weaken them sufficiently that they can't resist me."

"You don't like the idea of having to torture them, do you?"

"Not particularly, but I'll do it, and you'll help me if it comes to that."

It wasn't a question, and it wasn't a particularly challenging statement. He wasn't trying to draw any kind of rise out of me, he was just stating a fact that we both knew.

"I guess you're right at that. If it comes to it, I'll do even worse than torturing one of the Coun'hij's trained killers in order to save Ben."

"I think we understand each other quite well, Jasmin. That's the way that I feel about Melody too. Can you find a way for us to capture one of these guys?"

"I think so. Let me make a couple of calls."

I tried Alec first, but he didn't answer. I left a message asking him to give me a call and then hung up feeling more than a little betrayed by his failure to pick up. I debated among the remaining options open to me and then dialed Isaac's last known number.

"Jasmin, is that really you?"

"Hi, Isaac."

"You don't have any idea how good it is to hear your voice. Everyone else has pretty much gone dark lately."

"I was afraid of that, I just tried Alec and he didn't pick up. Are you, Ash and Kristin all okay?"

He cleared his throat and I could tell he was trying to decide whether or not to lie to me.

"Tell me the truth, Isaac."

"Things are pretty bad here. Kristin got hurt and lost a lot of blood. I've spent weeks now worrying that she was never going to wake up from her coma. We got forced down to the territory claimed by Ash's old pack."

"What the crap were you guys thinking? You have to get out of there right now or Onyx and the others will kill you!"

His breathing picked up as he struggled to keep control of himself. I'd crossed a line and we both knew it. Back in the old days Isaac had always been clearly dominant to me. I hadn't particularly liked that fact, although he'd been better to me than James had been, but it had been one of those hard realities that I hadn't been able to get away from.

That was all up in the air now. He and I hadn't faced off against each other since I'd manifested my third shape. It was anyone's guess who would win a fight right now. I had size and strength on my side for the first time ever, but he had years of experience fighting as a hybrid in his corner. My beast was eager for that fight, hungry to prove herself the better fighter, but I shouldn't have let that push me into treating him like he was subordinate to me.

"I'm sorry, Isaac, that was out of line. I'm having a harder time keeping control of stuff lately."

His laugh was a bitter-sounding thing. "Join the club. It seems like I want to rip the head off of anyone who even talks to me lately. The truth is that it's too late. Onyx's people found us within a few hours of us arriving. Ash tried to shoot his way out, but this new guy just shrugged off all of the bullets and practically tore him in two."

My hands were shaking, but I couldn't have said whether it was rage or fear causing it. "He'll be okay, though, right?"

"I'm not sure. Normally I'd say yes, but you know Ash, he's not a very fast healer."

It was bad news on several levels. I'd always liked Ash. He was competent in a quiet, no-nonsense way and he'd been part of the glue that had held us all together when things had been at their worst, back when I'd been pretty sure that Alec was only days or weeks away from self-destructing and taking all of the rest of us down with him.

That would have been enough to make me want him to pull through his injury all by itself, but there was also the fact that with him and Kristin both injured Isaac was all by himself down there. Isaac was big and tough, but he wasn't going to be able to take on an entire pack all by himself.

"I'm sorry to hear that."

"Yeah, me too. How's Ben?"

"Weaker every day. I don't know how much longer he's going to make it, but Rachel seems to finally be helping me rather than just leading me on some kind of cross-continental wild goose chase. Have you heard from any of the others?"

"Just Andrew."

I wasn't sure whether or not to pursue that particular line of questioning. Andrew had practically adopted Isaac. The two of them were close, but Andrew was also Jess's biological father. I couldn't necessarily blame Jess for what she'd done over the last few months, but talking about Jess was going to re-open some pretty deep wounds for Isaac.

"He's okay. We only had a minute to talk, but he told me that Jessica phoned him. He said that she was being really evasive about where they are, but that she's found some kind of big secret."

"I'm not sure whether that's a good thing or a bad thing."

"I'm pretty sure it's a bad thing. Whatever Wyatt is involved in it isn't good."

Isaac paused to give me a chance to respond but I wasn't quite sure what to say about that either. He had an almost pathological hatred of Wyatt. I agreed that there was something off about Wyatt, Carson and Grayson, but that didn't necessarily mean that they were the villains of the piece.

"I'm serious, Jasmin. I'm starting to feel like I'm playing the wrong game, like I thought we were playing checkers and now it turns out that everyone is playing three-dimensional chess only I don't know the rules. Onyx has a new guy here, someone I've never heard of before, and he fights like Wyatt used to fight."

"That weird grappling style?"

"Yeah, that alone would pretty much make him unstoppable for the rest of us who don't know that kind of fighting, but that isn't all. Ash shot him, several times, and in all of the right places, but it didn't even slow him down. I saw bullets ricochet off of him after hitting places where I've been cut before. There shouldn't have been bone there, but there was."

I felt like throwing up. I could tell that Isaac was half convinced that he'd been seeing things, but I knew that he wasn't, only this wasn't just my secret to tell.

"Does he have blue eyes?"

"I don't remember for sure, but I don't think so. Why, how does that matter?"

"You need to do everything you can to stay clear of this guy, Isaac. You weren't imagining things. I can't explain, but your suspicions are correct, whoever he is he's going to be faster, stronger, and harder to kill than any hybrid has a right to be."

"Like Alec."

It wasn't a question, and I knew then that I'd just confirmed suspicions that he'd had for a while now.

"Yes, like Alec. If you could get around behind him and manage a good clinch you could still kill this guy, but otherwise it will be like fighting someone in armor."

"Where are his weak points?"

"I don't know, Isaac, I swear. I don't...I don't have it. Donovan might be able to tell you, but I'm not sure he'll be willing to give away Alec's secrets like that. Just stay clear of this guy, do whatever it takes."

"I understand, but I don't think that's going to be possible, Jasmin. Thanks for warning me though."

His voice was different. His words were fine, but the way that he was saying them made me want to cry. He hadn't given up, not exactly, but he sounded resigned. He was going to go down fighting, but he didn't expect to win.

Thanatas, the ancient king who'd been the last to rule as monarch over all of the wolves, had been a storied warrior, but very few people even suspected that his abilities had been more than just raw skill and the innate strength and speed of his hybrid body. I only knew because I was a direct descendant of one of his sons.

Thanatas had possessed the ability to mold his body, making it stronger and faster, but he hadn't stopped there. He'd gone on to reinforce many of the weak points that other hybrids attacked out of habit. Major blood vessels had been rerouted to be further away from the surface of the body and the shape of certain bones had been altered to provide additional protection for the vital organs.

All of that would have been astonishing enough by itself, but those changes had been passed on to Thanatas' sons. The rest of the moonborn at large didn't know why certain of our kind seemed to hit harder and move with blinding speed, but those of us who were the descendants of the monarchy knew it was because either our hybrid or our wolf form were blessed with the fruits of all of the tinkering that the old king had done.

Not every descendant manifested those special gifts, what we called the royal attributes, and nobody other than Thanatas had ever been both a royal wolf and a royal hybrid, but a royal wolf was nearly the equal of a normal hybrid and a royal hybrid had a decided edge over any normal hybrid. I'd been a royal wolf up until now, but it appeared that my manifestation of a third shape had robbed me of my royal attributes as a wolf without bestowing equivalent gifts on me as a hybrid.

Isaac was up against a fight he couldn't possibly win and there wasn't anything I could do to help him, not without at least temporarily abandoning my quest to save Ben.

"What if I came down there, Isaac? I could be down in New Orleans in a day or so."

"No, it's not worth it, Jas. There's no telling when I'll get backed into fighting this creep. You could arrive down here, and find me dead, and end up in the same position I'm looking at right now. Besides, I couldn't ask you to watch Ben die. You said it yourself. He doesn't have much time left."

"I want to tell you that you're wrong, but I can't seem to force myself to say the words."

"I know. It's because I'm right and you know it. Have you found this Geoffrey character yet?"

"Yes, it turns out he's a vampire and I'm going to have to help him before he'll save Ben for me."

Isaac considered what I'd just said for several seconds before responding. "I don't like the sound of that, Jas. Bloodsuckers can't be trusted. Everything I've ever read says that they are all cunning and amoral in ways that sometimes even the Coun'hij can't equal."

"I know, but Rachel says it's the only way."

"What do you need from me?"

I didn't want to say the words, but I forced them out. "We need the location of Puppeteer and the rest of the Coun'hij. You've spent time thinking about where you'd go if you had to leave because of the way things have been going with Jessica. I need a pack with ties to the Coun'hij that is small enough I have a chance of taking it over."

"You knew that? You knew I was looking at leaving the pack and making a run for it?"

"Yeah. I didn't have any evidence, but it's what I would have been doing in your place. I don't blame you."

Isaac sighed. "I figured if you all found out that you'd feel like I was betraying you."

"Like I said, I understand why you wanted out. Can you think of a pack that might fit the bill?"

"I'm not sure. I mostly was looking for packs that were more independent than that, since the Coun'hij tends to take a dim view of people coming in and deposing leaders who have an established history of toeing the line."

Isaac considered the problem for a few more heartbeats before going on. "You know, in some ways that could make things easier. The Coun'hij tends to scrape off the cream of the crop out of their allied packs, so there doesn't tend to be as much talent there as what you see in the independent packs."

"Right, a lot of the time they end up being on the smaller side too."

"I think your best bet is Duluth then. Between the cold and the snow it's one of the less desirable territories, so they haven't had anyone challenge up there for a couple of decades. You'll still be up against some stiff competition though. The alpha there isn't anything too special, but he's still got more than two hundred years of fighting under his belt. Your biggest problem is going to be a guy named Branson. He's practically an honorary enforcer for the Coun'hij. He's big and fast, not as big and fast as you, but he's good and you haven't been in very many fights as a hybrid yet."

"Yeah, I know. If you've got a better idea for finding the Coun'hij I'm all ears."

"Sorry, nothing comes to mind. I guess we've both got some impossible fights ahead of us."

"Yeah, I guess we do. I'll see you on the other side."

Chapter 10

Geoffrey
United Medical Implements and Supply
Toledo, Ohio

Geoffrey watched Jasmin disappear into the medical supply shop and wondered once again why he'd agreed to such a risky plan. Actually that wasn't fair, he knew exactly why he'd agreed. He couldn't bring himself to give up on Melody while there was even a slight chance that she was still alive and in need of his help. She never would have ended up in trouble if not for him. He owed her that much and more.

Even so, it felt very much like they were risking everything on a single throw of the dice. Jasmin had explained enough about shape shifter challenge law for him to understand that she couldn't just stroll up and challenge the leader of another pack to single combat. She was going to have to make her way through each and every member of the pack who was willing to fight her first.

Jasmin was confident that she'd be back up to full strength by the time they made it up to Minnesota, but Geoffrey wasn't stupid. By the time she'd fought two or three of her own kind she was probably going to be even weaker than she was now.

The entire plan was madness but Geoffrey didn't have a better one to offer up. They couldn't just hang around the other pack's territory hoping that someone from the Coun'hij would swing by for a visit. Jasmin was confident that the other pack would smell Geoffrey sooner or later and come after him, and even if that wasn't the case there was still the fact that Ben was getting weaker by the hour and there was no telling what kind of privations Melody was suffering through.

They needed the location of the Coun'hij soon and this seemed like the only way to get what they needed.

Ben started twitching and Geoffrey turned back to check on him. It didn't happen often, but sometimes Ben had to be physically restrained to make sure that he wouldn't pull his IV out. A few strands of thought reflexively slipped free of Geoffrey's skull, but he pulled them back before they could make contact with Ben.

He wanted to help Ben and Jasmin out, but it was just too dangerous right now. More and more he was coming to believe that Jasmin was who she said she was, but that didn't necessarily mean that Ben was who she thought he was.

There was no telling what kind of changes had been made to his mind. Even Rachel seemed to think that the kill switch that other vampire had implanted was nothing more than a construct designed to end Ben's life, but just because that was what they thought was going on didn't mean they were right.

The more Geoffrey thought about it, the surer he became that there was more going on than just a simple kill switch. Any vampire who was strong enough to implant a kill switch was going to be skilled enough to make it work like intended and Venice hadn't ever told Geoffrey any stories about lethal kill switches that took more than a few hours to complete their work. Ben, on the other hand, had been stuck in this coma for weeks if Jasmin was to be believed.

It was very much starting to look to Geoffrey like Ben was a metaphysical Trojan horse. If his suspicions were correct, then touching Ben's mind with his own would result in Geoffrey being sucked into a living trap that would slowly tear Geoffrey's mind free of his own physical body.

It wouldn't be an easy death, but Geoffrey still fully intended on living up to his promise. If

Jasmin and Rachel were able to take him to Melody and help him free her then he'd do whatever he could to help Ben. It might cost him his life, but once Melody was rescued that hardly mattered.

The angle was all wrong, but Geoffrey was strong and Ben's illness had left him incredibly weak. Geoffrey gently took each of Ben's wrists in his hands and stopped Ben from thrashing around. The twitching never seemed to last very long and this time it was over almost as soon as Geoffrey touched the cool skin of Ben's arms.

Once he was sure that Ben was calm again, Geoffrey released him and checked the IV bag hanging from the grab handle mounted above the passenger door. It was their last bag, and Jasmin had become increasingly distracted as her texts to someone named Donovan had gone unanswered. Apparently Donovan was her best chance at sourcing another supplier for everything needed to keep Ben's fragile body from shutting down completely.

Twenty minutes earlier Rachel had texted an address, a name and a passphrase to Jasmin's phone. The address had led them to this medical supply store and presumably someone willing to bend the rules enough to get Jasmin everything she needed.

It would be good to know that Ben wasn't in imminent danger of starving to death, and not just to eliminate a distraction that Jasmin didn't need as she prepared to fight multiple bouts to the death. Geoffrey would rest easier too knowing that Ben was taken care of, but medical supplies, especially black-market medical supplies, didn't come cheap, and Jasmin was already getting evasive about how much cash she had left.

The cash that Geoffrey had saved up before his capture had all disappeared sometime before he'd woken up in his cage, so once Jasmin was out, they were all out. It was one more thing to worry about. Geoffrey supposed that they could always steal or con someone out of cash if things got bad enough. He didn't like the idea of preying on innocents like that, but he also wasn't going to let a few hundred dollars in gas money stop him from rescuing Melody.

Geoffrey looked to his left once again, past the empty driver's seat, but while he could see through the windows of the medical supply store he couldn't see Jasmin or the clerk she'd been talking to. Geoffrey knew he was being paranoid, but he also knew that in their line of work that wasn't a bad thing. He was just about ready to send out mental probes when a knock on his window made him jump.

A casual gesture confirmed the presence of the knife he'd pulled off of one of the dead guards back in the facility where Imastious had caged him. Reassured that he was as ready as he could be in case the situation became hostile, Geoffrey lowered his window a couple of inches.

The young man standing next to the car looked like he was in his early twenties. He had a shaved head and skin that was as dark as any Geoffrey had ever seen, but there was something subtly different to his facial features that made it seem like he didn't fit in with any ethnic group Geoffrey could name.

"Hey, man, can you help a guy out?"

Geoffrey shook his head. "Sorry, I wish I could, but I'm tapped out myself. I got robbed a couple of days ago."

The panhandler didn't look convinced. "You really think people are going to believe that when you're sitting in that kind of a ride?"

Geoffrey looked at the luxurious leather interior of the Mercedes and then shrugged. "It's not my car, I'm just along for the ride. Besides, it doesn't really matter if you believe me. It's the truth."

"Might be you could cough up a twenty if it meant that your friend's ride wasn't going to be wrecked."

"Don't threaten me."

"Why, what are you going to do? Kill me?"

The words could have been nothing more than idle talk, but there was something about the way that they'd been said. Geoffrey's internal alarms all went off at once. Being stuck inside of a car was enough of a disadvantage when dealing with some punk kid, it was an unacceptable position to be in if he was up against someone who knew what they were doing, a real killer.

Geoffrey grabbed the door handle, intending on opening the door hard enough to knock the panhandler off of his feet, but there was an odd, half-imagined flare of light like an arc welder and the car shook slightly. When Geoffrey pushed against the car door nothing happened, it was like pushing against solid stone.

"We're not done talking yet."

The expression on the other man's face hadn't changed and Geoffrey suddenly realized that it was the kind of expression that could take on almost any meaning the viewer wanted to see in it.

"Who are you?"

Geoffrey's question earned him a frown of disappointment. "That's the wrong question. You should be asking who *you* are, Geoffrey."

"I already know who I am."

"Do you? Do you really? Has the hunger started up again yet? Have you started looking at the boy behind you with an eye to how much blood he could spare yet?"

"How do you know that? How do you know *what* I am?"

The words were meant to serve simply as a distraction. Geoffrey had already extended his mental feelers. He got a single probe into the surface of the other man's mind and accessed a kaleidoscope of images in the split second before his probes were all sheared away by crackling whips of power.

Geoffrey was still trying to process what he'd seen, it was little more than impressions of a bright light and beings that seemed made out of glowing crystal. The other man shook his head at him before Geoffrey could ask another question.

"So you invade the minds of those around you? Don't you think that's wrong?"

"I see nothing wrong with defending myself. There's obviously more to you than meets the eye and you're holding me inside of my friend's car against my will."

"I suppose there is some validity to that argument, but you spend more time inside of people's minds than just when you're threatened. You've made it practically a way of life, haven't you?"

"I won't be judged by you. You have no idea what I've been through."

"That's the thing about principles, Geoffrey. They exist independent from our circumstances. When was the last time you fed?"

There was something about the question that compelled Geoffrey to answer. "It was just before I was recaptured."

"Tell me about it, did you kill whoever it was?"

"No, it was a girl, her boyfriend was an addict and I told her that I'd cure him in return for her letting me feed on her. I took just enough to beat back the hunger and then I released her."

"How did that feel?"

"It was amazing. It's been a long time since I've taken blood from someone without providing some kind of value in return, but that was the first time that someone gave blood to me voluntarily."

"Was it? What about Melody?"

"How do you know about Melody?"

The man shook his head. "That's not for you to know right now. I find you worthy of life, but alas, you aren't the one who will be waking those who sleep."

Geoffrey opened his mouth to ask what that meant, but at that second Jasmin's phone started ringing. Geoffrey looked towards the phone in an involuntary gesture and when he looked back out the window the man was gone.

The car door opened without any problems, but getting out of the car and looking around didn't make any difference, there still wasn't any evidence of the panhandler. Geoffrey reached back inside of the car and picked up Jasmin's phone as he sent probes back out in an effort to try and locate the man.

"Hello, Jasmin's phone."

"Geoffrey, is that you? It's Rachel."

"Yeah, it's me. What do you want?"

"Are you okay? Is Jasmin okay?"

Geoffrey stretched his probes out as far as he could. He could feel Jasmin and the clerk both, and a light brush against the surface of the clerk's mind seemed to indicate that Jasmin wasn't in any kind of danger, but there wasn't any sign of the man who'd imprisoned him inside of the car.

"Yeah, we're all okay, Ben too."

"What just happened?"

"What do you mean? I thought you could see the future."

"I can, just not all of it, you jerk. What just happened? One minute I could see all of you and then all of a sudden you were gone."

"Interesting."

Rachel tried to press for more information, but Geoffrey hung up on her. It appeared that there was more going on here than even Rachel knew about.

Chapter 11

Jasmin Bianchi
Sleep Deep Hotel
Duluth, Minnesota

Things felt more than a little weird when I got back to the car. Geoffrey handed me my phone without saying anything, but when I checked the call history the only activity was an inbound call from Rachel.

I stacked most of the supplies in the back seat next to Ben and then put the rest of everything in the trunk and climbed back into the car. Just before I turned the key in the ignition I got a text from Rachel's number.

Find out what just happened with Geoffrey!

I looked over at Geoffrey and he met my eyes with a stubbornness that dared me to ask him what had happened, but I decided that I didn't want to get into a pissing match with him inside such a tiny space while I was trying to drive. I promised myself that I would try and get it out of him later, but by the time we made it up to a small town in Minnesota called Marshall I was too tired to play conversational chicken with him.

Paying for two hotel rooms used up the very last of my cash, but I wasn't going to spend the night in the same room as Geoffrey, not if I could avoid it. I told myself that I would deal with my lack of funds later, but I knew that was just a lie. I didn't have any way to replenish them, not without help from Alec, and he still hadn't returned my last call.

Ben had a restless night. I heard him moving around in the darkness. Even after I strapped his arms down to the bed so he wouldn't pull out his IV, he still twitched and even occasionally moaned. I sat there listening to him for nearly an hour before I broke down and started crying.

I didn't cry very often. Crying was a sign of weakness and I wasn't weak, at least that was what I'd been telling myself for years. It turned out that crying couldn't make me weak though because I was already weak. I'd been operating on borrowed time in almost every way for days now.

I was out of cash, I had a vampire sleeping less than a dozen feet away from me, and every time I pulled Ben out of the car I risked someone realizing that he wasn't just drunk and calling the cops on me. Alec's people had mostly managed to keep the Coun'hij off of my tail, but he wouldn't be able to stop the police from swarming all over me if they got involved.

Nothing but sheer dumb luck and Rachel's behind-the-scenes machinations had kept me in one piece so far, and even they had only let me scrape by a couple of times. There wasn't any possible way for me to fight an entire pack one at a time and survive the experience. I'd come to the end of the road. I didn't want to die, but I couldn't see any other route that had even the slightest possibility of letting me save Ben.

I cried myself to sleep and when I woke back up a few hours later things weren't any rosier, but I was once again ready to do what needed to be done. I pulled myself out of bed, checked on Ben, and then jumped in the shower.

I was down to one change of clothes, the black boots that Geoffrey had looted for me, and a single pair of sneakers. Flash shifts were always hard on clothes, and the subsequent fight was usually pretty rough on the ha'bit we happened to be wearing at the time.

I pulled out all three of my ha'bits, but none of them were in very good shape, so I bit the bullet and got out the black needle and thread that Donovan had packed in the bug-out bag he'd prepared for each member of the pack. I stitched up the worst of the tears on the ha'bit that had seen the least amount of use, and then hand-washed it and one set of clothes in the bathroom sink. I figured I had another couple of hours at least before Geoffrey would wake up. Unlike shape shifters, who only needed three or four hours of sleep each night, vampires seemed to need just as much sleep as normal humans.

There wasn't anything I could do physically to prepare myself for the fight I knew was coming. There were some energy bars still left in the bug-out bag, enough for a modest breakfast for Geoffrey and me, but beyond that I was as strong or fast as I was going to get.

There was however one thing I could do, and that was to prepare mentally. I was still just wearing a towel while I waited for my clothes to dry, so I didn't particularly feel like yoga. Besides, I'd never been into yoga enough to get into the mental and spiritual aspects of it anyways.

Instead I knelt down on the floor next to my bed and focused on my breathing. My old instructor always said that the inside followed the outside and the outside followed the inside. I controlled my breathing, forced it to be calm and steady, and as the minutes slowly passed my mind and emotions did start to mirror my breathing.

Even my beast became less restless and at one point my body, and even the world around me, dropped away. It wasn't enlightenment like the eastern disciplines preached, but it was something better than I'd ever experienced before and it left me feeling like a still pool.

Emotions and thoughts were both distant, quiet things, but eventually I felt ready to be done. I opened my eyes feeling like a different person.

I couldn't remember for sure when I'd started meditating, but it didn't really matter how long I'd been at it, it had taken as long as it needed to take and I was ready to do what needed done. My hair was mostly dry, which was perfect because that meant it hadn't 'set' yet. I still had a few minutes in which it would more or less do what I wanted it to, so I combed it out and then pulled it back so that it would be out of my face.

My clothes weren't quite dry yet so I grabbed the hotel hair dryer and used it to dry everything out enough that I wouldn't freeze once I stepped outside. I was just about ready to leave my room when my phone rang.

"Is that you, Rach?"

"Yeah, how are you feeling, Jasmin?"

For a second the words didn't have any meaning to me. Identifying my feelings required separating myself from them in some way that I'd never noticed. I would have rather continued walking around without having to put that kind of distance between them and me, but it was too late. Rachel had asked the question and something inside of me had been only too happy to tear me in two so that I could answer her.

"I feel better. I meditated for a few minutes earlier and I'm okay. I'll do my best and just have to hope that will be good enough."

Rachel was silent for a few seconds while she processed what I'd just said. "You haven't meditated for a really long time, Jasmin."

"I know. I guess things were just so bad that I had to do something."

"I didn't expect that."

For some reason that struck me as being funny. "I thought you saw everything that was important. I guess that means this wasn't important."

Rachel cleared her throat. "I thought I saw everything that was important, but I didn't see this and it was important. You, Ben, Geoffrey, you all disappeared from my sight yesterday just before I called and talked to him. You only just barely became clear enough that I could really see you again."

A few hours earlier that would have been enough to send me back into tears, but it was curiously unimportant to me now.

"Is there still a course that you can send me down that results in Ben surviving all of this?"

"Yes, I mean I think so. The original route forward is still there and it still seems to lead to Ben's survival, but it's different. I can't really explain it though, it's like trying to explain the color orange to a blind person. It's like the world just shifted, like it was just hit by a giant meteor and everything moved from the impact, only some things moved more than others and some of the pieces still haven't settled back down yet."

"I guess just call and tell me if things change and there's no longer any point with going forward. In the meantime I've got a protein bar waiting for me."

"Wait, Jas, I can help with that. I'm going to text you a bank and an account number. Send Geoffrey there and they'll let him withdraw pretty much any amount you guys need. You should at least have a good breakfast before you go into a fight like this."

"Thanks, Rach, I appreciate that. Any words of advice before I face off with Branson and the others?"

Rachel was silent for so long that I thought for a moment that she'd hung up on me again.

"What is it, Rach?"

"I'm not sure what I can and can't tell you. You're going into another decision point and I'm not sure what things will help you win it and what things will harm you. The margin of error is as small as anything I've ever seen before."

"Then just tell me the truth, Rach. I'd rather go into it knowing what I'm getting into. I'm tired of running around with blinders on."

"Isaac told you that Branson is pretty much an honorary enforcer for the Coun'hij, right?"

"Yeah, he said that Branson is the one to beat inside of the pack, which I thought was kind of odd. I would have expected for him to be top dog if he's really that tough."

"You're right, it's uncommon, but it's not unheard of. It just means that the alpha has something that the more powerful hybrid wants more than they want to lead the pack."

"You're stalling, Rach. What is it?"

"Branson was one of the hybrids Agony brought with him when he killed my dad and sundered the rest of the pack."

My mouth went dry. Donovan, Andrew and the rest had always been reluctant to talk about that night, the night that the dreams of everyone in the pack had been destroyed. When pressed they had recounted the barest details, but they'd never gone so far as to tell us who else had been there other than Agony. Adri had told me once that Oblivion had also been there, but she'd been pretty evasive when it came to how exactly she knew that.

"You're making this personal."

Rachel sighed. "Yeah, I guess I am. Maybe that will be the extra little push you need to be able to take him down."

"It's not going to make any difference. If I need an extra push to beat Branson then I'm already screwed because it means I'm not going to be able to beat the alpha, whatever his name is."

"Stekensbridge, Samuel Stekensbridge."

"Yeah, him."

"I know things look grim, Jas, just remember that none of them realize that you're a hybrid. If you can use that to your advantage then you have a chance."

"Okay, I've got to go now, Rach. You're screwing up my internal balance."

I hung up on her without waiting for her to say goodbye, and then looked around the room. It wasn't home, there was no reason to dwell on it, taking mental pictures, but I did regardless. A second later Rachel texted me the banking information that she'd promised.

I checked on Ben one last time and then left the room. Geoffrey answered the door within a second or two of my first knock. His sword was unsheathed and for a second I almost thought that he was going to attack me, but instead he turned his back and walked over to the bed.

"Are you and Ben ready to go?"

He picked up a scrap of material that he'd apparently been using to polish his sword, and then sheathed the weapon in a move that looked so easy and natural that I knew he was even better with a sword in his hand than I'd suspected.

"Just me. I'd like to leave Ben here for now. If things go badly then the Duluth pack will rip him apart. It's a small chance, but I'd still like to leave him here so someone else can come get him if the worst comes to pass."

"You're just filling me with confidence."

"That's me, ever the optimist."

I tossed my phone to him. He caught it with his left hand and then looked back up at me questioningly. "What's this?"

"A present from Rachel. She says that you've got some kind of numbered account in a bank near here. I don't know how she set up a fake account for you, or why she did it in your name instead of mine, but it means that we should have enough cash to at least buy Ben a few more nights here."

Geoffrey swallowed a couple of times and then shook his head. "Rachel didn't set it up; at least I don't think she did. I suspect that *I* set it up before I lost all of my memories. I don't have very many things from back then. This sword, my vendetta with Imastious, and now a bank account."

"I'm sorry, it must really suck not to remember so much of your past."

"Yes, and no. I feel so incredibly isolated from everything that sometimes I just want to scream. I don't have any ties to anyone or anything. I've been completely uprooted from the person who I once was, but it's not all bad. By all indications the man I used to be didn't have a single redeeming quality to him. I'm probably better off without those memories."

"I just assumed that it was something Rachel arranged, but if it's your money then I shouldn't go presuming as to how you'll be spending it."

"No, I think your plan of buying a few nights for Ben is a good one. It's not like you haven't kept me fed and with a roof over my head for the last couple of days. I owe you for that. Besides, I don't want to see anything happen to Ben either."

My nod was choppy and probably revealed more of what I was feeling than I would have liked it to, but at least I managed a response. I left Geoffrey to finish his packing and went back into my room and grabbed my stuff.

Leaving Ben there in the bed by himself was every bit as hard as I'd known it would be. He looked so tiny, like the smallest tremor would shatter him into a thousand pieces. The bubble of calm I'd surrounded myself with earlier helped a little, but it was mostly faith in Rachel that gave me the strength I needed to leave.

I already knew that I didn't have a plan of my own that would save Ben. The only way forward was to trust Rachel and help Geoffrey. I picked up Ben's free hand and cupped my face in his palm for several seconds.

I could hear Geoffrey outside in the hall. He was pacing, which meant I was out of time. I turned my head and kissed Ben's palm as I stood to go. I grabbed my stuff and forced myself to leave without looking back. We put the 'do not disturb' sign up on my room, on Ben's room, and then we stopped at the front desk and explained that we would be calling back in a couple of hours to pay for a few more nights. Technically that put us a bit past the normal checkout time. The clerk seemed like he was going to balk at that, but then suddenly nodded and said that he'd make sure my room wasn't disturbed.

I waited until we were back to my car before asking the obvious question. "That was you who convinced him, wasn't it?"

"Yeah. It seemed like a good cause, I just hope he doesn't get into some kind of trouble as a result. That's the problem with being able to play with people's minds, it's too easy to take what you want and not consider the possible consequences to them."

"That's surprisingly decent."

"Just because I'm a vampire doesn't mean I have to be like all the rest of them."

I looked up the address to the bank from Rachel's text and then we set off. The trip to Minneapolis went by faster than I'd expected it to, and almost before I knew it we were pulling into an underground parking structure underneath the bank itself.

It felt like we were entering Fort Knox, although, come to think of it, I wasn't actually sure that they still kept any gold there. With the way that the Federal debt figure had been ballooning for the last decade or so, it was entirely possible that all of the country's gold reserves had been sold off years ago.

The ramp we drove down didn't initially go under the bank. Instead we drove down a series of declines that seemed to put us under the vacant square next to the bank and went through three different check points before we were allowed to enter the main parking area underneath the bank.

Rachel's text had contained three different codes and Geoffrey had to provide the first code before we were allowed into the second checkpoint where they proceeded to check my car for surveillance devices, bombs and weapons. Geoffrey's sword didn't even cause the guards to raise an eyebrow, they simply brought out a long metal canister with a complicated combination lock on one end.

Geoffrey input a code of his choice and then locked his sword up inside of the case and it was taken away for holding with a promise that it would be waiting for us when we left. Once the car was vetted and the guards were satisfied that neither of us had any weapons, we were escorted out of the car into a series of man traps which isolated us from each other and from the guards who'd been escorting us.

Less than three seconds after I realized the doors on either side of me were locked, a speaker above me clicked on without even a hint of static.

"Good morning, sir, madam. I apologize, but our procedures generally allow for only the account holder to access the deposit vault in question. I've pulled up the physical description of the account holder, which the gentleman matches. The next step in the authentication process is for you to provide the second numerical password and then we'll conduct you back to the vault."

I would have expected for the speaker to talk to us from the anonymity of some windowless control room, but apparently that wasn't classy enough for Credit Suisse. Instead the man addressing us was doing so from behind what looked like a six-inch pane of Plexiglas. While I was busy taking in the luxuriously-appointed room behind him, the bank employee continued.

"I've left the lady's speaker on so far as a courtesy so that she knows what is going on, but in a moment I'll be turning her sound feed off and we'll be proceeding with the exchange of the passcode. Assuming that the gentleman correctly provides the passcode he will be allowed to proceed into a secure area to which his deposit box will be conveyed. The lady will remain in her present location until the gentleman returns."

The thick glass in front of me didn't do anything to hide the determination on Geoffrey's face. "No, you'll see on your screen that there is provision for me to bring one other, previously selected individual in with me. My companion's name is Lucy, and as you've no doubt already determined, she matches the description I left with you at the time the account was set up. Please leave the audio feed on and allow her to accompany me back to the secure area."

The banker nodded, and then Geoffrey read off the second code that Rachel had sent us. A couple of minutes later we were being escorted down a long, stainless steel corridor by a man in a suit whose shoulders were much too broad for him to be anything other than another guard.

We were shown into a six-by-six room that held a table and two chairs and then told that the door would be locked until we were ready to leave. Twenty seconds later the dumbwaiter-like device on the far end of the room conveyed up a metal container roughly the size of a briefcase.

Geoffrey looked at the case for several seconds before walking over and picking it up. Once it was on the table and he was back in his chair, he started entering the final code into the tumblers.

"I don't know what's in here. Maybe it's just money, but I could have left money anywhere. Please remember that I'm not the same person as whoever left this here."

It took me a minute to realize what I was seeing on his face. "You're scared. Is that why you wanted me here with you?"

"I guess. As much as I hunger to know more about my life before the amnesia, links like this terrify me. By all accounts I was everything you hate about vampires."

"Go ahead and open it up. No matter how bad it is you're better off knowing rather than continuing to wonder."

"Yeah, and time's running short. We still have to go buy some kind of prepaid credit card and call back to the hotel for Ben."

Geoffrey slid the release over and opened the case. There was cash, hundred-dollar bills, but Geoffrey simply pulled that out and stacked it on the table. Underneath the money was a series of US Treasury bearer bonds with amounts in the millions, and a single picture of a girl who was a few years younger than me.

"Who's that?"

"I'm not sure, but this face has haunted my dreams almost as long as I can remember. This is what Melody looks like, but I'm pretty sure it's not her. You heard Rachel tell me that the girl I remembered from before, the one Melody reminded me of, was named Lucy, but the clothes are all wrong. The girl I remember lived and died decades before this picture could have possibly been taken. She met her fate on the dusty American Frontier."

"So there are three girls, all of whom look the same?"

"Yeah, three, where up until a few minutes ago I thought there were only two. It's a problem for another day. We need to get moving."

Geoffrey walked over to the door and pushed the call button.

"Yes, sir?"

"We're ready to leave."

"Very good, sir, we'll have someone down shortly to escort you back to your car."

We stuffed the money into our pockets and the bearer bonds disappeared underneath the front of Geoffrey's shirt, but he left the picture of the girl out, holding it in his left hand. I saw him stealing glances at it when he thought I wasn't looking, but I didn't say anything. He deserved at least a measure of privacy.

Our escort arrived a few seconds later. He was another big guy, blond this time, dressed in a suit and wearing a wire in his left ear.

"Right this way if you please."

We started down the hall, headed towards the opposite set of doors, with our guide a few steps ahead of us.

There was no way of knowing what caused our escort to stumble, but it was a spectacular trip. I started towards him, thinking that I would be able to catch him, but I'd spent years learning not to move with my full speed when there were normal humans around.

That hesitation was all that was required to make it so that even I couldn't catch him, and the blond guy crashed into the wall on our left. His arms had been flailing in an effort to catch himself, but all he got from that was a long slash on his left arm where it ran into the metal frame that held the 'occupied' sign next to the closest door.

The wound wasn't immediately life-threatening, he hadn't opened up any of the major blood vessels, and for a second I thought the worst of the damage had simply been done to his pride. That stopped as soon as I looked over and saw Geoffrey's face.

Geoffrey had gone completely rigid as though every muscle in his body was fighting every other muscle. It took me only a heartbeat to realize that it was the sight, possibly even just the smell of the blood that had hit him so hard.

My beast screamed nine kinds of rage at him as she tried to break free and force a transformation. Both she and I knew just how messy things were about to become if Geoffrey couldn't get himself back under control.

Geoffrey was unarmed, but he was still going to be faster and stronger than any normal human. I could stop him, but not without changing and if that happened every single person watching the cameras pointing at us would get a show that would blow their minds.

I watched as Geoffrey's nostrils flared and his jaw dropped slightly, no doubt giving his teeth room to lengthen. He was in full-blown predator mode, as dangerous as he could possibly be, but I couldn't just sit there and do nothing.

I grabbed Geoffrey's arm and stepped between him and the guard.

"Fight it."

My words came out as something less than a whisper. They were too faint for a human to make out, but I was pretty sure that Geoffrey's hearing would be keen enough to pick them out.

"It's hard."

"I know it is, but you have to fight it or we're both as good as dead. If you lose control they'll seal this place up and we'll be stuck rotting here until some government agency comes to collect us."

Geoffrey brought himself back under control with a visible effort that left him wrung out and shaking. I waited a heartbeat to make sure that he really had himself pulled back together and then let go of his arm and looked over at our escort.

The poor guy had his right hand clasped tightly over the wound and had gone bright red out of embarrassment.

"My apologies, I'm not usually so clumsy."

I managed what I hoped was a winning smile. "Not at all. We're just fortunate that the damage was limited to your suit jacket. Hopefully the rest of your day is less fraught with peril."

My words brought a relieved smile to the face of the guard. He had no idea how close he'd come to death.

Chapter 12

Jasmin Bianchi
I-35
Duluth, Minnesota

"So what else should I expect from this challenge match?"

Geoffrey's tone was casual, but I knew he was worried. If I failed to win there was a very good chance that he wouldn't make it out either. Shape shifters hated vampires, and him having arrived with me wouldn't make them like him any better.

"They'll either honor my challenge or they won't. If they do then you'll have to just stand there and watch while I work my way through the pack, fighting anyone the alpha has been able to intimidate into standing between him and me. If they don't then all bets are off. Bring your sword and be ready to try and cut your way free if that's the case."

"How will I know they aren't honoring the challenge match?"

"They'll probably say something to that effect, but if all else fails more than one person attacking me is a pretty good sign that they aren't holding to the challenge rules."

"What about if someone attacks you from behind?"

"That too, probably. Unless my opponent is dead and I'm in the middle of whatever they are using for a circle, then it's still part of the challenge."

Geoffrey nodded and leaned further back in his seat. I waited for a few more minutes, but he didn't seem ready to volunteer anything else. We'd made it safely back to the car, purchased the prepaid credit card we'd needed, and called the hotel to pay for a few more nights.

We'd done everything we needed to do, including stowing away all but one of the bearer bonds inside a safety deposit box at a much less prestigious bank than the one where they'd been secreted before, and then we'd climbed back in the car and started for Duluth. Things hadn't necessarily been strained between us, but the events inside of Credit Suisse hung between us.

I'd been hoping that Geoffrey would broach the subject on his own, but apparently that wasn't to be. I took a deep breath and then asked the question that had needed asking for the last hour.

"So what happened back there at the bank? It looked for a second like you were going to rip that guard's throat out."

"It looked that way because I very nearly did lose control."

"It couldn't have just been the blood. You bandaged me up without losing control of yourself, and I saw you run a new IV for Ben."

"That's different."

"Different how?"

Geoffrey waited for so long to respond that I almost repeated the question by the time he opened his mouth again.

"When you were hurt it hadn't been quite such a long time since my last feeding. Not only that, you had just finished rescuing me from Imastious. It's easier to control myself around someone I care about or someone I owe a debt to."

"Easier, but not easy?"

"No, not easy, at least not when it's been so long between feedings. It gets progressively harder as each day goes by."

"So what do we do about that?"

"*We* do nothing. Have no fear; I'm still able to control myself. I'd just been too long with nobody but you and Ben around. All of that blood caught me by surprise. I'll be fine for another day or two and then I'll make some kind of arrangement to deal with the hunger. Possibly there is a blood bank nearby that I can raid."

"Possibly?"

Geoffrey turned on me with the kind of suddenness that usually presaged an attack, but he didn't escalate further than that.

"Yes, possibly. I'm sorry, but I don't have any better answer than that. I understand your fears, but I will take whatever steps are necessary to ensure that I'm capable of continuing our quest. One way or another I'll feed enough to make sure that the hunger doesn't cause me to turn on you at an inopportune moment."

I'd had an abstract, distant understanding of what Geoffrey's existence must be like, but in that instant I got a true taste of what he went through.

"You do this every time, don't you? Wonder whether you'll be able to feed without killing?"

Geoffrey's nod was curt. "Yes, but it's not just about killing anymore. My control has grown, but I still worry about what I'm taking from them. I don't like being a parasite, don't like taking without providing some kind of value in return."

I considered that for several long minutes before responding. "You know, a few days ago I would have said that it wasn't possible for a vampire to be anything other than a parasite. You're starting to convince me."

"Don't get too caught up in the possibilities. I'm not even sure myself whether it will be possible for me to provide enough value on a long-term basis to convince people to voluntarily open up their veins for me."

We passed the rest of the drive in silence, and all too soon were pulling up to the large stone house that was the headquarters for the Duluth pack. I'd made three separate calls and six texts to drag that particular address out of Alec.

As nearly as I could tell it wasn't that Alec didn't want to help, but it was looking very much like he was having problems of his own, big problems. That wasn't something designed to make me feel very good about the medium-term future. If Alec fell then the rest of us were all as good as dead.

That probably wouldn't make any difference to me, I was likely going to die before the afternoon was out, but there were a lot of other people I really cared about who were depending on Alec for survival. I pushed all of those worries aside and rang the doorbell to the manor house. What I really wanted was another slice of the serenity I'd achieved earlier in the day, but that continued to be soundly out of my reach.

The man who answered the door looked like a younger, unscarred version of Donovan. "Hello, my name is Cruthers, how may I be of service?"

Geoffrey looked over at me and I forced out the words that I'd been dreading since before I'd talked to Isaac.

"Please tell your master that I'm here to challenge for leadership of this pack."

The butler's expression didn't change in the slightest, but I could feel the disapproval radiating off of him. Things only got worse when the wind shifted and he was able to smell Geoffrey.

"You may enter, but that thing may not."

I grabbed him by the throat, moving too fast for him to react, and slammed him into the door. "He'll enter into your damn house and you'll like it. He's my witness, so unless you want the dispossessed to find out that you're not living up to challenge law, you'll back off and let him in."

It wasn't exactly a bluff, but the truth was that I didn't want to involve the dispossessed any more than the Duluth pack did. The dispossessed normally didn't take much interest in the comings and goings of the rest of us, but the one thing guaranteed to make them coalesce into a ravening horde was news that one of the packs wasn't living up to the long-established challenge law.

Geoffrey held up my phone, which already had a rather long, detailed text on it ready for him to hit the send button.

"I'd rather not have to send this."

The butler looked at me with hate in his eyes. There was no guarantee that the dispossessed would come here in response to a text from me of all people, but if they did, if my message was convincing enough, then they'd kill every man, woman and child in the pack and torch their homes.

"Fine, it can come, but you're responsible for it."

We followed Cruthers into the house and to a sitting room less than two dozen feet from the front door.

"I'll inform Mr. Stekensbridge of your presence."

"Fine. You've got twenty minutes. Anyone you can't get here by then can't face me across the circle."

He knew the rules as well as I did, possibly even better, but it didn't hurt to make sure that he knew I wasn't going to cool my heels while they called in people from two states over.

Less than fifteen minutes later Cruthers returned and conducted us deeper into the house. We went down two flights of stairs before arriving at our destination, a large room nearly two stories tall and half as big as a football field. It had been carved out of the bedrock that the house rested on, and obviously served as the place of challenge for the Duluth pack.

Geoffrey acted unimpressed as we walked through the house, but I knew him well enough to realize that he'd been shocked at some of the artifacts we'd seen before being led downstairs. The Duluth pack was as old as any. They'd fallen on hard times as of late, but the Stekensbridge family had led the pack for more than three generations. A thousand years was a long time to gather up pretty bits of art, but I'd grown up around better in Sanctuary.

The Graves family had been in power in one form or another since the monarchy. Alec could have bought and sold the Stekensbridges out of little more than petty cash. Not only that, the house itself was less than two hundred years old while parts of Graves Manor were much, much older than that.

I was in the middle of reflecting on the irony that Geoffrey, who potentially had been alive for longer than any of the rest of us, was the one most impressed by the ancient air of our surroundings, when the first of the Duluth pack started trickling in.

What started as a trickle quickly grew into what felt like a flood and I had to tell myself over and over again that the Duluth pack was on the smaller side, that they were my best chance of saving Melody and thereby saving Ben.

When all was said and done, there were eleven men and women gathered along the far wall. There were a few other people as well, young kids who weren't old enough to have manifested a second shape yet and a single human spouse, but those eleven were the ones I had to worry about and I knew it. They gave off an unmistakable aura of power.

Some were weaker, some were stronger, but all of them were moonborn and therefore dangerous. I took a deep breath, held it for a three-count and then stepped forward to the edge of the thin circle that had been cut into the cold gray stone.

Geoffrey was a reassuring presence at my back, but ultimately this was all up to me. I had one card up my sleeve, and one card only. None of the wolves and hybrids here knew that I was a hybrid.

Every pack in North America maintained files on every other known moonborn. The flow of information between packs was far from perfect with packs routinely withholding information where they thought doing so might give them an advantage, but the files were still maintained with the best information available to the pack.

Eventually word of my manifesting a third shape, long after it should have been possible, would trickle out along the grapevine and everyone would know that I was now far more dangerous than I'd been before, but for now everyone here was underestimating me by a great margin. It was an advantage, but when stacked up against the possibility of having to fight my way through ten other wolves and hybrids just to have a shot at the alpha, it wasn't worth much.

As I stepped forward to the edge of the circle the moonborn across the way also stepped forward, forming a partial circle that left the two members on each end only a few yards away from me. The circle here in Duluth was smaller than the one back in Sanctuary.

"I'm here to challenge for the right to lead this pack."

The man standing directly opposite me shook his head. "What, no fancy words? I would have expected someone so ready to threaten us with the wrath of the dispossessed to be more anxious to hold to the old forms."

I didn't need to be told that I was looking at Stekensbridge. He was big, but no bigger than James. With any luck that would mean that his hybrid body was roughly the same size as James'.

"Very well, my name is Jasmin Bianchi. That's all you really need to know, that's all you really wanted."

My accusation was met with a hint of a smile, and then a barely-perceptible ripple of calm spread out from the center of the other pack, working its way out to the submissives. They'd all been assuming the worst-case scenario. They'd been worried that I was some hybrid with a powerful ability, one who was virtually guaranteed to defeat them all. Now they were confident that any of their hybrids and some of their wolves could defeat me without too much effort.

Stekensbridge opened his mouth to name his first champion, but before he could get the words out the man on his left, a big, redheaded brute who had to be at least six-three, stepped forward.

"A moment?"

For a second I thought that Stekensbridge would refuse, but he didn't. That one fact told me everything I needed to know. I was looking at Branson, and Stekensbridge and Branson both knew who was truly dominant between the two of them. Branson allowed Stekensbridge to remain the pack alpha for some reason known only to himself, but he was the one who should have been ruling in Duluth.

I watched as Branson crossed the circle, walking slowly towards me, and it was obvious just how dangerous an opponent he would be. He moved well, much better in human shape than most people that big, and there was a lazy confidence to him that told me he was used to winning fights, which considering that he'd clawed his way into an honorary position with the Coun'hij's enforcers said quite a lot about his skill.

I shifted my weight slightly forward, moving more onto the balls of my feet. The challenge match hadn't officially started, but that didn't necessarily mean anything. A guy like Branson was more than capable of attacking without warning and I was determined not to go down from some cheap shot.

I didn't make a show, but once you've been in a few dozen fights you get very good at reading people's body language. Branson could tell that I was ready for him to attack, and that just made him smile.

You had to worry about sneak attacks from a hybrid more so than from a wolf. For a wolf to attack they had to shift, let gravity pull them down to the floor so that they had something to push off of, and then lunge upwards and lock their jaws around someone's throat. In a sense, for wolves the change worked against them.

Hybrids were exactly the opposite. When a hybrid changed, from human or wolf form either one, there was a natural upwards motion as their body grew up to the full measure of a hybrid's stature. That meant there was not real pause between when the hybrid started transforming and when an attack could land. All that was required was for the transforming hybrid to do a kind of modified uppercut as they transformed and their claws would be driven deep into their enemy.

It meant that that the only true safety when you were dealing with a hybrid was to make sure that you were far enough out of reach that you'd have a chance to react before they could get close enough to hurt you. Branson was purposefully stepping too close to me, threatening me with his presence in a way that he thought I couldn't match.

"Jasmin Bianchi, of the Sanctuary Bianchis, I presume?"

I nodded, but I didn't let my eyes look away from his hands. He smiled even wider.

"I guess they finally told you then."

"Told me what?"

He shook his head in much the same way that Stekensbridge had done a few seconds earlier, but his gesture was even more mocking.

"Don't play dumb. This is exactly the kind of grand, juvenile gesture that I've been expecting from you for years. They finally told you about the night that Kaleb Graves died."

"You were there. So were a lot of others. The Sanctuary pack was nearly as big as the Chicago pack back then and Agony brought enough men to make sure that he outnumbered the Sanctuary pack by a huge margin. Are you looking for a medal for having participated in one of the biggest massacres in recent history?"

His smile flickered slightly, he hadn't lost his sense of superiority, but it was obvious that I hadn't provided him with the response he'd been expecting.

"They didn't tell you then. You have...anger issues, everyone knows it. If you really knew what happened back then you wouldn't be so calm. Why are you here then?"

"I already told you, I want to take over this pack."

"You can't possibly hope to win, and you know it."

This time it was my turn to smile. "You might be surprised."

I could see the ripple of unease move through the Duluth pack. I hadn't been lying, which made them all nervous, it even made Branson a little worried. I'd just told them the truth and they'd been able to tell it was the truth because my body hadn't given off any of the normal signs of a lie. My breathing hadn't sped up, my pulse hadn't changed, my body temperature had remained even, there were a host of clues telling them that I believed what I'd said.

They were shape shifters, so they knew that the 'truth' they'd thought they'd just heard might not be quite the truth I'd been telling them, but it was still the kind of thing that made people wonder what else was going on.

"Bold words for a third-rate wolf from a pack that's been scattered to the four corners of the continent."

I cocked my head to one side. "Have you heard reports of the battle in Sanctuary already up here in Minnesota? I'm betting not. That's just what your contacts on the Coun'hij told you was going to happen, isn't it?"

"We've heard all about it. Graves Manor is a smoking pile of rocks. You all evaporated like a desert mirage before the might of the Coun'hij."

"That's an interesting take on events, but I was actually there for the fight. Puppeteer brought in dozens of werewolves backed up by a couple dozen worthless bullies like you. By the time the night was over the house was destroyed, but all of the werewolves were dead and the enforcers died within seconds of the last werewolf falling."

Again, they knew I was speaking the truth, but it was a truth that their minds couldn't accept for many reasons.

"That's right, Puppeteer brought werewolves in to destroy the massed strength of four packs.

He did what the Coun'hij has threatened to do for decades. They are so scared of Alec and what he represents that they risked a mass revolt by every other pack in North America to try and kill him."

Branson didn't like that, both my telling his pack mates just how far the Coun'hij had gone, and the fact that his contacts hadn't bothered to tell him about our having killed all of the werewolves.

"You lost people too."

A collage of faces swam past my vision and I found myself nodding.

"Yes, too many, but not as many as your side lost."

Branson had been just barely within striking range before, but now he stepped in closer, sticking his mouth just inches away from my ear.

"Your mom died that night when Agony came calling, but he didn't kill her. I did."

My beast tore free of the metaphysical chains I'd used to bind her, but it wasn't like anything I'd ever felt before. I didn't change, at least not immediately, but Branson's words had hit me with the strength of a wrecking ball. A verbal blow like that should have devastated me, but that titanic force bounced off of something in my core, something that refused to give into the blow that he'd expected to crush me.

My inner landscape seemed to be composed of huge walls of ice and my beast's anger perfectly offset the force of Branson's barb, canceling it out and leaving me motionless inside. It wasn't an enduring kind of stillness, it was nothing more than a pale shadow of the peace I'd found earlier during my meditation, but it was still enough to channel the power from my beast with brittle walls that still refused to give way before her.

Branson had stepped forward and to one side, trying to flank me, and I'd turned with him. Even while in a state of profound shock, I still reflexively made sure that the biggest threat was where I could see him. As I turned my hand moved forward without any conscious decision on my part, but rather than the impotent blow I'd been expecting to land on Branson, my hand exploded outwards with the deadly, semi-retractable claws of my hybrid leading the outermost edge of the change.

My claws went through the soft flesh of his human body like it wasn't even there. One second we were standing there looking each other in the eye, and then his corpse was lying on the ground in front of me as his blood dripped off of my hand.

I was still in shock, I could feel it, but I knew I needed to do *something*. I reached for my beast, begging her for the power required to do a full transformation, but for a split second nothing happened. My beast was shocked too, she hadn't realized we were capable of a partial transformation and she had to pull deeply on the golden thread that fed *her* power before she could turn around and offer me the energy I needed.

A whisper of sound behind me brought me around, but despite the fearsome form of my right hand, I was still just a human, still too slow to have any chance of surviving against the enraged moonborn of the Duluth pack. I turned just in time to see a large gray wolf sailing towards my throat.

I couldn't dodge, not in this body. My one hope was to shift, to move my throat out of range of the attack by the simple virtue of growing more than a foot, but my beast was still depleted. In the instant before my attacker would have fastened his jaws around my neck, a blur of silver flashed past me.

The wolf still hit me, but Geoffrey's strike had killed him. Rather than gray snapping, clawing death, I was hit by nothing more than dead weight, but the collision was still more than enough to send me sprawling backwards.

As I tumbled through the air my beast finally found the energy to force my body through the sweet pain of a transformation. I hit the floor as a hybrid and then rolled over backwards and landed on my feet.

The Duluth pack was moving towards us, fanning out to make sure that they could surround us, but a second corpse was already resting at Geoffrey's feet and they were obviously not eager to come within range of his sword.

The other pack was down to eight living moonborn, but that would still be more than enough to kill the two of us unless I was able to come up with some way to stop them from coming after us all at once.

"Stop!"

I'd opened my mouth without a clear plan, with no real idea how to save Geoffrey and me, but as the words came out I realized that there was a single pretext under which what I'd done might not be considered a gross violation of everything the challenge law stood for.

I didn't actually expect my yell to give pause to any of the wolves or hybrids stalking towards me, but Stekensbridge echoed the order a split second later.

"What do you want, Bianchi?"

"He killed my mother in an unlawful attack nearly two decades ago. My killing him was nothing less than the king's justice."

"We don't have a king now."

Stekensbridge's words came out low and angry, but some of his pack members were backing away, slowly, almost as if they were hoping that he wouldn't notice what they were doing.

"You may not have a king, but I do, and it's only a matter of time before Alec overthrows the Coun'hij. When that happens, anyone who treats what just happened as anything other than justice will pay the ultimate price."

"How will he know? Your pet vampire isn't going to have a chance to text him before you're both dead."

I shrugged. "These things have a way of coming to light sooner or later. It's always a surprise when you actually figure out who spilled the beans. For something like this Alec would grant a pardon to whoever steps forward first, but he'll only grant a single pardon, everyone else will be killed."

I could see wolves and hybrids alike looking at each other out of the corner of their eyes. It was time to drive the knife in a little more.

"All I'm trying to point out is that attacking Geoffrey and me would be running an awful big risk to avoid having to face me in the ring yourself."

Hybrid faces didn't show quite the same range of emotion as what a human face could, but there was no mistaking the fact that Stekensbridge was pissed. I'd just mousetrapped him quite handily, but that didn't stop him from trying to weasel his way out.

"You'll never make it past my challengers. Either way I won't have to bother with putting you out of your misery."

"Are you so sure of that? Wasn't Branson your best fighter?"

"You killed him through trickery, you couldn't have beaten him in a fair fight."

I couldn't help it, I grinned at him as I responded this time. "I guess we'll never know. Personally I think he would have been easy meat, but I couldn't take that risk. An execution, the delivery of justice, couldn't be allowed to interfere with this particular challenge match."

He opened his mouth to rebut that, but I didn't give him a chance. "The law is on your side, Stekensbridge, if you want to get some more of your people killed trying to save your own throat and they are willing to die for you then there's nothing I can do about it other than to kill each of them. When *was* the last time you all went up against a hybrid powerful enough to shift just their hands? Were they as big as I am?"

That had him. In a strong, unified pack the alpha could afford to exchange barbs with a challenger, but they rarely needed to. It was only a weak pack, one beset by divisions where the alpha had to trade insults. Refusing to hear the challenger out could be construed as a weakness and weakness invariably made the submissives less willing to fight in your behalf. If you matched wits and came out ahead you could motivate your people to make an even stronger showing, but if you did poorly then wolves and hybrids who otherwise would have fought for you decided that they weren't willing to risk their skins on your behalf.

Stekensbridge had gambled and lost. He could order people to fight me, but that would just make things worse for him in the long run. He needed to beat me and it needed to be a decisive win, especially now that he'd lost his main enforcer.

"Very well, I'll kill you myself. I don't care how big and strong you are, you haven't been a hybrid for long enough to be worthy of my time, but I'm not opposed to proving that with fang and claw."

I waved Geoffrey back outside of the circle and then watched as the rest of the Duluth pack withdrew as well. It was time to control my breathing once again. Our circle back home was sand. We had another circle cut into the floor of one of the caves below the manor, but we rarely if ever used it. I couldn't remember the last time I'd fought on stone, but I knew it was going to be tricky. Stone didn't absorb the force of your lunges the way that sand did, but it was so slick that in some ways it was worse.

With sand if you wanted to move faster you just had to push harder. With stone there was a practical limit to how quickly you could change direction. It didn't matter how strong you were, talons only gripped so well.

Stekensbridge moved towards me across the scarred surface of the rock and I told myself for the final time that it didn't matter how little experience I had fighting in this form. I was bigger and stronger, I just needed to keep him at arm's length long enough for him to start getting tired and then I could end the fight all at once when he couldn't keep up anymore.

I feinted forward and smiled when Stekensbridge darted back with more speed than the attack justified. He was scared. It was starting to look like he was out of practice. Branson had been fighting too many of Stekensbridge's fights over the last couple of decades.

My moment of moral superiority was short-lived. I moved forward, trying to force him even further back, but he changed directions with impressive speed, springing forward and raking me across the outside of my left arm.

I countered, slashing at his face, but that was a mistake, his head was too mobile and he managed to avoid my attack. I took another slash, this time to my left leg before I managed to land a blow of my own on him.

His shoulder was dripping a slow flow of blood, but I was bleeding in two spots and starting to realize that he was doing to me exactly what I'd been planning on doing to him. If he continued to land two blows for every one of mine then it wouldn't matter how much bigger and stronger I was, I'd still end up bleeding out.

I tried to push the tempo of the fight. I couldn't change direction much if any faster than him, but I was stronger, which meant that he couldn't match my upper body speed. I drove him back before me with a barrage of slashes. High and low, left and right, I worked every possible angle of attack, and I was rewarded with a host of cuts to his arms, but he just kept backing away from me, denying me the critical wounds I was going for as he led me around the edge of the circle.

He was tiring, he had to be under the fury of my assault, but I was tiring too, and even my massive hybrid muscles weren't going to be able to continue to keep up this level of aggression forever. My lungs sucked air in with big gasps, but I was still managing to keep him off balance and on the defensive right up until he saw an opening and charged me.

I tried to get out of his way, tried to knock the cruel edge of his claws away, but neither effort was fully successful. He scored a deep slash along the outside of my leg and a tremor of weakness raced up the damaged limb.

I could still walk on it, but I could tell that it was nearly done for. Any additional blows to that leg would put me down on the ground for sure and there was a possibility that even too sudden a move would cause it to collapse underneath me.

Stekensbridge should have pushed the attack and capitalized on my new vulnerability. It was what I would have done, but apparently he felt the need to recapture some of the credibility he'd lost before we started fighting.

"Maybe next time you'll all do your job and take down the challenger rather than making me deal with them. I can promise you all that you're going to regret standing down today."

The words were just a distraction. Even as the last one left his lips he sprang at me with the force of three hundred pounds of raging hybrid. I wanted to dodge out of the way. Every instinct I'd been born with, every reflex I'd spent so many hours as a wolf wiring into place said that meeting that kind of charge head-on was just asking to be killed, but I couldn't move and I knew it.

I tried to move to the side regardless, but my leg started to give way and instead I was forced to step forward to avoid falling. My left hand went down, claws digging into the rock floor beneath me in an effort to convert all of that shaky momentum into something I could use.

I hadn't realized just how outclassed I was until that instant, until I saw Stekensbridge dart to the side. He was still going to hit me, he was still leading with the claws of his right hand, but rather than just crashing directly into me he'd changed his course enough that he would bury his hand in my stomach and then use it as a fulcrum to swing around behind me. Once he was behind me, I would be as good as dead, but I didn't have the mobility required to get out of his way.

With all other options closed to me, I did the only thing I could think of. I let his fist sink into my guts, but I drove my own claws into his shoulder and then I pulled with every ounce of strength I had. My left hand pushed off against the rock at my feet to give me a little extra rotational momentum, but what happened next still shouldn't have been possible.

Stekensbridge curled around to the right just as he'd intended, his fist sending bright ribbons of pain through me, but he moved with incredible slowness. Instead of him snapping around behind me and grabbing me, I used the force of his charge to pivot around on my uninjured right leg, and a second later I was behind him and my left hand was sinking into his back.

My right arm was a single bar of fiery pain, but I refused to let go of his shoulder until I had a better grip on him with my left hand. I sank the talons on my left foot into the back of his leg. I couldn't use that to lever myself up any higher, not with my leg weak and shaking like it was, but it served to help reduce his mobility.

The metallic snick as my left hand closed around a pair of ribs was all the reassurance I was going to get. I let go with my right hand and buried it in the meat where his neck and shoulder met. If I'd been fighting a werewolf I never would have been able to climb up high enough to put him down, but Stekensbridge was shorter than me by a few inches and it only took a few more seconds before I was able to end him with two violent motions that left me exhausted and shaking.

I looked out at the remaining members of the pack, meeting each set of eyes until they'd looked away, acknowledging my greater strength. The wolves were all too submissive to question my claim, and I could practically read the thoughts of the remaining hybrid.

Challenging me right now would go against every unwritten law the moonborn believed in, but doing so would practically guarantee he'd win and become the new alpha, only his tenure at that point would be painfully short. He wasn't intimidating or deadly enough to stem the tide of dispossessed hybrids who would be headed this way in the next few weeks.

"I rule here in Duluth now. You all live by my sufferance, you all shelter under the strength of my arm."

Chapter 13

Geoffrey
Stekensbridge House
Duluth, Minnesota

Geoffrey stood guard outside of Jasmin's suite of rooms, the suite that had belonged to Stekensbridge until she'd killed him, for nearly twelve hours before she finally stumbled back out dressed in what he was pretty sure was her last change of clothes.

"How are you feeling?"

"Like I nearly lost my first hybrid-on-hybrid fight and almost died in the process, but other than that I'm okay. What about you?"

"I'm getting tired…and hungry, but I'm okay for now. The rest of the pack has been milling around in the house. They are staying just out of sight, but apparently haven't realized that I'm a mentalist so they haven't been staying far enough away to stop me from sensing their presence."

"How much hungrier are you?"

"A lot hungrier. I didn't realize how much of a relationship there is between using my gift and the growth of the hunger. Don't worry though, I've still got things under control."

Jasmin had been walking towards the long hall that led to the front door, but Geoffrey's admission made her stop and look at him.

"You used your power on Stekensbridge, didn't you?"

Geoffrey would have been much happier if that particular fact hadn't ever come to light, but he wasn't about to lie to Jasmin, not when she asked him a direct question.

"Yes, right after you killed Branson. I helped tip the scales so that he ordered everyone back. I knew he needed to listen to your justification. If I hadn't pushed when I did, then he would have had the rest of the pack just rip you apart."

Jasmin pursed her lips. "I didn't think you were that strong. Invading the mind of a shape shifter like that is no small accomplishment."

"Honestly I wasn't sure that I would be able to pull it off either, but I knew I had to try something. There was no way that we were going to cut our way out of there."

"I won't deny that it cheapens the victory a bit to know that you had your hands in it, but the truth is that you're probably right, so thank you for saving my skin—several times as I recall."

Jasmin seemed to sense that Geoffrey wasn't particularly comfortable with the direction of the conversation. She only let the silence stretch out for a couple of seconds before continuing.

"How much have you been able to pull from the minds of my pack? Have any of them started spreading the news of what happened yet?"

"Mostly I've just picked up surface thoughts. I haven't wanted to penetrate too deeply, not after you warned me that your beasts are able to sense intrusions and then help you fight. Still, nobody seems to be in a state of mind to do anything other than just wait and see what kind of an alpha you're going to be."

"Nobody?"

"The hybrid, Jorge, seems like the one most likely to give you trouble, but you don't need me to tell you that."

"Right, he's the next most dominant, but is that the only reason?"

"I'm not sure. If you can get the two of us alone with him for a few minutes I might be able to get more out of him. Are you ready for another fight if he realizes what I'm doing?"

Jasmin rubbed her side absently for a couple of seconds before nodding. "Yeah, I can take him if it comes to that. It won't be pretty, but it should be doable."

The seven remaining original members of the pack were waiting in a large solarium that was mounted on the south side of the house. Geoffrey followed Jasmin into the airy, sunlit space and found, not to his surprise, that they were all standing, uneasily watching the two new arrivals.

"Please be seated, all of you. We have a lot to discuss and not much time to do it in."

A tall, slender guy who looked like he was in his late twenties shook his head. "We'd all just as soon stand."

Geoffrey's mental probes confirmed that this was Jorge, the one he'd felt, the one who'd spent the last two hours trying to work up the courage to confront Jasmin. This close it was easier to pick up more of what was skittering across the surface of Jorge's mind and Geoffrey wasn't surprised to find out that Jorge had been trying very hard to follow in Branson's footsteps and win himself a spot on the Coun'hij.

"Jorge, is it?"

Jorge stuck his chin out truculently. "Yeah, that's me."

Jasmin smiled and then backhanded Jorge hard enough that the older hybrid fell back over a heavy black metal chair. Before Jorge could claw his way back up to his feet, Jasmin stepped on his right arm and looked down at him with a face that had suddenly gone colder than the snow outside.

"Unless you've got a mouse in your pocket you should probably stop using the royal we. Based on the fact that your friends are all sitting politely in their chairs just like I asked them to, you don't speak for them anymore than you speak for me."

"I'll see you dead for that!"

Jorge looked like he wanted to spring to his feet and rip Jasmin's throat out, but her other foot was poised just inches away from his throat. Geoffrey knew they were in every bit as much danger as they'd been down in the circle after Jasmin had killed Branson, but Jasmin seemed completely unconcerned about what the rest of the pack might choose to do, her focus was on Jorge and only Jorge.

Geoffrey rested his hands on his sword's hilt and forced himself to turn away from Jasmin and Jorge so that he could keep an eye on the other five shape shifters. It wasn't something that he liked doing. Jorge was the single most dangerous person remaining in the pack and having him at his back made Geoffrey's shoulder blades itch.

There was nothing to do but just suck it up and trust that Jasmin could control the confrontation. The sense of hot prickles dancing across his skin suddenly increased as he heard Jasmin lean forward.

"I don't think that you have the spine to try it, but any time you want to take a shot at me just say the word. I'd like nothing better than to kill you and rid myself of the incessant headaches that I suspect you're going to cause me."

"You wouldn't dare. Without me there's nobody between you and any challengers."

"Yeah, I saw how much help you were for Stekensbridge, I'm sure I would be completely lost without you. Now are you going to toe the line or should we just get this out of the way right now?"

The heat behind him was exponentially hotter than it had been a second before. Geoffrey couldn't help himself, he stole a glance back at Jasmin and Jorge and saw that Jorge had gone almost completely white. Jasmin stepped away from Jorge and then waved Geoffrey to a chair.

"You too, Jorge, sit down."

Jorge obviously wasn't very happy about the order, but he took a seat next to the rest of his pack mates and didn't say anything else.

"Things are going to change around here for as long as I'm in charge. Firstly, we're switching to the other side of the war. You will all do everything in your power to support Alec Graves as the rightful king and ruler over all wolves everywhere."

For a second it looked like Jorge wasn't going to be able to hold his tongue. Even worse, Geoffrey could feel the hybrid's thoughts shifting. He'd been mostly happy with passively resisting before, but he'd just gone over to having decided to actively resist Jasmin as far as he was able without endangering his own skin.

Jasmin continued, unaware of the silent drama being played out inside of Jorge's mind. "Next, I don't know how the dominants have been treating the submissives, but as of right now I won't permit any of the abuse that is such a routine part of pack life in most places. If someone who is dominant to you asks you to fetch something then go do it. If we're in a combat situation then the dominants, me mostly, will be calling the shots, but beyond that I expect you to treat each other like actual people. No physical abuse, no stealing, basically no doing anything that would get you sent to jail if you did it to someone in the outside world."

There was obvious hope on many of the faces in the solarium, but it was equally obvious that they weren't sure whether they could trust Jasmin to live up to what she'd just said. Geoffrey knew little of pack life, but it was already plain that the alpha's word was law in a way that normal people couldn't ever hope to understand.

The alpha held the lives of every member of the pack in their hands and there wasn't any higher authority to appeal to if it turned out that they said one thing but behaved in a completely different manner.

"I'm not interested in any kind of witch hunt. By and large I'd like to just give everyone a clean slate and judge you on your behavior from here on out, but I may make an exception if somebody has done something truly heinous."

That last bit was said looking at Jorge, but Jasmin wasn't quite done making her point. "I will however take past action into account when doling out punishments for current actions. If someone has a history of poor behavior in some way or another, I'm not going to let you work up a list of infractions as long as my arm before I deal with you."

She looked around at the pack, at her pack, and then raised an eyebrow. "Any questions?"

When nobody responded Jasmin rubbed the side of her head with one hand and then pointed at a slim fifteen-year-old red-headed girl.

"You, what's your name? Out of the remaining members of this pack who has the closest ties with the Coun'hij?"

The girl cleared her throat nervously and looked around at her friends and family, but there was obviously no help going to come from any of them.

"I'm Sally, ma'am. In answer to your other question, it's Jorge you want. He's got a couple of the enforcers he talks to on a regular basis. The rest of us have been involved in the occasional operation with them to kill a vampire or hunt down one of the dispossessed who had crossed some line or another, but it was just the hybrids the Coun'hij were interested in talking to when they were here."

Geoffrey had wormed a couple of hair-thin tendrils of thought into Sally's mind when it became obvious that Jasmin was going to pump her for information. It was a risk, but he figured it was offset by the need to know whether or not she was telling the truth. He expected Jasmin to look back at him for confirmation, but Jasmin just nodded.

"What do you have to say for yourself, Jorge?"

Jorge pushed dark black hair out of his eyes and then shrugged. "You just got finished telling us that you weren't going to hold the past against us. It doesn't seem like I really have to say anything."

Geoffrey didn't even see Jasmin move. One second she was sitting in a chair like everyone else, and in the next she was standing over Jorge and her hand had been replaced with hybrid claws which now rested along the side of Jorge's neck.

"Don't push me, Jorge. I did say that, but I also said that this pack was now going to be resisting the Coun'hij and helping Alec. Your history seems to indicate that might be a problem for you. Will it?"

"I'm not going to help you, if that's what you mean. You can torture me if you'd like, but you're not going to kill me. I can already see that you don't have the stomach for it. You'll threaten, but threats won't stop the Coun'hij when they come to put you down for killing Branson. You can't stop them from coming, and when they arrive you're going to die."

Jasmin's face had gone cold and remote again. "Geoffrey, there is something I need. Go ahead and pick that particular thought out of my mind and then take one of the submissives with you so they can find it for you. The wolf can tell you where it is when you're safely out of hearing range."

As Geoffrey cautiously reached a thought out towards Jasmin she turned back towards Jorge. "You've got things all wrong. I'm actually hoping that the Coun'hij will be along soon. My associate and I have some unfinished business with them."

Geoffrey's probe skimmed off the thought Jasmin was sending in his direction with so much force that he almost wouldn't have had to be a mentalist in order to know what she wanted. She wanted wire, thin wire, or barring that a heavy-gauge fishing line. Geoffrey was so curious that he couldn't help but probe just the tiniest bit deeper to find out what she wanted it for.

What he saw made Geoffrey's stomach heave unexpectedly. He wasn't sure whether his respect for Jasmin had just grown or decreased, but he no longer had any qualms about working with her. He couldn't have asked for a more ruthless partner when it came to his quest to save Melody.

Chapter 14

Jasmin Bianchi
Stekensbridge House
Duluth, Minnesota

Geoffrey had done his job with the signature competence that I'd come to expect from him. He took Sally with him and when they came back fifteen minutes later they didn't just have the wire, he had a multi-tool and he'd fashioned one end of the wire into a noose.

I spent the entire fifteen minutes they were gone convinced that Jorge was going to find his courage and transform, but I'd angled my claws so that if he did the natural movement of his head and neck as he shifted would rake my claws through his throat. I didn't actually want to kill Jorge, but I hadn't been lying when I said that I was pretty sure he was going to cause me more problems than he was worth.

Geoffrey prepared our little surprise while he was still well out of sight of Jorge and the rest, so Jorge had no heads-up as to what I was planning before Geoffrey stepped around behind him and slipped the wire over his head.

It was a nasty trick, the kind of thing more suited to one of the Coun'hij than it was to someone from Sanctuary, but I didn't have a choice. I couldn't babysit Jorge twenty-four hours a day and I didn't want to kill him, until I was sure that he couldn't be saved. It was the lesser of the evils facing me, so I let Geoffrey slip the wire noose around Jorge's neck and then held the now-terrified hybrid there with my claws while Geoffrey tied the ends off so that the loose wire loop wouldn't have any give in it.

We put more loops around his upper arms and then we wired his hands together behind him and put another loop around his waist. Once that was done Jorge was as close to being harmless as I could make him without putting him inside of a cage.

Putting him inside of a cage would have actually been my first preference, but I knew there wasn't any way I was going to make that happen. No healthy, conscious hybrid would ever let themselves be locked up, but by putting the wires around him I put him enough in my power that he wouldn't have any choice but to do whatever I wanted, up to and including voluntarily locking himself up.

I actually felt sorry for him. If he transformed to a hybrid with those wires on him he'd bleed to death in a matter of seconds as the wires cut into his expanding flesh. If he transformed into a wolf he might not die, it all depended on the relative size of his wolf neck as compared to his human neck, but the wires around his wrists would dislocate both of his front legs and leave him crippled even if the wires around his neck didn't get him.

It was nothing less than cruel. Jorge had been around long enough that he should have a pretty good mastery of his beast, but even so all it would take would be a momentary loss of control on his part, the briefest instant where his beast took over and forced a transformation, and he'd be dead.

Once Jorge was neutralized we pulled his phone out of his front pocket and rehearsed the call that I wanted him to make. He blustered and tried to avoid agreeing to my demands, but he never really had a chance. Between my ability to smell his lies and Geoffrey's ability telling us exactly what Jorge was planning, it was easy to cut off all of his avenues of escape, one by one.

It took nearly an hour, but by the end of that time Jorge was a hollow shell of a man. By the time we finished he'd lost the last of the hope he'd held onto as he'd watched me kill his alpha and his best friend. I felt dirtier for having done it, but I just kept telling myself that this was the only way to rescue Melody and therefore the only way to save Ben.

Even before we'd started breaking Jorge I sent two of the other wolves off with instructions to go pick up Ben. Before they left I promised them that they'd suffer if anything happened to him, and extracted a promise from them that they would do exactly as I'd asked them to in this particular instance.

Under normal circumstances that would have been plenty of reassurance, but when it came to Ben I seemed to need more reassuring than normal. Geoffrey's barely-perceptible nod indicating that they weren't planning on making a run for it was heaven-sent. I'd hated vampires for as long as I'd known of their existence, but it was incredibly empowering to be working with one, especially such a powerful mentalist.

I called to check in with Sally and Jeff, a skinny twenty-year-old who looked like he should be wearing glasses and a pocket protector, and then Geoffrey, Jorge and I made the call to his contact on the Coun'hij.

Jorge spent the whole conversation sweating like a pig, but he didn't try to pull anything on us. By the end of the five-minute call the Coun'hij enforcer was convinced that the Duluth pack had captured me. The guy wanted to talk to Branson to confirm the story, but Jorge was very convincing when he said that Branson had been gravely injured in the process of capturing me. Apparently I was a hybrid now and positively huge, nearly as big as a werewolf.

I could practically hear the eagerness dripping from the enforcer's voice as he hung up. There was no doubt in my mind but that he thought he'd just scored big by being the one who was going to turn me over to Puppeteer and the rest. It even sounded like he was only planning on bringing a couple of guys with him due to the fact that the Coun'hij's people were spread out all over the country trying to deal with the cats coming up from Mexico while at the same time trying to hunt us rebels down.

Geoffrey and I had everything we needed and all it had cost was one little piece of my humanity.

Chapter 15

Geoffrey
Stekensbridge House
Duluth, Minnesota

It was obvious to Geoffrey that Jasmin was having second thoughts about Ben being in Duluth now that the Coun'hij's men were on a plane headed their direction. She'd put Ben up in a tiny hotel six miles from the pack's headquarters, but that wasn't going to ensure Ben's safety if the Coun'hij sent more men than expected.

Geoffrey had taken Ben to the hotel himself, but if the Coun'hij wanted to find Ben they could always just torture the information out of him. Geoffrey had been tortured before, the only difference this time would be that he wouldn't be up against anyone who could read his mind. It should mean that he would take longer than normal to start bleeding information, but it was still only a matter of time before he broke.

There had been quite a lot of debate about the best way to deal with the Coun'hij's people once they arrived, but in the end there hadn't been much in the way of viable options. If there'd been a way to get the enforcers to Stekensbridge House then there would have been a few different ways to ambush them, but Sally and the others had indicated that the Duluth pack traditionally provided transport to and from the city's small airport.

Geoffrey hadn't been entirely surprised when Jasmin told him that there was no way to get the pickup squad from the airport to Stekensbridge House. Apparently shape shifters could smell nervousness as well as they could smell lies.

Jasmin seemed to think there was a chance she or Geoffrey either one would have been able to avoid making the enforcers suspicious, but for the fact that they would smell that Geoffrey was a vampire and Jasmin was the one that they were there to carry away.

No, they were all in agreement that the attack would have to take place at the airport. Every member of the pack knew the code required to enter into the section of the airport where the pack's private plane was parked, so getting past the tall fence was no problem.

Once inside Geoffrey walked casually towards the small control tower. Before he'd even crossed half of the distance Jorge's phone vibrated with an incoming text.

It does look like Hangar Thirteen is the best bet, direct the plane there.

Geoffrey nodded to himself. Jasmin's text had hardly been a surprise, but it was nice to know that the Duluth wolves had been right in their assessment of the best place for the attack to take place.

The rest of the trip to the control tower passed without problem and then Geoffrey was standing in front of a heavy steel door. He briefly considered checking to see if it was locked, but he walked over to an especially deep shadow and sat down instead.

He was better off doing his work from outside of the building. The distance would make things difficult, but it would also eliminate the very real risk otherwise that he'd run into one of the air traffic controllers. If that happened he'd almost certainly be forced to kill someone. Even at his best he wasn't capable of destroying someone's memories and it would be far better for all concerned if he were able to avoid leaving any evidence that anything unusual was happening.

Geoffrey reached out with feather-light strands of thought, insinuating himself into the two minds currently situated only a couple dozen yards away from him. It was only a moment's work to determine which of the two was currently in charge of the arrivals, and then

Geoffrey began to work himself deeper and deeper into the man's psyche.

Ten minutes before the arrival time that Jorge's contact had given them, the phone in Geoffrey's pocket lit back up. This time the text was from that same contact.

Still on schedule, make sure that you have your people there waiting for us.

A cold smile worked its way onto Geoffrey's face as his traffic controller, the one that he'd burrowed so deeply into, began working through the final approach exchange with the pilot of the Coun'hij's plane.

Hangar Thirteen. That's right, you want to direct them to Hangar Thirteen once they've landed.

It was a simple mantra, but Geoffrey repeated it over and over with the conviction of a recent convert praying. It took only a minute or so before the suggestion started to take root, but Geoffrey continued to keep the pressure up on his controller.

Geoffrey waited until the plane had touched down and he 'heard' the arrival controller direct the pilot to Hangar Thirteen and then the vampire stood and started back towards the spot where Jasmin and the others were waiting for him.

The plane had to taxi across half the distance of the airport to make it to Hangar Thirteen, so Geoffrey was able to make it there a minute or so before the large doors started sliding back out of the way of the incoming plane.

Jasmin met him at the small door he used to enter.

"Everything is a go. The wolves are all here and positioned out of sight. We'll wait for the plane to power down and the doors to close and then Sally will cut the power and the entire structure will be plunged into darkness."

Geoffrey nodded. "Thereby making sure that we don't have to worry about the pilot seeing something he's not supposed to. That works."

"Will you be able to see well enough to fight?"

"Probably, but even if I can't, it won't be the end of the world. I'll still be able to sense them."

Jasmin looked surprised. "I never realized that was even possible for you."

Geoffrey hoped that his shrug was sufficiently noncommittal that she wouldn't be able to smell the lie on him. In theory it should be possible, but he'd never tried it before and wasn't actually sure if he would be able to fully compensate for the disorientation that was an inherent part of trying to see out of someone else's eyes at the same time that he saw out of his own.

A second or two passed in which Jasmin seemed to be waiting for him to expound, but then she just shrugged. "Just be careful. This all is pretty much pointless if you're not around to heal Ben afterwards. We need to take at least one of these guys alive, so our best bet is to kill one quickly and then we can overwhelm whoever is left with enough numbers to make capture possible."

Geoffrey took up station behind a pile of tires. Jasmin disappeared behind a large tool chest, and then there was nothing left but the wait. A few minutes later the plane, a shiny Gulfstream, taxied into the hangar and the large doors behind it began closing.

It looked for a second as though the plan might come apart completely. Geoffrey could hear the enforcers exiting the plane and not only were the lights still on, the doors hadn't finished closing.

"Do you hear that?"

"Yeah, heartbeats."

Geoffrey knew that the wolves would be able to hear the enforcers even better than he could, so he wasn't surprised when the lights died immediately after that. The hangar was dark, but not completely dark. Between the running lights from the plane and the five-foot gap in the main doors there was sufficient light for Geoffrey and he started off towards the open door at a full sprint.

Now that the main breaker had been thrown the doors had stopped moving and Geoffrey knew that everyone else had doors they were covering. It would be up to him to make sure that the enforcers didn't get out that way.

Geoffrey arrived at the door, katana in hand, ready to fight, but the enforcers didn't particularly seem worried. There were three of them, and they'd all shifted to hybrid form and stood in a loose triangle a few feet away from the plane as Jasmin and the wolves slowly collapsed inwards.

"Geoffrey, we need to break them up, as long as they hold together we're at a disadvantage because the wolves can't come at them from multiple directions."

Jasmin's yell told him everything he needed to know. Geoffrey started worming tendrils into the mind of the closest hybrid, but he immediately ran into resistance from the man's beast which seemed stronger and more aggressive than Jorge's had been.

One of the hybrids swore when he got his first sniff of Geoffrey. "Really? I never would have thought that even Stekensbridge would stoop to working with vampires."

"Stekensbridge is dead, I killed him and Branson too. Actually I'm starting to feel a little jittery from not having killed anyone in the last twenty-four hours. It's a good thing you boys decided to take the bait and fly into town."

Jasmin's voice didn't sound jittery, it sounded malevolent in a way that Geoffrey hadn't heard out of her before. He didn't have the advantage of being able to hear her heartbeat or smell her perspiring, and he was too occupied with the battle inside his hybrid's mind to send a tendril her direction, but he was pretty sure that she wasn't bluffing.

"That's too bad about Stekensbridge and Branson, but it does make things easier. We were going to raze your little pack to the ground no matter what once you ambushed us, but the fact that you killed them and are working with a vampire means that I won't have to explain myself to Puppeteer or any of the others."

Three of Geoffrey's probes were ripped away, stealing a little of the energy he knew he was going to need later, but he had two more probes that he'd done a better job of camouflaging and the hybrid's beast hadn't managed to find them yet. Geoffrey fed more power into those two, growing them and sinking tendrils into more and more of the hybrid's mind even as he sent more tendrils, these less cleverly disguised, to serve as a distraction.

Jasmin darted forward, slashing at the hybrid closest to her, but the attack was mostly a feint designed to draw him out of position and he didn't take it. One corner of Geoffrey's mind realized that this could very easily become a standoff unless he or Jasmin were able to make something happen.

The wolves were milling around in the near darkness, just outside of striking range of the hybrids, but Jasmin was right, none of them could go up against a hybrid by themselves. A bolder set of wolves might have still been able to create openings of their own, but not these.

One of the hybrids laughed, no doubt having come to the same conclusion that they were three lions cornered by half a dozen kittens, and then suddenly the hybrids exploded into motion. It was obvious that these three particular enforcers had worked together before, they supported each other too well for their actions to be a coincidence.

One of the hybrids managed a long, raking slash across the side of one of the Duluth wolves and when two other wolves tried to get in close enough to retaliate they found that the opening they thought they'd seen had evaporated almost instantly as the hybrid's companions had stepped into the gap.

Jasmin took advantage of the shuffle as the hybrids repositioned to rip a chunk out of her opponent's arm, which caused her opponent to advance towards her in an effort to bring her to bay. Each movement by any of the hybrids required covering movements by the other two which tended to create tiny, transient openings which the wolves did their best to exploit, but they weren't being very successful.

One of Geoffrey's probes expanded into a new section of his hybrid's mind and was shredded like it had just encountered a buzz saw. It took a second for him to realize that he'd just impinged onto the beast's home turf. The beast was going through the individual threads of Geoffrey's probe with remarkable speed, but there were a lot of threads.

Having the threads ripped away so quickly caused Geoffrey a level of pain that was only a shade away from a migraine, but he forced himself to work through the pain and took advantage of the beast's preoccupation to seed half a dozen new, heavily-camouflaged mental tendrils into the hybrid's mind. Instead of trying to expand back into the same area that had just wakened the beast that was so busy tearing through his work, Geoffrey instead focused on increasing the number of threads in the safe area.

The Duluth wolves were fully engaged now. The hybrids having attacked had pushed the more numerous wolves into defending themselves, but for all the motion and fury of the wolves' attack, they weren't actually doing much damage to the hybrids.

Geoffrey had been moving along with the flow of battle, keeping himself just outside of range, but now that his penetration of the hybrid's mind was nearly complete he moved in and slashed at his hybrid. Geoffrey knew what his opponent was thinking as soon as the other man's thoughts occurred, but it wasn't helping as much as it should have.

In a normal fight most of what happened was nothing more than reflexive movements, things that happened without conscious thought on the part of either of the combatants. Even so, Geoffrey usually was able to tap into enough of the ripples of thought to anticipate someone's actions.

Defensive actions were the hardest because they had the least amount of conscious thought associated with them. Offensive attacks were slightly easier because they tended to be more premeditated in nature. Monitoring the thoughts of a hybrid mid-fight was unlike anything Geoffrey had ever attempted before.

Everything was reflexive. There wasn't any thought of *feint* or rudimentary strategy, even something as simple as switching up tempo. The hybrid sprang at Geoffrey and he was forced back several steps while beating away slashes from those steel-like claws. Geoffrey was half convinced that his opponent was operating on nothing more than instinct, and even that was too alien for Geoffrey to get a good read on it.

Geoffrey pushed even harder on the mental side of things. The threads he'd planted in the hybrid's mind had grown into thick roots with an interlocking set of tendrils that touched every aspect of the enforcer's conscious mind. Geoffrey still couldn't access memory, that was always the hardest thing to breach, but he'd opened up everything else.

One of the wolves got too close to Geoffrey's hybrid and he swatted her aside. She hit the ground bloody and didn't get back up. There was something there as the hybrid attacked that time, a surge of something that was more than just reflex, a trail of thought that originated from inside the section claimed by the enforcer's beast.

The balance of the fight was tipping away from Jasmin and the Duluth pack. It would still be a few more minutes before things ground to their inevitable conclusion, but Geoffrey could feel the change, could see where things were headed.

Another wolf was ripped out of the air and limped away on three legs. There wasn't any time left for half measures. Geoffrey pushed more energy into his probes and sent more tendrils growing into the beast's territory from every direction, hundreds, thousands of tendrils that burrowed into the last remaining area of privacy, the last mental redoubt.

It was all there, all of the thoughts that Geoffrey had been looking for but been unable to find. The hybrid's beast tore through Geoffrey's probes trying to destroy them, but Geoffrey grew new ones, sprouted them almost as quickly as the beast could rip them free.

The thoughts that Geoffrey was tapping into were still subtly alien, but he could see what he needed to see now. The man and the beast were joined into something that was nearly one organism now that they were in the middle of a fight, but that wasn't sufficient to stop Geoffrey from anticipating the next few attacks before they even happened.

Geoffrey ducked under a slash that had never really been meant to hit him, and then brought his sword up and around in a spray of blood. As his hybrid fell to the ground, Geoffrey stepped into the gap where he'd been standing and cut the hybrid on the right across the leg with a slash that would have taken the leg completely off of a human.

The hybrid on the left drove Geoffrey back with a lightning-fast swipe of his claws, but the remaining four uninjured wolves had piled on the now-immobile hybrid and Jasmin was yelling for them to leave one of the hybrids alive.

Less than a minute later the last surviving hybrid shifted back to human form. He hadn't liked it, but even he hadn't been able to think he could survive against five-to-one odds. When faced with death or surrender he'd picked surrender.

Once the fight was over, all of the blood painting the floor was nearly more than Geoffrey could take, but he closed his eyes and forced himself to think of other things. It wasn't appealing blood, warm, from the vein, it was little more than liquid garbage. Geoffrey promised himself that he would feed soon and then opened his eyes and went back to cleaning up.

They had the captive they needed, now it was just a question of whether Geoffrey could break him in time.

Chapter 16

Geoffrey
Stekensbridge House
Duluth, Minnesota

The final butcher's bill was worse than Geoffrey had hoped, but better than it had almost been. Geoffrey ran through a list of Jasmin's wolves as he walked down the hall. It wasn't strictly something he should have been thinking about right then, but it had the benefit of distracting him from what he was about to do.

Jeff's right leg had been shattered in more places than Geoffrey even cared to think about, and he'd lost an incredible amount of blood, but he should make a full recovery given enough time. Sally and most of the other wolves had made it through the fight more or less okay, but the last wolf, the one Geoffrey had seen go down in a spray of blood, was in fact dead.

Geoffrey hadn't been sure what to expect out of Sally and the others, but what he got was a kind of tired acceptance of their friend's death. None of them liked it. They felt like they'd been dragged into a war that had nothing to do with them, but they also weren't ready to stand up to Jasmin and tell her what they were really thinking.

It turned out that restraining a hybrid was more challenging than Geoffrey had realized. They'd restrained Jorge just fine, but only by putting him in a position where he could die at any time. They couldn't let the enforcer die, at least not until after they'd gotten the information they needed out of him, so just tying him up with wire wasn't a suitable option.

After being restrained by Imastious so many times, Geoffrey was practically an expert when it came to tying people up, but he didn't know very much about hybrids other than the fact that they were insanely strong and that shifting would cause them to get much bigger. Jasmin, on the other hand, knew quite a bit about hybrid anatomy and abilities, but not very much about tying people up.

It took a little while, during which time the enforcer, Jeete, was tied up with wire just like had been done to Jorge, but eventually the pair of them hit on a solution. The Duluth wolves rounded up two of the cages used to restrain wolves or hybrids who'd been injured too badly to control their shape, or who'd otherwise displeased their alpha. Geoffrey had thought that the cage Imastious used on him had been heavy-duty, but it had nothing on the monstrosities that Sally and the other two wolves scared up for them.

The bars were thicker than Geoffrey's arms and the spaces between the bars were only about two inches wide. The whole thing was made out of hardened metal and not only was it small enough that a hybrid wouldn't have very much room to move around inside of it, the key surfaces were all angled so that from inside of the cage you couldn't get leverage on anything.

The steel bars were marked up from the claws of the hybrids who'd spent time in them, but apparently even hybrid claws couldn't shear through that much metal, at least not without the room required to build up some serious inertia.

Geoffrey, Jasmin and the others put Jorge and Jeete in separate cages and then put human-style restraints around Jeete's wrists and ankles. Jasmin was fairly certain that the restraints would simply tear if Jeete shifted, but just to make sure, she had bolted them to the wall using a section of metal that was too strong for a human to break, but which a hybrid should be able to tear away from the stone without too much trouble.

By adjusting the distance between the cage and the wall, they were able to make sure that the restraints were too tight to fall off while Jeete was in human form, but once he shifted and the bolts tore through the scrap metal holding them to the rock wall, then the restraints should loosen and fall off rather than cutting his hands and feet off.

Once they had both hybrids satisfactorily restrained, Geoffrey took a pair of pliers and removed the loops of wire around each of their necks, wrists, waist, ankles and arms. Jasmin came back from retrieving Ben about the time that the vampire had started hunting around the house for the things he would need to break Jeete. By the time Geoffrey headed back down to the basement, Jasmin had gotten Ben comfortable in the master bedroom and caught back up with Geoffrey.

"Have you done this kind of thing before?"

"Not that I remember, but based on some of the things that I've been told it's likely. The toughest part is figuring out how far you can push someone without killing them. That's the part that gets most humans in trouble when they start out."

Jasmin worked her mouth a couple of times like she was trying to get words out but unable to make her voice function.

"Don't worry, I shouldn't have to push him nearly as close to the edge of death as you would. I just have to lower his natural resistance to my mental probes to the point where I can get in and find the information we're after. The fact that he's a shape shifter and naturally tougher than a human should only give me a bigger margin of error."

"That's true, but you're also going to have to watch out. If he gets too close to death he'll more than likely shift despite his best efforts and I suspect that you'll have a harder time ransacking his mind once he shifts."

"I guess it's a good thing that we aren't restraining him with wires then."

Jasmin looked away from Geoffrey for several seconds and then cleared her throat. "Does it bother you? I mean what you're about to do?"

Geoffrey shook his head. "No. I'm ready to play my part. Does it bother you?"

"Not in the slightest."

Jasmin stepped around him and pushed open the door to the rock room where Jeete was being kept. Geoffrey followed her inside. He'd lied, apparently well enough that Jasmin couldn't tell, but he was fairly sure that she hadn't.

He was still planning on upholding his word, but he'd started to see the glimmer of a possibility that he'd have to put Jasmin down before that day came. They would do what they had to do in order to save the ones that they loved, but that didn't mean that either he or Jasmin were going to be safe enough to run free once that was done.

Geoffrey had already seen too much of what happened when someone stopped viewing other people as anything other than objects. Imastious had already done plenty of evil. Geoffrey wouldn't be part of turning Jasmin into something like that, not without trying to clean up after himself at least.

Sally and two of the other wolves had been left down with the cage to make sure that Jeete didn't try anything. Jasmin didn't seem to think anything could go wrong, but she also wasn't going to take any chances with Jeete, not when they weren't likely to get another chance to capture one of the Coun'hij.

"You can all go; Geoffrey and I will take things from here."

Sally looked at the knives, batteries and wire in Geoffrey's arms and then licked her lips. "What are you going to do with him?"

"We need to know where the Coun'hij is. Once we know where their base is located then we can bring Alec and Grayson in and kill all of them in just a matter of minutes. In order to get that information out of him we're going to have to hurt him enough to bring down his natural resistances to Geoffrey's gift."

"You're going to torture him?"

"Yes, I won't argue with you if you want to call it that. You can leave now."

Sally shook her head. "That's not right. Jeete deserves better than that. Any person would deserve better than that. I'm not going to just stand by and let you do something like that."

"You don't have to stand by, just leave. I've already told you that."

The other two wolves had stopped moving. They hadn't stepped up to offer overt support to Sally, but it was obvious that they weren't any more comfortable than Sally with what Jasmin was going to do.

"No."

Jasmin moved so quickly that Geoffrey didn't even realize that she'd stepped closer to Sally until after she had her fist around the shorter girl's neck and was dangling her several inches off of the ground. "This isn't a democracy and you should thank your lucky stars that it isn't."

One of the other wolves, Chad based on the name that Geoffrey plucked out of his mind, stepped forward and crouched slightly almost as though preparing to spring at Jasmin. "Democracy is the highest form of government. You're nothing more than a tyrant."

Jasmin grabbed Chad, also by the throat and slammed both of her captives against the wall hard enough that their teeth clicked together from the force of the impact. She glared back at the third wolf with an intensity that made him take a step backwards.

"You're right, I'm a tyrant, but you're giving way too much credit to a democracy. The only way for a democracy to survive is to value the rights of the individual. Democracy runs based off of blind justice. Democracy values everyone's rights, but in the process it sometimes treats the murderer better than the victim."

Geoffrey stepped slowly towards Jasmin. "Jasmin, they can't breathe, you need to let them go."

For a second it looked like she was going to ignore him, but then she threw both of the shape shifters to the ground in disgust.

"You can keep your damn democracy. You may have not noticed yet, but it's already turning into something only a bare step up from mob rule out there. Your precious democracy is already violating human rights, it's just the rights of the minority that are being violated and the unwashed masses are fine with that."

Sally and Chad were both scooting away from Jasmin like a pair of hermit crabs that had just lost their shells, but Jasmin didn't even bother watching them.

"Give me an empire any day of the week. You should be grateful that I'm here. I don't have to follow the same rules as blind justice. I can weigh things that blind justice can't take into account and therefore my judgments can be better than what you'd get otherwise."

There was something there that resonated with Geoffrey, but he wasn't sure which parts he believed. Regardless, it was a dangerous philosophy, one that would easily lead someone over the edge without them realizing just how far they'd gone until it was too late.

"What if you're wrong, Jasmin? What if torturing Jeete is a mistake? You know that you're not perfect, you can still make mistakes."

Some of the air seemed to go out of Jasmin. "Yes, I can make mistakes. Democracy has built this country into what it is, but a good king or queen could have done better, slightly better at least."

"But wouldn't a bad monarch be *a lot* worse? Everyone in this pack is completely at your mercy."

Jasmin nodded choppily. "Yes, my personal code of conduct is the only thing protecting them, the only thing keeping me from being even worse than the Coun'hij. They're stuck though now. The only way to get out from under my thumb would be to trade me for a different tyrant, that or rise up against me. They won't do that though, that's why they are submissives, because they aren't willing to take responsibility."

The wounds that Jasmin had taken in the most recent round of fighting had already started healing, but they seemed to have washed her out. In the dim light the two of them were standing in she looked like an old woman who was covered with scars.

"They'll risk life and limb if they are ordered to, but they won't do the same to guarantee their freedom. People like that aren't worthy of living in a democracy or a republic, or whatever it is that rules us outside of these walls. They have to have a ruler because they're too weak to rule themselves and too dangerous to be allowed to run around ungoverned."

Geoffrey had stopped approaching Jasmin when she'd released Sally and Chad, but he almost went over to her now.

"This isn't just about the Duluth wolves, is it?"

"I don't know. It is at least a little bit about them. Jeete is a conscienceless killer, all of the Coun'hij enforcers are. He doesn't deserve any more mercy than he gave the people he killed."

The temptation to send tendrils of thought over to Jasmin so that he could sample her thoughts was nearly overpowering, but Geoffrey forced himself not to do so. There was a chance he would get caught and he knew that Jasmin would never forgive that.

"You said that the personal code of the king is the only thing that protects his people. How honorable is this Alec that you keep talking about?"

Jasmin laughed, a bitter, mocking sound. "More honorable than me, hopefully honorable enough. A few months ago I would have told you that he'd make a terrible king, but he's better now that he has Adri."

"Are you second-guessing your support of him?"

Jasmin shook her head. "No, he's better than any of the alternatives. Even if he does a terrible job he'll still make life better for the average submissive wolf. I think he'll do okay though. Maybe I'm just realizing that there's less difference between a submissive like Jessica or Sally and me than I used to think. Now I'm the one sitting on the throne and having all of my decisions second-guessed. Even at my best I don't think I'm ready to rule over anyone else. I can hardly rule myself."

"You're tired and injured. You've been through something like six fights in less than two weeks. You need some time to get your feet back under you."

"What if you're wrong, what if I'm a terrible alpha, what if I'm completely wrong about Alec and he's a horrible king?"

Geoffrey sighed. "I don't have many answers when it comes to this kind of thing, Jasmin. I'm about to torture Jeete and the fact that I feel bad about it isn't going to stop me. If you turn out to be a bad leader then I think you'll still be a good enough person to realize it. If that happens then just step down. Find a better leader and hand the pack over to it."

"What if I get to the point where I like the power too much to let go of it?"

"Then I'll hunt you down and kill you. It won't be the first time that I've executed someone for their sins."

It was the kind of statement that was almost guaranteed to strike sparks off of her beast, but Jasmin didn't look mad, there wasn't any barely-perceptible surge of energy, she just looked relieved.

"That's actually a relief. I think you might even be able to do it too."

"Hopefully it never comes to that."

Jasmin looked away. "What about if Alec turns out to be worse than the Coun'hij?"

"I actually have fewer worries there, at least where you are concerned. You've already proven that you're not the kind to just sit back and wring your hands and ask why this is happening to you. If Alec turns bad then you'll fight to overthrow him or at least check the worst of his excesses in some fashion or another."

"You're not half bad, at least not for a vampire."

"Thanks. You're not so bad either. Let's get this over with so we can go get Melody."

Geoffrey turned back to the cage where Jeete had been quietly watching their exchange, but before he could get close enough to set down the grisly tools he'd gathered upstairs, Jeete snorted at the two of them.

"You guys are too weak to stay in power. You're right about the submissives deserving whatever they get, but power is meant to be used."

Jasmin looked like she was ready to yell at him, but Geoffrey got his words out first.

"If you really believe that then you'll have no problem with what I'm about to do next. You're in my power and I'm going to exercise that power in ways that will hurt you."

Geoffrey started with the wires and the batteries. The current sizzling through Jeete's body caused him to scream and beg for Geoffrey to stop, but it didn't seem to noticeably weaken Jeete's beast or his natural defenses around the section of his mind that contained his memories.

After nearly an hour Geoffrey finally unclipped the wires from the batteries and picked up the knife that he'd been hoping not to have to use. Bleeding Jeete was even harder than Geoffrey had been worried it would be. The act of cutting the enforcer wasn't difficult, but seeing so much blood sent the hunger raging to new heights.

The shape shifter's natural healing ability meant that Geoffrey had to make new cuts on a regular basis to continue bleeding Jeete out, but it also meant that he was able to compress the torture down into something that lasted only a couple more hours.

With a human Geoffrey couldn't have opened up any wounds that would have bled too quickly because a human would have bled to death before the wounds closed on their own. With Jeete, Geoffrey made some fairly serious cuts to bleed him out most of the way and then once those had healed, Geoffrey proceeded more slowly.

Geoffrey sent probes into Jeete's mind on a regular basis to check on their progress, but found that Jeete was weakening physically at a much faster rate than he was weakening mentally. Jasmin took the news better than Geoffrey had expected her to.

"So what do we do? I'm not sure that you can bleed him out much more than you already have. He's already shaking, which probably means that he's nearly to the point of an involuntary shift, at which point you're probably going to have an even harder time bypassing his defenses."

"I think you're right. The last time I scanned him it seemed as though his will had weakened nearly to the point of not being able to contain his beast."

"What about if we starved him? Maybe that would weaken his beast."

"I'm not sure. It might work, but I don't think we have that kind of time."

Jasmin's frustration was obvious. "You're right, but what other choice do we have?"

"I can just throw my entire strength at him now and hope that he's been weakened enough to get what we need out of him. I won't be able to see everything, but I'll be able to see *some* things. There's a decent chance that I'll see where their base is."

"And if you don't? What's the downside?"

"I'm nearly at the end of my strength. If this attempt isn't successful then I'll have to rest for a day or two before I can try again. Also, I'm going to need to feed soon, almost certainly after doing what we're talking about. If I fail to feed then I'll lose control of myself and try to feed on whoever is closest."

"Okay, I think we go ahead. It's no worse than starving him. If you fail we can still try again in a day or two. Even if it takes us a couple of tries and they realize he's been missing too long, we'll still know where they are. It means that they'll be waiting for us, or possibly that they might even relocate, but Alec can always send in more guys, and even if they relocate that will still give us a trail to follow."

"And the other problem?"

"Just go ahead and feed off of Jeete."

Geoffrey forced himself not to give into the anger spidering across his mind. Jasmin was still equating him with all of the others of his kind, but he'd never actually told her that he'd stopped feeding on the unwilling.

"I won't feed on him. I only feed on the willing, or at least those I can adequately compensate in return for their blood."

There was a new respect for him in Jasmin's eyes. "That must make things difficult."

"It does, the last time I fed I wasn't sure that I was going to find an appropriate donor in time."

"What about bagged blood?"

"That's an acceptable alternative if it can be found, but it's getting harder and harder to get hold of bagged blood these days."

"Don't worry about that, every pack has whole blood stocks. We can't exactly make a run to the hospital if something goes wrong, so there are always at least one or two people who can transfuse blood and a stock of supplies on hand so that they can do their job." Jasmin already had her phone out. "Hey, Sally, go round up two or three bags of whole blood and bring them back down here."

As she slipped her phone back into her front pocket, Jasmin gave Geoffrey a sad smile. "She won't like me for the foreseeable future, but she'll do it. You can start whenever you're ready."

Geoffrey took a couple of deep, calming breaths and then closed his eyes and knelt down next to Jeete's cage. The enforcer had passed out from the blood loss and torture more than half an hour previously, so the initial infiltration was relatively easy.

The surface thoughts came first, pouring into Geoffrey's mind like a torrent of images and feelings that were alien but still incredibly compelling. Geoffrey's fingers had been curled inwards and he'd been flexing them for almost two full seconds before he realized that it wasn't him chasing Jasmin through the woods trying to tear her to ribbons, it was merely Jeete's dream, an overpoweringly vivid dream.

The realization allowed Geoffrey to pull back mentally enough to stop from losing himself inside of Jeete's psyche. This was something new, something stronger than Geoffrey had ever felt while linked mentally with someone. It was nearly enough to cause him to abandon the search, but he pushed on.

Geoffrey didn't want to lose himself inside of someone else's mind, but the stakes this time were simply too high for him to give up.

The mental probes cored down through the conscious mind like a taproot, minimizing the amount of contact between Geoffrey's mind and his victim's dream. All too soon the leading edge of Geoffrey's probes bumped up against the hard barrier that separated the conscious, present mind from accessible memories.

It was like cutting through solid rock, but Geoffrey forced tendrils of thought into the wall before him, digging and coring with diamond-hard tips. The shield that Jeete's mind had thrown up wasn't a uniform structure and before too long Geoffrey started finding softer spots, flaws in the barrier that he was able to exploit.

With each new fissure he created Geoffrey shoved his probes a little further inside and then he fed power in the hair-thin threads so that they grew, creating ever-larger holes. A few seconds passed, but it seemed like hours before Geoffrey felt the first of his probes slide through the barrier and touch the goldmine of memories on the other side.

Geoffrey was expecting for things to get easier once Jeete's natural defenses had been breached, which they did, but it still felt like he was swimming against a vast current. The first tendril was followed by others until Geoffrey had half a dozen taproots sunk deep into the short-term memory that he expected would hold the location he and Jasmin needed.

The taproots spread out, branching thousands of times as Geoffrey tried to access as much as possible before his strength gave out. It was like bathing in a sewage pond. He'd known that Jeete was an unsavory character, but he hadn't realized just how much liberty the Coun'hij allowed its enforcers. As long as the hybrids who made up the Coun'hij's shock troops showed up when called and killed whomever the Coun'hij needed killed, nothing was denied them.

Nearly unlimited funds was only the start of the perks for someone like Jeete and those perks didn't end short of murder. Geoffrey saw a string of killings that Jeete had been involved in or covered up and was nearly ill at just how docile the humans in that part of the country had become, but try as he might he couldn't get ahold of the location.

He got images, but nothing cohesive, no name, nothing that would allow him to find the town where Jeete had lived for the last forty years. It was inexplicable. Geoffrey had been hoping for success, but he'd been expecting to fail in his efforts to breach the barrier if he was going to fail at all.

He'd never expected to successfully breach the barrier and then be unable to find the location of the Coun'hij base. Something small, something hidden like the location of Jeete's first kill would have been harder to ferret out, but not the address of his home—that should have been easy simply by virtue of the fact that it formed a continuous narrative inside of Jeete's mind.

With something like that, Geoffrey didn't need to form any kind of comprehensive picture of what he was accessing, he just needed to stumble into one of the many places where Jeete thought about home in enough detail to include an actual location or address.

Geoffrey felt his strength bleeding away and knew that he only had a few more seconds in which to find the base's location. There were only two routes open to him. He could either expand back into longer-term memory, or he could push into the section of memory that was claimed by Jeete's beast.

There wasn't time to second-guess his decision or make a tentative, half-hearted effort, so Geoffrey inserted his tendrils into the beast's domain, branching them out to access as many memories as possible in the time he had left. It was like trying to drink acid from a fire hose.

The beast, which had been quiet, almost listless even, up until that point tore into Geoffrey's probes with a fury that he'd never seen before. Three of the probes were sheared away in short order and the loss of each sent Geoffrey reeling away so badly that it was all he could do to process the flow of information coming from the remaining tendrils.

The destruction of Geoffrey's last probe dumped him back into his own mind with enough force that for several seconds his body stopped breathing. Geoffrey fought the terror that threatened to overwhelm his mind, desperately trying to force his lungs to draw air in without any success.

When the first gasp of air finally streamed into his body he had only a scant two or three heartbeats before a new survival imperative roared to the top of his consciousness.

"I need the blood, right now, where is it?"

"Sally just called back down. They only had a small supply and they used it all on Jeff after the fight with the Coun'hij."

Chapter 17

Jasmin Bianchi
Stekensbridge House
Duluth, Minnesota

Geoffrey looked at me with eyes full of the kind of mind-numbing terror that I hadn't been sure he was even capable of feeling. He was shaking and sometime in the last few minutes he'd gone so pale that I could clearly see the blood vessels underneath his skin. I'd never realized that there were so many of them so close to the surface of the body.

"You've got to restrain me. I'm fighting with all I have, but there just isn't time."

Between one heartbeat and the next Geoffrey's sword materialized in his hand. I thought for a second that he'd lost it already, that he was about to attack me, but he just spun in place as though looking for salvation that he knew wasn't there.

"Wait, Geoffrey, I'll send Sally for some more blood. They've got a supplier, multiple suppliers actually."

"Not one that can have the blood here in the next five minutes."

Geoffrey hurried over to Jeete's cage, opened the door, and then his sword licked out multiple times, severing each of the restraints that were holding the enforcer inside of the cage. He pulled Jeete out of the cage and then grabbed the roll of wire that we'd used earlier to restrain both of our rogue hybrids with.

"What are you doing, Geoffrey?"

"Help me by wrapping a loop around his neck while I do his arms. We don't have much time. You can restrain him with the wire until you decide whether or not to kill him, but the wire won't work on me. You're going to have to stick me inside of the cage."

I was desperately searching for another option as I cut a length of wire and then looped it around Jeete's neck. I'd known that Geoffrey's worries about blood starvation were serious, but I hadn't ever even considered the possibility that the Duluth pack might not have spare blood on hand.

Geoffrey tightened the wire he'd tied around Jeete's wrists, and then threw himself into the cage, pulling the door shut behind him.

"This is crazy, Geoffrey. You'll be able to keep things together until we can get more blood."

"I'm afraid not. I'm already hallucinating. I did the wrists by feel, but you'd probably better double-check them. At this point I only have a few more minutes at the most before I lose control. From there I've got less than an hour or two before the blood starvation is fatal. Hopefully Sally's blood supplier is faster than I suspect they are."

"This is stupid. Feed off of Jeete or let me go get Jorge. I'm not letting you die because you don't want to be a parasite like the rest of your kind. Neither of them is worth the air they're breathing right now."

Geoffrey pressed up against my side of the cage, but his eyes were too unfocused for me to be sure he could see me.

"I'm not going to be able to stop you, Jasmin, not when the blood starvation sets in. Once that happens I'll feed on anyone I can get my hands on, but this rule is the only thing stopping me from diving headfirst into the kind of depravity that Imastious tried so hard to push me into. If you do that to me I'll never forgive you and I'll let Ben die."

"I'm supposed to just stand here and let you die? Either way it sounds like Ben's a goner."

"Like I said, we'd better hope that Sally's supplier is nearby."

I watched the transformation come over Geoffrey a second later. I hadn't really believed him, not deep down, but he hadn't been joking.

The guy I'd spent the last few days helping look for Melody wasn't looking out of his eyes now. The *thing* wearing his body had more in common with my beast than it did with me.

Geoffrey threw himself at the cage with enough force that the cage rocked slightly back and forth. I wouldn't have said that he had enough body mass or enough room to make that happen, but he hit the bars a second time and for a second I thought he was really going to manage to tip it over.

I put a hand on the top of the cage to help steady it as I pulled my phone back out. I started dialing Sally again, but I nearly dropped the phone when Geoffrey threw himself at me. The space between the bars wasn't wide enough for him to get his hands through, but he raked the outside of my arm hard enough to draw blood.

"What do you want now?"

"How long before you could have more blood here if you pulled out all of the stops? Can you be back here in an hour and a half?"

Sally was on the road already, I could hear her signaling as she passed someone. "I've got to make it all the way down to Minneapolis, there's no way to make it that quickly. Maybe if I took a helicopter there and back, but even then I'm not sure it's possible."

I could see the light in Geoffrey's eyes changing. I'd thought he was savage before, but that wasn't anything compared to what he was becoming before my eyes. There wasn't time to call anyone else, I knew what I was going to have to do.

"Listen, Sally, please listen very carefully. When I'm done talking I need you to hang up and then call Chad and the rest. Geoffrey has already entered the final stages of blood starvation. They need to lock the doors so that no matter what happens he can't get up to them. I'm really sorry about nearly losing control earlier. I know it's a lot to ask, but if the worst comes to pass I hope that you'll help Geoffrey rescue his friend. It's the only chance that Ben has."

I hung up before she could respond. I didn't want to know what her answer was going to be. If I heard her say no then I wasn't sure that I would able to force myself to go through with what I was about to do.

Geoffrey had continued to savage my arm while I was talking to Sally. It felt like my arm was on fire, but that didn't matter, I hadn't lost enough blood to make any kind of difference and the wounds should heal enough to stop bleeding once I shifted.

I reached up to the top of the cage with my free hand and pushed down the release. The door flew open with enough force to knock me across the room. I shifted in midflight, but I still hit the rock floor at a bad angle and with enough force that I was stunned for a split second. That was all that Geoffrey needed, he was on top of me before I could make it to my feet.

He went for my neck, trying to tear out my throat, but I managed to get an arm up in his way and he latched onto that instead. The pain was intense, even with the muted pain sensors that were part and parcel of this form. Geoffrey wasn't just trying to feed, he was worrying at my arm the way that a dog works over a bone.

It went against every instinct of self-preservation hardwired into my being, but I reached up with my left hand and grabbed the back of his head. He fought me the entire time, but I pressed his head down against my arm, forcing him to feed instead of just tearing the flesh of my arm.

"Let me know when you've had enough, Geoffrey."

He didn't respond, but after a minute or so I could feel myself starting to get dizzy from the blood loss. I was about to try and force him away when I felt the most incredible sense of peace settle over me.

I was basking in the feeling for several seconds before I realized that the tranquility was coming from somewhere *outside* of me. There was only one explanation, it had to be something that Geoffrey was doing. I half-expected for my beast to fight the feeling, but she seemed more than happy to just observe without interfering.

The peace deepened into something incredible, a two-way link with Geoffrey that was more intimate than anything else I'd ever before experienced. I couldn't read his thoughts or access his memories, but I could feel him, feel his nature and character and I knew he was experiencing the same thing.

The connection between us felt simultaneously right and wrong. Right because I could feel his iron-hard determination, and taste his commitment to saving Melody, but wrong because for all of his good qualities I knew that he wasn't the one for me, not in the way that Ben was.

It was the kind of unreserved honesty that I wasn't sure even best friends could share. It was exactly what I wanted with Ben, and it was something that I knew would destroy Geoffrey and me if it continued for long enough.

I came back to myself enough to realize that I needed to get Geoffrey off of me or I was going to bleed to death, but while I was still trying to come up with a way to do that without hurting him, I realized that there wasn't any need. Sometime in the last few seconds Geoffrey had stopped thrashing about and trying to fight me. He was completely relaxed and when I pulled my arm away from him he didn't try to stop me.

"That was a very dangerous thing you just did, Jasmin."

I snorted as I shifted back to human form and applied direct pressure to my arm. "You didn't leave me with any other choices, at least not choices that I could live with. You needed blood and it had to be from a willing donor. I was the only donor around that you couldn't say that I forced to volunteer. Did you find where Puppeteer and the others are?"

Geoffrey nodded. "I think so, but there are complications."

Chapter 18

Jasmin Bianchi
Just outside of Fort Loudon State Park
Tennessee

I'd already been on the phone with Alec for five minutes and the conversation was getting progressively worse the longer it went on.

"We aren't going to get another chance like this, Alec. We know where something like a fifth of the Coun'hij are and we can kill them all in one fell swoop. Mobilize your people and get out here before it's too late."

"Jasmin, you don't *know* where they are, you *think* you know where they are. You said it yourself that this vampire…"

"Geoffrey."

Alec obviously didn't like the fact that I'd interrupted him. Our beasts hadn't had it out with each other since I'd manifested my third form. Intellectually I knew that he could just use his power to drop me to the ground at any point if I was to fight him, but my beast wasn't convinced. Despite the fact that his beast had to be giving him hell because I wasn't acting submissive enough, Alec managed to keep his wits about him.

"Right, you said it yourself that Geoffrey only got bits and pieces of information out of your captive. You think you've found one of the Coun'hij bases, but for all you know he's misreading the information."

"What if he isn't? We aren't going to get another chance like this, Alec. We need to just accept the risk and go for it."

"I'm sorry, Jasmin, but it's just not safe. I'm still not sure how the Coun'hij is managing it, but they know way too much about everyone's movements. You seem to have fallen off of their radar, but most of my other people are under constant attacks. If I pull everyone together to come support you in some kind of massive attack on the Coun'hij then Puppeteer and the rest will know that you're coming."

"That's fine, let them come. Grab Grayson and you and bring half a dozen other hybrids and we'll clean them all out. It's not like we need an army, not when you and Grayson are practically armies all by yourself."

Alec sounded tired. "I know you've got a lot riding on this, Jasmin. I don't know how all of the pieces fit together, but in hindsight it's obvious that the best way to heal whatever those vampires did to Ben is with another vampire."

"Yeah, he's my ticket to healing Ben, but in order for that to happen we need to flush out Puppeteer."

"Right, but if you flush out Puppeteer we could find ourselves going up against dozens of werewolves and you know as well as I do that the only reason we won our last confrontation against that many werewolves was because we had the Coun'hij enforcers in the mix too. I can short-circuit Puppeteer's control over the hybrids, but all that does is make them attack whoever happens to be closest to them. If it's just our people around then we're still pretty much screwed. They'd bury us."

I was tired of talking and I could tell that Alec wasn't going to give me a straight answer, not without me forcing the issue. "What are you saying, Alec? Are you going to help me or not?"

"I want to, but I can't justify running that kind of risk with the rest of my people. We haven't even addressed the fact that this might be a trap."

"How could this possibly be a trap, Alec? Geoffrey ripped the information out of Jeete's mind. There isn't any way they could have anticipated that."

"No, I agree, they didn't set out to make this a trap when they sent Jeete, but the Coun'hij has access to way better information than they should be able to pull together. They may already know that you have him and that Geoffrey has gotten ahold of their location. This could definitely be a trap."

"So we're just supposed to sit here and do nothing with the single best piece of intelligence we've ever had?"

"No, you're not going to just sit there, you and the others need to leave Duluth and come meet up with me. The Chicago pack has been through a meat grinder over the last little while, but I think I can convince Ulrich to shake loose four or five hybrids to escort you back here. Once you get back here, we'll put Geoffrey to work interrogating everyone we can get our hands on who has any kind of link to the Coun'hij. In a couple of months we'll know so much about their operations that we'll be able to launch a decisive blow, one that will end this fight overnight."

"Ben doesn't have a few months, Alec. He's got a few days, a week maybe at the outside."

"Geoffrey can fix Ben, that's why you freed him."

"Yeah, but Geoffrey and I have a deal. He isn't going to help Ben until I've helped him find Puppeteer."

The silence was more eloquent than anything Alec had said so far. I could tell that he wanted to tell me to *force* Geoffrey to help, but Alec wasn't stupid. There wasn't any way to guarantee that Geoffrey would do what we wanted, not when working under compulsion. Not only that, once we started trying to use force on Geoffrey he wouldn't be any use to us when it came to interrogating the people Alec was hoping to capture. Besides, it was wrong.

"Look, Alec, if you're not going to help me then I need to go. I've got a lot of arrangements to make and this isn't putting me any closer to saving Ben."

I hung up on him before he could respond and then looked over at Geoffrey and the others, all of who had been able to hear both sides of the conversation.

"It looks like we're on our own. I'm open to ideas on how we proceed."

Geoffrey gave me a long, serious look. "We've been inside of each other's minds, Jasmin. You know as well as I do that I'm not going to let Ben die. All you had to do was stall another couple of days and I wouldn't have had any choice but to see what I could do to reverse the damage to his mind."

"Yeah, I know, but a deal is a deal. Besides, I can't imagine that the Coun'hij's prisoners have a very long life expectancy after they are captured. Melody may not have a few more days. This is our chance to save her; we may not get another one."

None of the Duluth wolves, my wolves, seemed to have anything to volunteer, so I pointed to the map of the park that we'd purchased earlier in the day.

"I still think that our best bet is to take this trail in. We can buy or rent a couple of Jeeps and it should get us around behind the section of the park where the Coun'hij have set up. The prevailing wind here is from west to east, so once we're on the east side we should be relatively safe from detection."

Geoffrey nodded. "What do we do though once we are there?"

"We'll work our way in close enough for you to start reading some thoughts and see what we come up with. I know, it's a terrible plan, but it's all I've got right now. Once we're there we should be able to find some weakness that we can take advantage of. If needs be, we'll kill them one at a time whenever they step out into the forest."

"I don't have a better plan. You know that I'm onboard. It doesn't matter how long the odds are, I'm still committed to trying to free Melody."

I smiled my thanks at Geoffrey and then turned to the rest of my people. "I could order you all to come help us, but I won't. This isn't your war, and I treated you poorly yesterday, for which I'm sorry. I would welcome your help, but I release you all to do as you please. Stay here or go to some other pack, it makes no difference to me, but before I leave I'll have a ritual promise, a beast-bound oath, that you won't go to our enemies for at least the next three weeks. I mean to have your silence for at least that long or our mission won't have any chance of success."

Silence reigned supreme for several seconds as the uninjured wolves looked around as though trying to read each other's thoughts. It was Sally that finally stepped forward and spoke for the group.

"You're not safe to be around right now, Jasmin. As long as Ben is at risk it's obvious that there isn't anything that you won't do. Torture, murder, anything."

It wasn't something I could argue with. "You're right. We both know it would be futile for me to lie to you and try to pretend otherwise, but even if that were possible I still wouldn't try to deceive you there. Ben has to live or everything I've done so far is for naught."

"I don't appreciate being manhandled, choked and thrown into a wall, but the truth is that it's no worse than Branson or Jorge used to do to me. I'm not eager to trade one worthless alpha for another, but you're the first to have apologized afterward for mistreating me. Right now you're not better than Stekensbridge or the Coun'hij, but you have the potential to be better if we can save Ben for you. I'll come with you. It's a small chance, but it's one I'm willing to risk my life on in the hope of a better life down the road for me and any children I might have."

One by one the other wolves nodded their agreement, and it was all I could do to keep from tearing up. It took me a couple of seconds to get myself back under control, but then I cleared my throat and pointed at Geoffrey.

"You're the money man, so if you could please see to getting us a transport it would be much appreciated. I'd like to start off first thing tomorrow morning, so we'll have to move pretty quickly to make all of the arrangements that need squared away before we can leave."

My phone cut me off. I half expected it to be Alec with one more argument why I shouldn't be doing this, but it wasn't his number, in fact it wasn't any number that I recognized.

"Yeah?"

"Jasmin, it's me, Rachel."

"Calling to tell me that we've got the wrong spot?"

"No, at least I don't think that you do. I know that you aren't planning on leaving until tomorrow morning, but it's important for you to go now, as soon as you can tonight."

"Why, what do you see?"

"That's the problem. I can see you guys going out into the mountains, but once you get there you disappear. Something is interfering with my ability to see you past a certain point tomorrow morning. If you leave now I can see what happens for at least part of the time you're there hunting for Puppeteer."

"So you don't have any idea whether or not we're going to win?"

"None at all. If you leave within the next couple of hours then things go pretty well up until you're shrouded from me, but no matter what happens I can't see you come out of the other side. It's like you and all of the Coun'hij just cease to exist and the world goes on without you."

"So we're going to die then."

"No, I saw this happen once before. There's someone out there who can defeat my ability, he's going to be there with the Coun'hij tomorrow. Once he's gone then the future will snap back into place and you'll all reappear, but until then I'm as blind as you are."

Chapter 19

Geoffrey
Fort Loudon State Park
Tennessee

Jasmin was driving the lead jeep with Geoffrey in the passenger side next to her. He'd tried to convince her to ride in the back and get some rest. She'd lost a lot of blood and he'd figured that it wouldn't hurt and might very well help for her to take it easy for at least the duration of the drive, but she'd refused to let anyone else drive.

Instead, the little caravan was slowly making its way down the bones of a trail that even back when it had been well-used hadn't been meant to be driven by jeeps in the dark. For all that the vehicles were only moving at something barely faster than Geoffrey could have run, it was faster than most people would have believed possible given that they were driving at night with no lights on.

Vampires had incredible night vision, which combined with the shape shifter's ability to see living things outlined in light meant that Jasmin was able to see trees and fallen logs from quite a ways off and Geoffrey was able to pick out rocks and other inanimate objects and warn her away from them.

The group had been driving for more than two hours and had settled into a well-oiled routine which required only minimal amounts of talking and which left Geoffrey plenty of time for thought. Since her people had all agreed to come along on the attack against the Coun'hij, Jasmin hadn't ended up needing to swear any of her people to silence, but Geoffrey had asked her about the ritual promise anyway and been astonished to learn that it was possible for shape shifters to bind their beasts to honor a given promise.

It was a useful thing, but it was obvious to Geoffrey at least that they'd never understood quite how useful it actually was. The binding didn't just force them to comply with their promise, he was sure it also was what had caused Jeete's memories of the base to be moved into the memory space claimed by his beast. Jeete could still access those memories without problems, but anyone else who tried to get at them would have to fight off his beast to get what they were looking for.

The only logical answer for what Geoffrey had seen inside of Jeete's mind was that Puppeteer and the rest of the Coun'hij had sworn their enforcers to secrecy where some of the more sensitive areas of their operations were concerned. It helped explain how the Coun'hij had managed to keep their base secret for so long.

The true extent of their achievement hadn't become apparent to Jasmin until Geoffrey had explained that the Coun'hij didn't have just one base, they had several, possibly as many as five, although that was pure speculation on Jeete's part. Jasmin told Geoffrey that there was also a suspicion held by those on the outside that the Coun'hij was more fractured than it appeared, but nobody had realized that each of the major powers inside of the Coun'hij had their own base and by and large had their own people as well.

For the most part everything Geoffrey had learned, other than the actual location of the base, had been nothing more than colorful background, but the more he thought about it the more apparent it was to him that finding Puppeteer wasn't going to be as easy as they'd hoped. Jeete might have known for sure which Coun'hij member he was serving. In fact it was likely that he did know, but Geoffrey hadn't known enough to be looking for that particular piece of information.

"You know it's possible that this camp we're headed to isn't even one that works for Puppeteer directly."

Jasmin nodded without taking her eyes off of the road. "I know. I figured that out as soon as you told me that there was more than one camp, I just figured that once we got to the camp we could nab somebody who knew where to find Puppeteer and go from there."

"It's still possible that we could do that, but given the sheer depth of the care they've taken around the area of operational security it's not very likely that they have very many people moving back and forth between camps."

"Yeah, I know. Unfortunately we don't have any better options."

They made the rest of the drive in silence but for the occasional word of warning when Geoffrey saw an unexpected rock in their way, and soon enough they were all climbing out of the two vehicles. Jasmin pointed off towards the sound of moving water, but Geoffrey already had his tendrils out and he could feel minds out on the extreme edge of his sensory range.

"I can feel them, you're right, that's the direction we need to go."

"Is there anyone else around?"

Geoffrey shook his head. "I can't feel anyone, but my range isn't usually very big, less than half a mile inside of a city. Out here where there isn't so much in the way of background noise it's probably better, but I don't think it's much better than a mile, maybe a mile and a half."

Jasmin frowned at him. "I can smell them. They are at least a couple miles away from us right now, maybe three miles, it's hard to tell exact distances just from smell."

"I'd say that my range has increased, but vampires don't just undergo sudden surges of power growth like that. Our growth is so slow as to be imperceptible."

"And thank goodness for that. I shudder to think of what the world would be like if every hundred-year-old vampire was able to set me on fire from a mile away."

"I guess you're right there. Most of my kind aren't worth the blood they steal to keep themselves alive."

Jasmin's pack stripped out of their clothes and shifted with only a hint of the tingling rush that Geoffrey had come to associate with shape shifters. One second there was a cluster of pale, naked forms standing only a few feet away from him in the darkness, and a heartbeat later they'd all been replaced with wolves that were more than half again as big as any natural wolf ever grew.

Geoffrey looked over at Jasmin, but she hadn't transformed yet. She finished stuffing her clothes into the jeep, smoothed her ha'bit down over her thighs and then patted him on the shoulder.

"Don't worry, we're going to find her."

"You don't know that any more than I know it."

"I've known Rachel for a long time; she wouldn't send us off on a wild goose chase. There is still a chance for us to save Melody or Rachel would have told me otherwise."

Geoffrey managed a smile and then started towards the minds he could feel off to the west. Jasmin shifted and caught up with him in just two steps. They ranged through the forest, tall trees all around them and leaves and other detritus crunching under their feet. After a few seconds Jasmin let out a faint growl.

"I can smell them a little better in this form, not as well as when I'm a wolf, but they are definitely more than a mile and a half away."

Geoffrey didn't bother with a response other than to speed up his pace to something very nearly a jog. Jasmin snorted and then passed him, her huge hybrid legs eating up as much ground in one bound as he managed in three steps. Eight minutes later as Geoffrey was jumping over a fallen tree, Jasmin slowed down and held up a hand. She whispered to him, barely audible as he stopped next to her.

"We're close. Sally and the others aren't ranging as far afield as they were before and I can make out more in the way of individual scents now."

Geoffrey pointed up ahead. "You probably can't make it out since it's not living, but there is camouflage netting hung from the trees up there."

"You're right. It's hard to make out, but now that you've pointed it out I can see it. From here on out we'll follow you in. Don't burn yourself up trying to work from too far away, but don't get any closer than you have to. The wolves will all collapse back into a half-circle behind us. You're our eyes and ears out here, you've got to let us know when we're about to get into trouble, if someone circles around behind us we're all dead."

Geoffrey patted Jasmin on the arm reassuringly in a conscious mimicry of her gesture from a few minutes earlier and then started towards the closest mind, a bright flare of thought only a hundred yards away.

Their timing seemed to have been perfect. Shape shifters needed so little in the way of sleep that it would have been impossible to ever catch all of them slumbering at the same time, but more than half of them seemed to be abed, either sleeping or headed that direction.

Geoffrey tested the mind before him, weaving some threads of thought into it and tasting the vibrancy of the images and feelings he was then able to access. It had become second nature now to camouflage his probes and once again he was able to sneak past the beast that otherwise would have shredded the gossamer threads that connected him to the hybrid.

They were still too far away, but Geoffrey had expected that. What he hadn't expected was how much easier the contact was to sustain than it should have been. The evidence was starting to pile up in support of Jasmin's assertion that his abilities had strengthened dramatically sometime over the last couple of days. If that was indeed the case then he was going to be able to get a lot more out of the enforcers than he'd expected to be able to.

Geoffrey severed contact with the hybrid and then started moving forward again. His progress was painfully slow, but that was what was required for him to move with the same kind of silence that seemed so natural to Jasmin and the others. It took him another fifteen minutes to move twenty more yards, at which point he decided that he'd gotten as close as he could without risking exposure.

Geoffrey knelt down behind a fallen tree that he figured would serve to conceal him from anyone in either of the two closest houses, and then reached out with his mind again. There were three minds close enough for him to work with. He picked the one who was in the deepest sleep, and started subtly manipulating the fabric of the dream around him.

It wasn't something he'd done before, but he knew he wasn't going to get much information out of the hybrid's dreams otherwise—they were nothing more than a long series of bloody fights, none of which meant anything to Geoffrey.

Geoffrey inserted one of the hybrids from Duluth into the dream. Not Jeete, but the one Jorge had called, the one who seemed to have been in charge of the trio. The emotions that came flooding through the link were revealing.

This hybrid, Brad, and Jeete's companion, Stan, were rivals. Brad tried to push Stan out of his dream, but it wasn't a conscious decision, he didn't realize that the dream Stan was an artificial construct, he just preferred a world in which Stan wasn't around to cause him problems.

"We've been ordered to report to the boss."

The words were easy, Geoffrey's Stan construct spoke them easily because Geoffrey remembered what Stan had sounded like from the phone conversation with Jorge. Mannerisms were more difficult. Geoffrey hadn't ever observed Stan outside of combat. There wasn't anything to do but let his construct stand at ease and hope that Brad didn't notice the absence of Stan's usual mannerisms.

"Why did he call you instead of calling me himself?"

Geoffrey made Stan shrug. "I don't know. He sounded rushed though, like maybe he had a lot to do before he left. I can always head over there by myself and tell him that you want a personal invitation once I get there."

"Go to hell."

Brad stood up from the chair where he'd been sitting and opened his door. Geoffrey, positioned just behind Stan's eyes, followed Brad outside just in time to see Brad drop down to all fours and race off as a wolf.

Geoffrey had never run as a wolf, it was all he could do to keep up and he knew the movements of Stan's body weren't right. Luckily Brad didn't look back at him, and Geoffrey was still able to pay enough attention to their surroundings that he was confident of being able to retrace his steps later.

The 'boss' apparently didn't live in a house, he lived in a cave located more than five miles northeast of the town, but it wasn't just any cave. As Brad led him into the darkness and around a corner, Geoffrey nearly stumbled at the sight of not one, but two massive werewolves standing guard before a heavy metal door that had been set into the rock of the cave.

The urge to pull out of Brad's mind was intense. Geoffrey knew that Puppeteer was nearby and knew the route to his hideout, but it wasn't enough. Jasmin had said that none of Alec's people had any idea what Puppeteer looked like and Geoffrey finally had a chance to see the man who was one of the main lynchpins behind the Coun'hij.

Geoffrey forced himself to stay inside of Brad's dream, following now in human shape so that the two of them could open the doors set at intervals into the system of caves that Puppeteer had made his home. Passing within two or three feet of the massive werewolves posted throughout the cave was terrifying, even inside of a dream.

It took several minutes to make it to a lavishly furnished study where Puppeteer waited for them. Geoffrey reminded himself that individuals tended to dream in a kind of stylized shorthand. The face looking up at him from behind the massive oak desk was probably not a perfect match for Puppeteer's actual face, but it would be close.

Geoffrey studied Puppeteer as he stood and walked towards the two of them. Puppeteer was an old man. He looked like he was in his nineties, which probably meant that he was more than three hundred years old. He was small, so short and slender that it was hard to believe that he was capable of wielding the terrible power that Jasmin had attributed to him.

As Puppeteer opened his mouth to give whatever orders Brad was about to subconsciously put into his mouth, Jasmin started shaking Geoffrey.

"You need to disengage, something's happening."

Chapter 20

Jasmin Bianchi
Fort Loudon State Park
Tennessee

I had to shake Geoffrey three times, whispering into his ear each time, before he finally opened his eyes.

"What's going on?"

"There's a new smell. It's hard to describe, but it's the kind of scent we sometimes find associated with really old werewolves."

"No surprise there, I was able to confirm that Puppeteer is the one in charge of this particular camp. He's probably got at least a few dozen werewolves roaming around here. I know where we can find him though."

My hopes soared. This was the chance that we needed. There was no guarantee that Melody was in the same place as Puppeteer, but if we could break into his house and capture him then Geoffrey could invade his mind and find out where she was.

"Let's go, you lead the way."

"It's no use. He lives inside a series of natural caves and he had werewolves stationed inside, at least six that I saw in the dream. We'll never manage to fight our way in, not without more people, and even then it would be a difficult battle. There isn't enough room inside there to surround them."

I could taste the edge of despair to his words, but we'd come too far to give up now. I knew that even if he'd momentarily forgotten it.

"Come on, we need to at least go check it out. Maybe those are the ones that we smell coming this direction. Maybe he sent them here and his lair is undefended."

I could see that Geoffrey wasn't convinced, but he started moving, which was all the victory that I needed just then. We started back working our way to the northeast, skirting around the edge of the town.

We'd been walking through the forest for no more than five minutes before the faint lights inside of the houses started flickering. A few seconds after that the screaming started.

It took me several seconds before my mind was able to make sense of what I was seeing. Werewolves had materialized as if by magic out of the darkness, but they weren't hunting us like

I'd expected them to, they were attacking the enforcers who were just now stumbling out of their houses and shifting into their hybrid forms.

There were only forty or fifty houses, and some of them had to contain the humans who acted as servants to Puppeteer and the others, but that still left dozens of hostile hybrids that we were going to have to deal with at some point once Puppeteer got his werewolves back under control. We were outnumbered and outgunned and the smart thing would have been to fall back to the vehicles, but I couldn't bear the thought of leaving now.

We weren't likely to get another chance at Puppeteer, and even if we did try to get away, there wasn't a very good chance that we'd actually be able to outrun the werewolves. Geoffrey certainly couldn't stay ahead of them, and even once we made it back to the jeeps the odds would be against us. The trail we'd driven in on was simply too rough to allow for the kind of speed one would need to outrun a werewolf.

It was hard to tell whether Geoffrey followed the same train of thought and understood the sheer hopelessness of our situation, or if he just couldn't bring himself to abandon Melody again, but he continued to lead us around the town, ignoring the fighting taking place in some places less than a dozen yards away from us.

We were trying to balance the need for speed against the imperative of not being seen, but less than five minutes after the attack started the first hybrid stumbled into us. He was disoriented and obviously still in shock; he never even had a chance.

Geoffrey's sword took him against the outside edge of his left leg a split second before two of the wolves latched on to his arms. He was already falling by the time I hit him, and once he was on the ground with a wolf pulling on each arm it took only a single swipe to the throat for me to execute him.

I was thinking how impressed I was at the way that Geoffrey and my pack were working together as I stood back up, but before I could tell them that, a whisper of sound brought me spinning around in an attempt to fend off the attack that none of us saw coming. The werewolf hit me hard enough that I was picked up and thrown into a nearby tree.

An intense pain ripped through my shoulder, but I didn't even realize that the werewolf had its fangs buried into my flesh because I was too busy trying to stop the claws that were only a split second away from disemboweling me. I was big, bigger than any hybrid I'd ever seen or heard about, but this wasn't one of the younger, weaker werewolves; it took all of my strength, two hands against its one, to keep the werewolf's left hand from ripping me open.

I sank both sets of talons into the werewolf's left leg, savaging the appendage, but I knew it wasn't going to be enough. I didn't have the leverage to break free of its jaws which meant that I couldn't get away from its free hand which I knew would be coming to end my life within the next second or two.

I could hear Geoffrey and the others frantically repositioning to try and save me, but there wasn't time, we'd been too focused on the hybrid that we'd just killed; the werewolf had taken us completely by surprise. Something whistled through the air the way you only get when something very thin is forced to move very quickly, and I tensed up for the impact that would be the last thing I would ever feel.

The whistle ended in a meaty thunk and then the werewolf's blow landed but rather than the bitter tips of its claws I was battered by a blunt object. My back was soaked in the werewolf's blood, but I could feel it pulling its stump back for another strike.

Geoffrey had bought me a couple more seconds, but the werewolf's left hand was still inching towards my throat, and there were still ways that it could kill me with what was left of its right arm. The fangs in my shoulder were still grinding away in an attempt to get to something vital, but then all of a sudden Sally and Omar were there. They'd circled around the tree and they threw themselves at the werewolf, jaws fastening around the arm both of my hands were wrapped around.

The extra weight was more than enough to tip the balance and as the werewolf's hand finally started pulling back away from me, I released it with my left hand and raked my claws along the side of its neck. As the werewolf dropped away, dead or dying, I turned around to find that the other wolves from my pack were desperately trying to keep a second werewolf occupied.

Tyler only had a single long set of slashes on his left flank that were leaking blood, and Chad had so far managed to remain unmarked, but we all knew that they were only seconds away from being killed. It took a lot more than just two or three wolves to hold off a werewolf. I stumbled over the corpse of the werewolf we'd just killed, but Geoffrey had already moved, gliding forward into engagement range of the werewolf.

Chad yelped in pain as the werewolf connected with a backhand that was fortunately more fist than claw. Geoffrey raised his sword for an attack, sliding to the left in an attempt to shield Chad, but he was too late. I could clearly see that nothing any of us could do was going to be enough to save Chad.

The werewolf spun around, but rather than following up on the opening it had just created, it stopped and for a fraction of a second that felt like eternity nobody moved. The werewolf was staring at Geoffrey and there was something in its eyes where I'd never before seen anything more complex than hatred or anger.

Sally and Omar resumed moving, trying to flank the werewolf, and that broke the spell, but rather than killing Chad, the werewolf turned and sprang away from us.

None of the wolves could speak in this form, but it was obvious from the way that Tyler was staring after it that he wanted permission to give pursuit. I stepped forward and bumped his shoulder with the back of my hand.

"Let it go, guys. We've got bigger worries than one vacuum that will hopefully take a few more Coun'hij enforcers with it before Puppeteer gets it back under control."

Even as I said the words I realized just how unbelievable it was that Puppeteer still hadn't brought his minions back to heel. Geoffrey apparently had the same realization.

"This can't be just Puppeteer, something else is going on here. Something or someone is interfering with his ability to control the werewolves."

"That's unprecedented, nobody has ever reported anything like that."

Geoffrey nodded. "I know, I can't explain it, but I've never seen a werewolf back away like that. They fled once or twice back in the city when we had them outnumbered, but this was something different. It was almost like that one recognized me."

"How? Like from the fighting in New York?"

"I guess that could be the case, but I killed all but two of the werewolves that I ran into. None of this makes any sense."

"You're right, but there isn't time to figure out what's going on. We need to take advantage of all of the craziness and get to Melody, how much further do we have to go?"

"She's not far now."

We set out again, but the Coun'hij enforcers seemed to be trying to make it to Puppeteer too. The battle was moving towards us now and despite our best efforts we couldn't stay completely out of things.

I saw three hybrids team up against a werewolf as Geoffrey took us out around a thick cluster of trees. The werewolf managed to bring one of them down before the other two swarmed it under, but we'd slipped back out of sight before they could decide whether or not they wanted to pursue us.

The darkness seemed positively alive with the sound of fighting. I caught additional flashes of violence as Geoffrey led us deeper into the forest. Usually we were far enough away that I couldn't even tell for sure who was winning a given fight before we dashed past at a run. Hybrids and werewolves bit and clawed at each other, circling, but I forced myself not to get involved.

I told myself over and over again that neither group was on our side. A part of me wanted to wade into the melee regardless, to kill as many of them as I could, werewolves and hybrids both, because each one we killed now while they were distracted with each other was one less we were going to have to face later, but I knew that Geoffrey was right to be leading us around the worst of the fighting. We couldn't afford to waste our strength here, not when we had no idea what we would be up against once we made it to Puppeteer's lair.

"We're getting close, but there's a group ahead of us fighting and there isn't any way to avoid them, not without stumbling into even bigger fights. We need to take these guys out or they'll follow us into the caves."

My beast flexed her claws inside of my head. She was past ready to kill more of our enemies. It was all I could do to restrain the bestial yell that she demanded from me, but I managed to just nod in agreement. My wolves spread out a little to either side as Geoffrey and I slipped through the underbrush and into a smoke-filled nightmare.

There had been so much else going on that while I had noticed the smoke on the air, I hadn't assigned it any importance. We'd just found the source.

Three of the hybrid enforcers had squared off against a single werewolf and they fought inside an artificial clearing that had been created by the fires that now flickered, barely living, at the clearing's edge. I'd never heard of a hybrid whose ability was strong enough to overwhelm the absorptive field of one werewolf, let alone the dozens that seemed to be fighting within a hundred yards of us, but one of these hybrids was some kind of pyromancer and he was nearly strong enough to use his power despite the werewolf that he and his friends were trying to kill.

The ash-covered ground was hot under my feet as I crossed it, but I ignored the discomfort as I sprinted towards the closest hybrid. The hybrids had backed the werewolf nearly all the way to the edge of the open space, and before I could cross the length of the clearing a tree directly behind the werewolf went up as though someone had poured gasoline on it.

The initial rush of heat was great enough to cause the trees on either side of the burning one to start smoking, but the fire died down almost instantly, leaving the original tree blackened and charred, dead, but not consumed. The heat scorched the back of the werewolf, which let out a roar that was answered by two more howls from nearby werewolves within seconds.

Under normal circumstances it was almost impossible to take a hybrid completely by surprise, and we were running much too fast to have any prayer of remaining silent, but I simply forced myself to go faster and hoped that the hybrids were all too involved in the battle at hand to notice us until it was too late.

The closest hybrid spun around just before I made it into striking range of him, but it didn't do him any good. He slashed at me, but I grabbed his wrist and spun, throwing him bodily into a nearby tree. Geoffrey hadn't been able to keep up with me, but his blade licked out as the hybrid stumbled past him. Geoffrey's sword came away red, but there wasn't any way to know for sure how badly he'd injured the enforcer because my wolves all jumped the hybrid before he could get back to his feet.

A hybrid was often a match for two wolves, but rarely could a normal hybrid take on three and never four, especially not when fighting from the ground after they already had both arms immobilized. I didn't stop to watch them tear the hybrid apart; I turned to go after another enforcer.

The werewolf was bleeding in a dozen different spots and had charred spots where it had gotten too close to one or more of the fires, but it took advantage of the shift in the balance of the fight with the kind of brutal suddenness that was so typical of its kind. One second there were two hybrids trying desperately to keep the werewolf busy, and then in the next the werewolf had one of the hybrids dangling lifelessly from its claws.

I'd expected the last hybrid to attack the werewolf while its back was turned, that or run away to join up with others from the enclave, but instead she turned towards me as I rushed forward. A blistering heat started to build just before I reached her.

"Scatter!"

My yell came only a split second before another intense fire exploded behind me, but I'd done all that I could to warn my people. I raked my claws along the other hybrid's arms and then ducked a blow that would have otherwise taken my head off.

As a wolf I would have probably stepped back then and waited for another opportunity. She'd turned slightly, enough to deny me a shot at her throat, but not enough to open up any of the other targets that I usually preferred. Retreat wasn't an option this time though because if I took the pressure off of her she'd launch another fire attack at one of my people. Besides, there was still the werewolf to worry about. A wounded werewolf was still more than capable of killing me, so I needed to finish off the hybrid now.

All of that went through my mind in a split second, but I'd already started moving, acting out of reflexes and an instinctual sense on the part of my beast of what needed to happen in any given fight. I stepped into the hybrid, slapping her arm out of my way to enlarge the opening that she'd left with her overeager slash, and then I hit her with my shoulder.

I didn't have enough momentum to send her sailing, but I hit her hard enough to knock her to the ground and I was on her before she could recover enough to regain her feet. I sank one set of talons into each of her arms, pinning them to the ground with my full weight, and then buried my right hand in her chest.

I looked over to the side, half expecting to find the werewolf half a second from pouncing on me, but it was looking at Geoffrey and slowly backing away from the vampire. It was impossible, but as the werewolf turned to disappear into the night a second werewolf crashed into the first one.

I was so shocked that I just stood there for a second. I'd never heard of two werewolves fighting each other. As Geoffrey had indicated, there were scattered records of them fleeing a fight that they couldn't win, but other werewolves seemed to be the only living things that they didn't view as their rightful prey.

Geoffrey stepped forward as though meaning to help the first werewolf, but in the dark they looked too similar to pick out one from the other, and even if he was inclined to guess, they were moving around so quickly that he'd probably have no better than an even chance of actually landing a blow on his intended target.

"We need to go, Geoffrey, now while they are distracted with each other."

"I know, it was just that I could almost read the first one's thoughts. There for a second when the fire started its absorptive ability was overwhelmed and I managed to get a couple of probes inside of its mind. It's alien in a way that I can't even begin to describe, but it was different somehow than the others that I've scanned. It was almost like there was a second presence there inside of its mind."

Geoffrey had started walking as he talked, but I checked first to make sure that my wolves were all okay before joining him. My people were all picking themselves back up off of the ground as I checked them over. The hybrid they'd been busy savaging had been what the pyromancer had ignited.

Omar had a pretty nasty-looking burn on his right side, and everyone else was singed around the edges, but they were still capable of moving under their own power. My warning must have come just in the nick of time, that or they'd been able to feel the hybrid starting to heat up.

"A second presence inside of that werewolf's mind would tend to gel with Puppeteer controlling it. That's no surprise."

I caught up with Geoffrey in just a few strides as he angled away from the snarling set of bodies that were busy tearing into each other with an abandon that I wouldn't have thought could be sustained for more than a few seconds.

Geoffrey shrugged. "I know. It's hard to explain, when it comes to werewolves their thought processes are so different that half the time I don't even understand what it was I saw. It comes down more to hunches based off of what I think it all means, but I just don't understand why Puppeteer would have backed away from us like that."

"Maybe he can't tell his own hybrids apart when he's controlling a werewolf?"

"Doubtful. You've indicated in the past that he's had werewolves and hybrids working together in some kind of limited fashion. Besides, he has to know that he doesn't have any vampires working for him, and from what you've said the Coun'hij doesn't make use of ordinary wolves very often."

Before I could respond another hybrid came crashing through the trees and threw itself into the fight. There wasn't any way to know for sure which side the newest arrival was on, but we were already nearly out of sight by the time the third softly-glowing figure started drawing blood from one of the other two.

Geoffrey found the entrance to Puppeteer's lair a couple of minutes later. It was exactly like he'd described it as we'd been ghosting through the darkness except for the fact that there were three dead werewolves outside of the first door.

I tried to pick out the separate scent trails, but it was just too hard. The air was so still and there wasn't any natural mechanism to wash away old scents so all I could really make out was the base smell of stone with other, fainter scents layered on top. There were dozens of 'people' who had crossed this way recently and dozens more who'd been there before them. Even worse, Geoffrey's overpowering vampire scent was washing out everything else even more than usual since we were in such an enclosed space.

The only real common denominator was that the corridor we were in was lousy with the aged, earthy smell that I'd sometimes found associated with some of the older werewolves. Geoffrey started to take the lead spot, but I stopped him with a word.

"You'll be second for this, Geoffrey. I'm more durable than you are. Just walk behind me and tell me which way to go. Oh, and keep your probes out looking for someone trying to ambush us."

We worked our way deeper and deeper into the complex and every step was a nerve-wracking ordeal. There was a very good chance that I'd be able to hear the heartbeat of anyone trying to get me with some kind of surprise attack, but nothing was guaranteed.

The heartbeats of my people stuttered along behind me at double-time and on top of that, sound seemed to be playing weird tricks as it bounced off of the stone walls. We walked down what felt like miles of gray-stone tunnels and found an unbelievable variety of different kinds of rooms at the end of them.

One room was as big as the entire west wing of Graves Manor and was filled almost to the brim with more art than I'd ever seen in one place at the same time. Greek sculptures, Renaissance paintings, blocks of stone that looked like they'd been lifted straight out of the crypt of one of the pharaohs, it was a display of plundered wealth that was somehow obscene in ways that I couldn't even begin to describe.

Alec and Rachel are rich in the way that some small countries are rich, and Graves Manor had been a very large and extremely luxurious home, but most of their wealth had been put to work making more money. This art collection could have purchased a hundred houses the size of Graves Manor and still had money left over.

It was somehow wrong for so many gorgeous things to be locked away where only one person would ever appreciate them, but it was more than that. Alec's money had largely been the result of creating value, but the Coun'hij hadn't ever done anything good. They had robbed and pillaged, scammed and extorted to get their initial chunk of working capital and I had very little doubt but that their business practices had remained essentially the same ever since they'd overthrown the monarchy.

Other rooms came and went without much in the way of rhyme or reason. A massive dormitory, a laboratory that looked like it was secure enough to work with pandemic-level infectious diseases, and a large kitchen capable of feeding a small army. It took twenty minutes for us to find the elegant study that Geoffrey had seen earlier when he'd manipulated the dream of one of Puppeteer's lieutenants.

It was empty, but a quick search revealed a wall safe that I was able to get open, which was odd in and of itself. Puppeteer had obviously known that this type of safe wasn't durable enough to stop a hybrid from getting in, so he hadn't meant for it to protect the contents from his people, but kitchens and dormitories notwithstanding we hadn't seen any signs of humans or others who would have been stopped by the safe.

The contents of the safe were practically a clone of what Geoffrey had left in his safety deposit box. Cash and bearer bonds, which I'd more or less expected, but it also had a small leather-bound book that seemed to be written in some kind of cypher.

Geoffrey emptied the safe, stuffing the contents into a small backpack that was also in the safe, and then we turned to the computers. There were two of them, a laptop that wasn't connected to anything other than the power cord, and a desktop that had an Ethernet cable coming out the back.

"I can't carry them both, not and still be able to fight."

I nodded at Geoffrey. "Grab the laptop. The only reason for him to have it here like that is that he's got something on it that he doesn't trust having hooked up to the internet because if it's connected to a network it's always possible for it to get hacked."

"You're right."

The laptop disappeared into the backpack too, and then we left the office, still hoping against hope that we'd either find Puppeteer or stumble onto Melody's location.

The next room we found was like something out of The X-Files. It had a door that would have put a bank vault to shame, which was plenty odd, but the inside was even odder. There were a series of metal loops set into the wall like the room had been intended for use as some kind of stainless steel dungeon. I checked the inside of the restraints and found them lined with thick rubber bladders that looked like once they were inflated would take the area inside of the restraints down to something roughly the circumference of a human wrist.

"Come on, Jasmin. We don't have time to waste, Puppeteer could be getting further away with each second that passes."

"All right, I'm just curious what Puppeteer might have been using these for."

Over the next ten minutes we passed a variety of laboratories, a massive library and a room full of weights and cardio machines, and then we found it. It was all clean stainless steel, but there wasn't any mistaking a torture room. It still had the feel of a room that had seen terrible things.

A huge, sturdy cage took up a third of the room and the rest of the space was dominated by a table and a variety of metal instruments.

"This is where she was."

I looked over at Geoffrey with a questioning expression. "How do you know? Can you smell her?"

"No, I can just feel it, but I know who can confirm my hunch."

Before I could ask him what he meant, Geoffrey walked over to a large floor-to-ceiling cabinet and unlatched it. The man inside of the cabinet was only about five-six and he couldn't have weighed much more than a hundred and ten pounds. If I'd seen him on the street, dressed differently, I probably wouldn't have given him a second look, but here, in a room that was so obviously constructed with the goal of breaking people, his white clothing proclaimed that he was the torturer.

I didn't have the telepathic advantages that made Geoffrey so dangerous, but even without them I could still practically feel the rage radiating off of him. Geoffrey pulled the little man out of his hiding place and slammed him against the wall.

"Was she here?"

"Who, who do you want to know about?"

The man's voice was a thin, weak thing that cracked at the end of his question. He screamed when Geoffrey spun and threw him down against the table. Moving faster than I'd ever seen him move before, Geoffrey snapped close the oversized metal restraints and then tightened the nylon loops that actually served to hold the tiny man to the table.

"I'm not going to ask you again. Where is she?"

"Which she? Which she does the man want to know about?"

I stepped forward, intending on clarifying Geoffrey's question, but Geoffrey's eyes were already closed and the torturer had started shaking. I'd seen Geoffrey rummage through Jeete's memories, but that had been nothing like this. Jeete had hardly seemed aware of the fact that Geoffrey had been inside of his mind, but the little man's eyes had rolled back into his head and based on the blood leaking out of the side of his mouth, he'd bitten his tongue.

"Geoffrey, you're pushing too hard!"

My yell got through, at least enough for him to open his eyes, but it was like looking at a different person. Geoffrey's nose had started to bleed and his eyes had skipped right past bloodshot and gone straight to dark red.

"Don't interfere or I'll let Ben die and I'll dance on his grave. This worm hurt her, she was here."

My beast wanted to rip Geoffrey's head off of his shoulders, but I forced her back into her corner. I couldn't afford to cross Geoffrey, not when he was the only one who could save Ben. My claws slid out to full extension and I tore furrows into the steel tabletop, but I forced myself not to take that final step that would have put me within striking range of Geoffrey.

Two more minutes passed before Geoffrey opened his eyes again and stepped away from the table. "He tortured her. His mind was too brittle, it shattered under the force of my attempts to access his memories, so I didn't get everything, but I know exactly what Puppeteer looks like and I know that Melody was here."

"Where is she now?"

Geoffrey wiped away the trickle of blood that was still leaking from his nose. "I don't know. That's one of the pieces that dissolved before I could access it, but he remembers seeing her walk away from him. She escaped somehow."

"The door."

His words were so faint that a normal person wouldn't have been able to make them out, but I leaned in closer to the little torturer to be certain that I'd be able to make out what he was saying around the coughs and gasps for air.

"The door…the key. All shiny and thick like a bank."

I reached for the closest ankle restraint and flipped the metal cuff open so that I could get at the nylon strap, but Geoffrey stopped me with a glare. I'd never seen him quite this furious before. I held up a calming hand, but I didn't step any closer.

"We need to let him go or he's going to choke on his own blood."

"Let him choke. You didn't see what he's guilty of. Death is too kind for someone like him.

He's told us everything he's capable of telling us. Let's go find that door, it's close to here, I saw the way there in his memories. Did you get Melody's scent?"

I wasn't the one who needed to fill my nose with her scent, but now wasn't the time to be telling Geoffrey that. I sucked in a lungful of air and nodded to Sally and Tyler. The scent of iodine was so strong that it even washed out Geoffrey's old-blood smell, but I thought I could make out someone else beneath all of that.

Tyler didn't look very sure of himself, but Sally gave me an unmistakable nod, so I turned back to Geoffrey and waved him out the door. "Sally has it. I think I can smell it, but it's pretty faint, so we'll follow Sally."

"Fine, she can go first then. Once we're back out in the corridor, we turn left to find the door he was talking about."

I nodded in agreement, but once we were back in the hall Sally turned a couple of circles and then whined softly as she looked back the way we came.

"Sally says that Melody went the other way."

Geoffrey shrugged as he pushed past us and started down the unexplored section of the corridor. "This door is important somehow. I can't explain it, not completely, but we need to get there and soon."

Geoffrey led us at something very close to a run, which meant that it took us less than five minutes to make it to the large circular door.

"It's just like that other vault we found."

Geoffrey nodded. "I know, which means that it's designed to hold werewolves. The metal straps are designed to hold them when they are in werewolf form, while the rubber compression ring holds them in place when they are in human shape."

I was astonished that I hadn't seen it myself. "The table in the room where they were keeping Melody had the same kind of mechanism. It used nylon straps instead of those heavy rubber bladders, but the principle is the same. Why would they…"

Geoffrey cut me off. "They probably have that kind of setup in every spot where they might need to restrain someone. It's not like cost is a consideration for Puppeteer, so it only makes sense to make sure all of his facilities could restrain humans or werewolves."

Before I could respond, Geoffrey reached up and unlocked the heavy door. It was the last thing I expected him to do, but in hindsight I could see why he might have thought that the werewolves would still be restrained inside of the manacles fasted to the walls. He was wrong though. No sooner did the bars inside the door slide back than the massive plate of metal was hit by the combined mass of three or four werewolves.

The door flew open with a speed that I wouldn't have believed possible, hitting Geoffrey on the side of the head with enough force that he collapsed like a rag doll. The werewolves that had thrown the door open were all on the ground, stunned from the force of their impact with the door, but others were lined up behind them and the first row jumped over the top of them in order to get at Geoffrey and me.

I yelled for Sally and the others to run, but instead of joining them, I stepped forward and grabbed Geoffrey's ankle. Without Geoffrey there wasn't any point in going back to Ben.

I meant to throw Geoffrey over my shoulder, but the first werewolf was too close for that. It was all I could do to tug Geoffrey out of the way of the massive foot that otherwise would have crushed his chest. Then the fight was on.

I knew I couldn't win, but neither my beast nor I was ready to just give up and let them kill us. I managed to knock the first slash wide and then ducked another one from the werewolf that was next to my main attacker, but the first werewolf was already bringing his hand back around in a backfist and I had almost zero chance of ducking under this blow.

I dropped down anyway, hoping that I'd be able to get my right hand far enough up to divert the claws headed straight for my head, but then, moving with a speed that left my head spinning, the front three werewolves turned around and started pushing against the flow of werewolves still trying to get out of the vault. It was impossible, but I didn't stay around to wait and see how long it would all last.

I slung Geoffrey over my shoulder and then started back down the hall at a full sprint.

Chapter 21

Jasmin Bianchi
Sixty miles outside of Fort Loudon State Park
Tennessee

I was dreaming. I knew that much, but I couldn't seem to recall anything else. There was something about a big fight on the very edge of my consciousness, and I had vague memories of running back to a Jeep, but no matter how hard I tried the details just floated away into deep space.

I'd been worried about someone, someone important, someone who had something to do with Ben, but those details were likewise inaccessible, so instead I took stock of my surroundings. I was underground, in some kind of cave apparently, which felt right on some levels, but wrong on others. The sheer amount of ice was astonishing. I'd heard of ice caves before, but I hadn't ever realized that there could be so much ice associated with them. The cavern I was in was almost as big as a football stadium, and when I looked down at the floor the ice was clear enough for me to see that it was at least three or four feet thick, except that I shouldn't be able to see anything because it should be dark.

My breath fogged the air in front of me as I bent down and tried to chip away at the ice with my claws. That gave me pause for a second, I couldn't remember shifting forms, and I'd been a human just a second or two before.

The ice proved impossibly hard, my claws skittered off of it without even leaving a mark, but before I could examine it further I felt the air move behind me and I spun around just in time to avoid losing my head.

The thing I was fighting was like a werewolf, but bigger, faster and stronger. I ducked away from another slash and suddenly realized that my opponent seemed to be eating the light around us like he was some kind of living shadow.

I tried to dance away to one side, tried to work my way around so that I could use his own bulk against him, but it was like I was moving through molasses. I was smaller than him, I should be more nimble, but instead I screamed as he sank the claws on his right hand into my chest.

"I've got an appointment with one of your friends, little wolf, but maybe if you prove to be enough of an entertainment I'll give your friend the night off and just stay here with you instead."

I got my right leg up between us and jammed it against his chest, blooding him for the first time, but more importantly throwing myself backwards and ripping his claws back out of my chest. Even that seemed to happen in slow motion, and as I hit the ground I looked up to find that my enemy was already waiting for me. He'd crossed the distance between us so quickly that I hadn't even seen him move.

He slashed down across my leg and I screamed in pain as hot blood splashed out of that wound to join the growing pool beneath me from my chest wound. I rolled back to my feet, ignoring the muted pain signals from my leg, but it was obvious that he was toying with me. I couldn't do anything without him allowing it to happen.

I'd never been so outmatched before in my life. Even when fighting Alec or Isaac, even when fighting the enforcers that Agony had brought to Sanctuary months ago. I'd never been at such a disadvantage because he was violating the laws of physics, laws that I'd spent my life learning to exploit right up to the ragged edge of what was possible.

It was a dream, I told myself that again, and again, but it was hard to believe. My injuries hurt, and I couldn't ever remember a dream like this, a dream where I'd experienced pain that hurt even more than it did when I was awake.

It took everything I had to strengthen that belief as I slowly backed away from the monster in front of me, but I forced my belief into something almost tangible, and as it grew into a certain knowledge I could feel the threads of liquid shadow that were restraining me.

I reached out and sheared through the dark cocoon surrounding me. It wasn't easy, but my beast woke at the last second and threw her efforts behind mine. I tore my way out and stepped forward into the attack that the monster had just started launching at me.

He was still fast, but no faster than a normal hybrid and he hadn't been expecting me to move at anything even approaching a normal speed. A thought strengthened my claws, making them even sharper than they were normally, and I tore through ribs and muscle like they weren't even there.

As the monster went to his knees I took his throat in my claws and shook him. "Who are you?"

"Don't you know?" The words came out choked and scratchy, but before I could respond he vanished and reappeared behind me. The pain as he cut through my spine exceeded anything I'd ever felt as a human, exceeded anything I'd ever thought was possible to withstand, but somehow I was still conscious as I dropped to the ground.

The monster kicked me, rolling me over, and then cocked his head at me. "I'm the Dream

Stealer, but then you already knew that. Congratulations, your recent exploit was finally sufficient to make me exert the effort required to find your dreams. You're lucky that I have bigger fish to fry, but I can promise that I'll be back later. You're obviously going to be a lot of fun. Don't worry, it only gets worse from here."

Chapter 22

Geoffrey
Stekensbridge House
Duluth, Minnesota

When Geoffrey finally opened his eyes he wished he hadn't. The light hurt, not the kind of excruciating pain that was a symptom of a concussion, but it still hurt. It was almost like his eyes had gotten even worse at adjusting to daylight than they'd been before.

Geoffrey managed a croak which alerted someone to the fact that he was awake, and they correctly interpreted the way that he was squinting to mean that the room was too bright. A second later the blinds had been drawn and the room was dark enough that he could open up his eyes without them tearing up.

"Where am I, and how long have I been out?"

"You're back in Duluth. You've been out for nearly two days and I had just about lost hope that you were going to wake up on your own. I even drew some more of my blood and fed it to you via a tube, but that didn't seem to make any difference in your condition. We're leaving again in an hour or two, we had to come back for Ben and Jeff, but it's not safe for us here any longer."

Geoffrey's eyes had finally adjusted enough for him to make out Jasmin standing on the right side of his bed.

"You shouldn't have done that. I appreciate it, but you look terrible, like you gave too much blood and nearly killed yourself."

"No, that wasn't it. Would you believe I had a bad dream?"

Geoffrey started to shake his head and then winced in anticipated pain, but moving his head didn't actually hurt.

"That must have been some bad dream."

"Yeah, you could say that. What do you remember from our trip to Tennessee?"

The question brought everything roaring back, and Geoffrey started to sit up in the bed. Jasmin made as if to stop him and then reconsidered and helped him by putting a pillow behind him.

"What happened? Did you guys find Melody?"

"No. I'm sorry. For a few minutes there I didn't think that we were going to ever have this conversation. There was something like two dozen werewolves inside of that vault. They should have torn through me like tissue paper, but at the last second they stopped and the ones in the front started trying to force the rest of them back into the vault."

"Why would Puppeteer want to save you?"

"I don't know, but it makes about as much sense as everything else that happened that night. I grabbed you and hightailed it out of there, but I could hear them behind us nearly until we made it back out of Puppeteer's complex."

"You never found him then?"

"No, but we didn't finish exploring everything so it's possible that he was still in there somewhere just hiding away until we left. I figured that following Melody's trail was more important than trying to assassinate Puppeteer."

Geoffrey nodded. "Agreed, especially since even if you had found him you probably would have been facing three or four werewolves. You couldn't have won that fight."

"Right. So anyway, Sally followed Melody's scent trail and that led us through an entirely new section of tunnels and rooms. It...well, there were humans down there, but they'd all been butchered by werewolves. They must have come in behind Melody and killed everyone. Sally said that Melody's scent trail wasn't noticeably older than the one the werewolves left, so she must have only been a minute or two ahead of them."

"It sounds like she was lucky that there were all of those people there to distract and slow down the werewolves."

Jasmin shrugged. "I guess. Do you think that she knew they were there? Do you think she's coldblooded enough to lead a pack of werewolves down there knowing that she was buying her own freedom at the cost of all of those deaths?"

Geoffrey wanted to bristle at the question, but it was obvious that Jasmin wasn't trying to provoke him.

"I don't know. A few months ago I would have said no, but being held captive changes a person, and if they really tortured her then that would have just compounded the pressure on her."

"Yeah, I expect that you're right. If that's the case is she still someone that you want to find?"

Geoffrey didn't even have to think about that one. "Of course she is. The only reason that she ended up inside of that complex was because of me. I was the one who led Puppeteer to her and I owe it to her to do whatever I can for her."

"We lost her trail a hundred yards into the forest. I'm sorry, Geoffrey. We spent a couple of minutes fanning out in an attempt to reacquire it, but it wasn't any use. We would have stayed longer, but the fighting hadn't stopped outside and I kept expecting for a dozen werewolves to come boiling out of the caves at any time."

The wave of disappointment that crashed through Geoffrey was almost completely debilitating, but he forced himself to respond.

"I understand, you did everything you could. Any sign of whatever had Rachel so freaked out?"

"I'm not sure. We didn't actually see anything concrete, but right before we headed back to the Jeep there were these weird flashes—only they weren't light, it was like pulses of darkness."

Geoffrey shook his head. "That doesn't make sense. Darkness is just the absence of light. How can an absence pulse?"

"I can't explain it, but there was something out there and it was the darkness that was pulsing, not the light. I thought maybe that one of Puppeteer's hybrids was still alive and fighting the werewolves, but even that doesn't make a lot of sense because we didn't see those flashes until after we came out of the caves."

Geoffrey closed his eyes and tried to process the fact that his search was over, that he'd failed, but Jasmin put a hand on his shoulder.

"Maybe we can try to go back there and pick the trail up in a couple of days."

Geoffrey's laugh was a bitter-sounding thing. "That will never work and you know it. There is almost no chance that a rain storm won't sweep through that area before then. Even if it didn't, you lost her when the trail was still fresh, we missed our chance. She's gone. I need to just accept that—at least I can be happy knowing that she managed to escape somehow on her own."

Jasmin had an unusually obstinate set to her mouth. "Maybe Rachel can help us some more. She knew that Melody was with Puppeteer before, there's nothing to say that she can't tell us how to find her again."

"Maybe, but the odds aren't good. Rachel seems to be less omniscient as time goes on rather than more omniscient."

Jasmin's mouth went tight at his observation, but she apparently couldn't disagree with what he'd said. Geoffrey put one hand up against the right side of his head. He could feel the beginnings of a migraine. It wasn't because he'd overexerted himself, this was something different. It was almost like his mind was working overtime trying to keep him from realizing something.

"You said that we're almost ready to leave Duluth. What are you doing with Jeete and Jorge?"

"I executed Jeete an hour ago. Based on what you told me you'd seen inside of his mind I figured he'd earned the death penalty several times over."

Geoffrey nodded. "What about Jorge?"

"I let him go. I made him swear a ritual promise that he wouldn't go to any other packs for at least three weeks. He's also prohibited from telling anyone anything about what's happened here during the last week or ever joining up with the Coun'hij. I didn't want to let him go, but I didn't have any proof that he needed to be put down."

Geoffrey reached over and clasped Jasmin's arm. Wordlessly conveying support and understanding of how hard it had been for her to make that call.

"That was the right decision. We'll still probably end up fighting him at some point, but it was still the right thing to do."

"I guess. I keep thinking how I'm going to feel if he ends up killing one of my friends, but I just couldn't bring myself to cut his throat. I guess I should be glad that I still have some limits. I was starting to think that maybe there wasn't anything that I wouldn't do."

Geoffrey started to turn away from Jasmin, but something stopped him. "What's going on, Jasmin? You're acting weird."

"It's Ben. He's gotten a lot worse over the last couple of days. I keep thinking that he's as weak as he can get and he keeps lasting a little longer, but I think this is the end. He's stopped breathing on his own. We bagged him and have been forcing air into his lungs for the last six hours. Sally is with him right now, but we can't keep doing that. I've been hoping that you'd regain consciousness before we had to leave Duluth, but now that you're awake it doesn't seem fair to ask you to help, not when we didn't find Melody for you."

"Take me to him. The deal was that I would do whatever was required to keep him alive. You've proved that you'll honor your promises. You and your people nearly died a number of times already. I couldn't ask for more than that."

Geoffrey was less steady on his feet than he would have liked, but Jasmin pulled one of his arms over her shoulder and they made it across the house without any mishaps. After having helped take care of Ben for so many days, it was hard for Geoffrey to see Ben lying there completely unresponsive like that. He could only imagine what Jasmin must be going through.

"He's still got a pulse?"

Sally nodded. "I've been checking it every few minutes. It's still there, but it's getting weaker too."

He hadn't wanted to say anything to Jasmin, but Geoffrey had been more than a little worried that the blow he'd taken to the head was going to get in the way of his mentalist abilities. Those fears fell by the wayside though as he sent out his first few probes and they slipped free of his body with an effortlessness that seemed to indicate that his mind was well-rested and ready to do whatever was asked of it.

"I'm starting now."

The words drifted out of his mouth out of little more than reflex and then Geoffrey shut down all of his other senses and focused solely on the golden threads connecting him to Ben.

The surface thoughts were much as Geoffrey remembered, but they'd become even fewer and weaker than they'd been before.

It was something he'd never seen anywhere else before, but it very much seemed as though Ben's higher brain functions had been almost completely suspended. Past experience had taught Geoffrey that there wasn't any reason to hang around in the outer layers of someone's mind for the kind of work he was about to try.

The surface could accept workings and even hold them for a short period of time, but what he needed to do with Ben was to create a powerful, long-lasting construct to counteract whatever the other vampire had done to the young man. Geoffrey gathered himself and then dove deeper into Ben's mind.

In some ways it was analogous to diving into water. The deeper Geoffrey went into Ben's mind the more he wanted to turn around and fight for the surface again, but as his strength started to trickle out of him, he knew that he wouldn't get a second chance at this. Ben didn't have the luxury of waiting for Geoffrey to rest up and try again in a day or two.

Time flowed differently when Geoffrey was this enmeshed inside of someone's mind. It seemed to take forever before he bumped up against the barrier that protected Ben's innermost psyche from intrusion, but only a second or two had actually passed. Geoffrey matched his probes up to the frequency of the barrier and slipped inside.

The first time that Geoffrey had entered the seat of someone's consciousness it had taken the form of a pool of water, but this time he was faced with hundreds of strands of living light. If not for the fact that he'd seen Ben gradually declining, Geoffrey might have been tempted to think that there was nothing wrong with the picture before him. The lights were so brilliant, so breathtakingly beautiful that it seemed impossible that they could be anything other than perfect, but Geoffrey kept sampling them and eventually he started to detect a pattern, dull threads that wound their way around the strands, robbing them of some of their brilliance.

It was almost more than Geoffrey could grasp. He could follow individual threads and even understand how some of the threads interacted with each other, but the complexity he was facing was almost more than he could hold inside of his mind.

Geoffrey built a theoretical framework inside of his mind, placing each thread in its place until he was finally able to see all of them together, but even then, he got the sense that there was something there he didn't understand. Making changes to a construct he didn't understand was risky, but he didn't have any other choice.

Simply destroying the constructs, dozens or even hundreds that there were, was the safest bet, so Geoffrey reached out and snipped the first of the threads, only it grew back almost as soon as it had been cut.

Geoffrey cut another, but the result was no different and he suddenly understood what he'd failed to see before. This wasn't a host of workings all layered together to create a single result, he was dealing with a single, multi-legged working with a complexity that exceeded anything he'd realized was possible. Even worse, it wasn't just designed to serve as a static working that only influenced Ben, it was actively drawing energy from Ben's thoughts to power itself and repair any damage done to it.

That was something else that Geoffrey hadn't known was possible, but the parasitic nature of what he was seeing turned his stomach. Most constructs had to be periodically refreshed or they lost cohesion. If they were set inside of the utter calm of the seat of someone's consciousness they could still last for years, possibly even decades, but there wasn't any possibility of outlasting this particular working.

Geoffrey realized he was going to have to uproot the entire working at once if he was going to have any chance of defeating it. He tried to work fast, severing the attachment points of one strand and then holding it away from the strands of light while he worked on stripping another thread away, but after only a few minutes he'd reached the end of his strength.

He still had energy that could be dedicated to the battle, but he wasn't strong enough to continue to hold the writhing threads away from the glowing tendrils, and he'd only managed to strip away roughly half of the threads.

There wasn't any way around it, Geoffrey had failed. The dull grey threads snapped back into place, ripping holes in Geoffrey's mental fingers as they did so, and the glowing pillars of Ben's mind darkened perceptibly as the working drew power into itself to heal the damage that Geoffrey had just done to it.

Geoffrey could continue to try and fight the construct, but it was obvious that doing so would just kill Ben even faster. Geoffrey backed up to the very edge of the pocket of calm in an attempt to take in the whole of the working and saw something even more amazing.

The guttering lights of Ben's mind strengthened, inexplicably growing brighter until the strands of light were almost as bright as they'd been before Geoffrey's latest attempt to rip away the construct. It took several more minutes before Geoffrey was able to figure out what had just happened, and even then it was mostly sheer dumb luck that allowed him to find the tiny golden thread that led from the base of Ben's mind out of the bubble of calm.

Geoffrey didn't follow it any further than that, he couldn't leave the bubble of calm or he'd be too tired to return for at least a day or two, but he was confident that the golden thread must lead to something or someone exterior to Ben. Geoffrey plunged one of his mental fingers into the golden flow and it was like bathing in a pool of warm water that rejuvenated and healed in a way that no water had ever been capable of doing.

For one glorious second Geoffrey felt his mental reservoirs being topped off with energy and then the thread seemed to recognize him as not belonging and pushed him away. The next time that Geoffrey tried to dip into that miraculous stream it twisted away from him. It appeared that he wasn't going to get another taste of the nectar that had kept Ben alive for so much longer than should have been possible.

Geoffrey had been surprised that the kill switch had taken so long to run its course, and one as powerful as what he'd actually found inside of Ben's mind should have finished Ben off in a matter of minutes, but instead of dying Ben had found a way to tap into a power source outside of himself and that had made all of the difference.

There was no way for Geoffrey to ever hope to replicate what Ben had done. He had no idea where Ben had gone in order to tap into such incredible power, but there was one thing that he could do still.

Geoffrey worked as quickly as he was able. The extra energy he'd siphoned off a few minutes ago was the only thing that even made what he wanted to do possible, but even so he was working at the very edge of his capabilities.

It was incredibly hard to force a better connection between Ben and the power source that was keeping him alive, but in the end Geoffrey managed it by creating workings on the far side of the link that forced the glowing tendrils of Ben's being down so that they rested more broadly against the glowing thread.

Once that was done, Geoffrey created another series of workings that boiled down to single-word commands designed to begin counteracting the construct that Ben's old vampire master had implanted inside of him.

Live. Thrive. Survive.

The workings were simple because Geoffrey knew that simple workings lasted longer, but they were strong, the strongest he could manage. They laced back and forth around the glowing pillars of Ben's psyche, forming a lattice of support that helped counteract the imperative that was draining his will to live.

There was just one last thing to do. It was risky and it would take every bit of energy remaining in Geoffrey's reserves, but it was what he would have wanted done if their positions had been reversed. Geoffrey reached out and fed his energy directly into Ben.

Chapter 23

Jasmin Bianchi
Stekensbridge House
Duluth, Minnesota

Geoffrey opened his eyes and I knew immediately that he hadn't been able to save Ben. He didn't look like someone who was about to deliver good news, he looked like someone who had given his all, just like he'd promised he would, but who'd failed.

"I'm sorry, Jasmin, the construct backing up the kill command is just too powerful. Maybe if there were two of me we could rip it out, but I'm just not strong enough."

"So we'll find another vampire. Rachel found you, you must know someone else you could trust, another mentalist who is strong enough to do what needs to be done."

Geoffrey shook his head at me. "I've never met another vampire, at least not another mentalist, who you would want to trust inside of Ben's mind."

I tried to stop the tears, tried to keep control of myself, but it was no use. They trickled down my face despite everything I could do.

"So there's nothing left to do but just sit here and watch him die?"

Geoffrey pulled himself to his feet and walked over to me, moving like an old man, like someone who had given more than they should have to the fight. He patted me on the arm.

"I did what I could; I bought him some more time. Sally, you can stop pumping now, he'll breathe just fine on his own for now. I know it's not much, Jasmin, but I thought that you'd want a chance to say your goodbyes."

I wanted to ask him what he meant, but it didn't matter. Even reaching up to wipe away the tears on my face was too much effort. I watched as Geoffrey ushered Sally out of the room and pulled the door closed behind him.

I'd been chasing Ben for years now; it just didn't seem fair for things to end this way. I'd done terrible things in my effort to save him, and now I was going to be left with nothing to show for it, no Ben, no hope for the future, just my sins and a knowledge of how much further I was capable of sinking than I'd ever realized before.

I reached out and took Ben's hand, but rather than remaining limp he squeezed my hand in return. I looked up to see that his eyes were open.

"Where am I?"

For a second I thought I was hallucinating, but then I realized that it didn't matter if I was. If this was some kind of grief-induced dementia then I never wanted to get better.

"You're in Minnesota. Isaac and I rescued you, but you went into convulsions when I carried you out of the shop so I knocked you unconscious and you've been in a coma ever since."

"How long?"

"I'm not sure, I lost count. Weeks, I guess, maybe a couple of months. I've been trying to bring you out of your coma since before we left Sanctuary. Alec paid for some of the best doctors to come look at you, but they couldn't find anything wrong, your body was just slowly shutting down."

"It still is, Jasmin. I can feel it like a shadowy spider sitting deep down inside of me, telling me to just give up and die."

"But you're here. Geoffrey said that he couldn't save you, but you're here, he succeeded."

"No, I could feel him trying to help me. He gave me a transfusion of strength, but it's already leaking away, I don't have much more time."

The tears that had been escaping my eyes one or two at a time were now a steady trickle, but I didn't care. It didn't matter that I usually prided myself on not crying, the only thing that mattered was that Ben was going to leave me again, just like he always did.

"You've got to fight it!"

"I am, and I'll go on continuing to fight it, but it's using my own strength against me. I'm sorry, Jasmin, this is all my fault."

"Don't say that, please don't try and take the blame for this. It's my fault. I'm the one that addicted you to my touch, if that hadn't happened then you would have been fine."

Ben shook his head, a weak motion, but a definite denial. "No, Jasmin, you saved me, just like you always have. It seems like as far back as I can remember you've been saving me. From my dad, from the drugs, from my own clumsiness, you're the one who's always pulled me back from the edge."

"No, Ben, you did that, I helped, but if you hadn't wanted it then nothing I did would have saved you."

"I know, but I wasn't strong enough to do it myself, I never have been. It's always been you who's given me the strength to do what had to be done. I think that's why I kept running. I never knew why you were willing to go to so much effort to save me when I knew I wasn't worth saving."

"But you are, can't you see that?"

"I know you think so right now, but I always figured that if I let you get closer to me, if I ever really let you in, that you'd realize that you were wrong all along. This is my fault. I knew that I was taking a risk when I let Jacque into my mind, but I didn't care. All I cared about was the fact that he made it so that I didn't crave your touch every single hour of every single day."

I started to let go of his hand, but he grabbed ahold of me with a kind of desperately weak strength that couldn't be denied.

"It doesn't bother me now. I love it, I love that I can touch you without hating myself for being so weak."

"I'm going to save you, Ben. Geoffrey said that he bought us some time, you just said as much yourself. Rachel knows things, she'll help, we'll find someone who can reverse what was done to you. I'll do *whatever* it takes to bring you back."

"No!" The denial was explosive, it seemed to take an alarming amount of Ben's strength, but he grabbed hold of me even tighter. "You have to promise me. The ends don't justify the means, I know that better than anyone else. You can try to save me, but don't do anything that you'll regret later. No torturing, no murder. I don't want any of that on my head."

"It won't be on your head, it will be on mine."

"You say that, but it doesn't change how I feel. Please, Jasmin, promise me. I don't want to survive if the cost is your soul. Survival isn't worth that to me."

"It is to me, not for just anyone's survival, but for yours it is."

"How would you feel if the shoe was on the other foot and I had to do those kinds of things to save you?"

I felt like he was ripping my heart out of my chest, but he was right. Nodding in agreement to his demand was the hardest thing I'd ever had to do, but I forced my chin, up and then down in jerky fits and starts.

It wasn't pretty, but it was enough for Ben. He gave me a tired smile and seemed to relax back into the bed.

"Thank you, Jasmin. I've never told you this, but I love you. I've loved you for years now. I wish things had happened differently and that we hadn't been forced to go through all of this, but I'm glad that I at least got one last chance to finally tell you how I feel."

"I love you too, Ben. I always have."

The words came out in a rush, but I was too slow. He'd already closed his eyes and there was no answering squeeze from his hand.

I wanted to stay there at his bedside and cry myself out, but there wasn't time for that. Geoffrey had bought me a few more days and I was going to find a way to save Ben. I wasn't going to let him slip through my fingers, not this time.

Author's Note

Getting to this point in the Reflections (and Dark Reflections) Series has been a real learning experience for me. When it comes to my stories, I think my writing has improved, but that isn't the only learning that has happened for me.

As I write this, I'm exactly 31 days past the release date for Bound. Hunted is basically finished save for the cover, Driven is headed out to my advance readers, Dark Reflections #3 is off for the first round of editing, and Isaac's book is in rough draft form. I've written a lot of words—more than 690,000—since I finished up Riven, but none of those words have been Alec and Adri Reflections words, and that has ended up mattering more than I expected it to.

To be honest, I gave lip service to the idea that some of my Reflections readers might not want to read the Dark Reflections books. I considered the possibility that with Driven, I'd be releasing another Trapped, another book in the main Reflections Series that was awesome, but which didn't get the same kind of uptake that I saw with Forsaken and Riven.

Intellectually I knew that all might happen, but I didn't believe it, not really. I still have faith that most of my fans will eventually pick up Bound and Hunted, and I'm confident that those two books will earn me readers who otherwise never would have even considered reading Broken or Torn. I know that eventually most of the people who loved Riven will buy Driven, but this note isn't about—or for—those people, this note is for the people who went out and took a chance on Bound before all of the 5-star reviews started rolling in.

This note is for all of the people who love the Sanctuary pack enough that they bought Driven on the first or second day that it was available. This is for my very best fans, the ones that I've taken to calling—inside the privacy of my own mind—my rabid fans.

Inside of Dean's world that's some of the highest praise I can offer, and I'm profoundly grateful to all of you. I know that there is a degree of trust every time you buy one of my books, and it requires even more trust for you to buy something when I do something unexpected like starting the Dark Reflections books. I will continue to do everything I can to make sure that each book is a compelling read, and I promise that I'll never write 'filler'.

These books, crazy though they might be, are the thing that's going to make Alec and Adri's story epic. I hope you enjoy the journey as much as I've been enjoying it.

Acknowledgements

The list of people who help out in this undertaking doesn't change much from book to book, but that doesn't mean that their effort is any less valuable as the months roll by.

RJ Locksley and Amy Jirsa-Smith continue to do outstanding work when it comes to the editing side of things, and their help is much appreciated.

My advance readers do great work when it comes to providing me story-focused feedback and finding the errors I introduce in the course of fixing some of Amy and RJ's finds. Mom, Dad, Shalese, Matthew, Mark, Mimi, Britney, Kim, Chris, Heather Tucker, Janelle Gordinier, and Jenine Anderson are some of the best readers a writer could hope to have and I consider myself incredibly fortunate to be able to work with them. Thank you all.

Lastly, none of this could happen without my wife, Katie. She edited, provided feedback on the story, and created the cover all while juggling a ton of other responsibilities. Thanks, Katie.

About the Author

Dean Murray is a prolific author with dozens of titles across multiple pen names and more than half a million copies of his work currently in circulation.

Dean started reading seriously in the second grade due to a competition and has spent most of the subsequent three decades lost in other people's worlds.

Things worsened, or improved depending on your point of view, when he first started experimenting with writing while finishing up his accounting degree.

These days Dean has a wonderful wife and two lovely daughters to keep him rather more grounded, but the idea of bringing others along with him as he meets interesting new people in universes nobody else has ever seen tends to drag him back to his computer on a fairly regular basis.

Keep up to speed on Dean's latest projects at www.DeanWrites.com.

Frozen Prospects

The invitation to join the secretive Guadel should have been the fulfillment of dreams Va'del didn't even realize he had. When his sponsors are killed in an ambush a short time later, he instead finds his probationary status revoked, and becomes a pawn between various factions inside the Guadel ruling body.

Jain's never known any life but that of a Guadel in training. She'd thought herself reconciled to the idea of a loveless marriage for the good of her people, but meeting Va'del changes everything. Their growing attraction flies against hundreds of years of precedent, but as wide-spread attacks threaten their world, the Guadel have no choice but to use even Jain and Va'del in their fight for survival.

Bound

The only thing worse than having no family at all, is having a family that is out to hurt you. That would all be bad enough for a normal 17-year-old, but it's even worse for Alec Graves. A shape shifter's pack, his family, is the only thing stopping the other preternatural creatures out there from killing them.

Alec's pack isn't just neglectful, he's pretty sure that his father wants him dead. Alec is about to be sent to the front lines of a war between his people and everything else that goes bump in the night. His only chance of survival is to convince everyone around him that he's the perfect soldier, but there are lines that Alec won't cross, not for any price.

Publisher's Note: *Bound is the first in Dean's new Dark Reflections novels, an alternate timeline set in the same world and featuring many of the same characters, but with a profoundly different backstory.*

CHET

By Larry Murray

Meet Charles Tucker, he has spent nearly 30 years living in denial, trying desperately to hide from his past and the events that shattered his heart beyond any possibility of healing. He can't let anyone close, for doing so would open him up to being hurt again, and there's no way he could survive another wounding.

Meet the Saunders family, new to the neighborhood and teetering on the verge of bankruptcy. Mark, the father, talks a good story but is that all he is? His plan could hold the key to reversing his family's financial misfortunes, or it could wipe out everyone involved.

Meet Chet, a battered old '64 Chevy pickup that was there on the night Charles' life imploded. For nearly three decades, he has been locked away in an old barn, safely out of sight if not completely out of mind. For 29 years Charles has blamed the old pickup for the destruction of his life, now he's about to find that the vehicle that destroyed his life might be the key to his healing and a journey of unexpected miracles.

www.ingramcontent.com/pod-product-compliance
Lightning Source LLC
Chambersburg PA
CBHW020933020726
47495CB00002B/477

* 9 7 8 1 9 3 9 3 6 3 2 7 5 *